SWIFT JUSTICE

D0808081

The Bob White Birder Murder Mysteries

The Boreal Owl Murder

Murder on Warbler Weekend

A Bobwhite Killing

Falcon Finale

A Murder of Crows

SWIFT
JUSTICE

Jan Dunlap

NORTH STAR PRESS OF ST. CLOUD, INC.
Saint Cloud, Minnesota

First Edition: September 2014

Printed in the United States of America

Published by
North Star Press of St. Cloud, Inc.
P.O. Box 451
St. Cloud, Minnesota 56302

www.northstarpress.com

CHAPTER ONE

I STARTED DRINKING COFFEE when I was twelve. The occasion was a pre-dawn drive to see a bird in southeastern Minnesota with Ken Kniplinger, an older fellow I'd gotten to know during bird walks at the Minnesota Valley National Wildlife Refuge in Bloomington.

Then again, everyone I met on bird walks was older than me when I was twelve, since birding was primarily the recreation of older people when I first got hooked on the hobby. Nowadays, though, I'm happy to report that birding is well on its way to overcoming age barriers; I frequently see young parents with babies in backpacks out on the birding trails in Minnesota. We still have work to do in spreading the hobby into more diverse cultural populations, but there are some awesome programs around the country that are picking up steam, along with birders of every race and cultural background.

But back to my first cup of coffee.

Since I wasn't legal for driving a car when I was twelve years old, my dad was my wheelman and regular birding companion, and almost every Saturday morning, he drove me to birding spots around the Twin Cities so he wouldn't have to listen to me begging to go birding all weekend. Dad and Ken, or "Nip" as everyone called him, really hit it off on the walks in Bloomington, and before I knew it, they were big buddies because they discovered a mutual passion for nature preserve projects around the state.

So when Nip called late on an October Friday night to invite us to chase a Mississippi Kite that had been spotted near the town of LaCrosse in Wisconsin, Dad said I could go with Nip in the morning, even though he wouldn't be riding along. I was thrilled— it was my first birding excursion out of town with a birder other than my father; I guess you could say I figured I'd finally earned my wings as a birder in my own right.

"What'll you have, Bob?" Nip asked me as he pulled his car into a Stop'N'Go gas station a few blocks from my home. "It's a drive down to LaCrosse, so I'm going to need some joe. How about you?"

"Sure," I said, "sounds good."

True, I wasn't quite sure what "joe" was, but I figured if Nip used it, it was clearly an experienced birder thing, and I needed to get on board with what other birders routinely relied on when they took off in search of rare species.

When he returned to the car with two cups of steaming hot coffee in his hands, I casually took the cup he offered me, then secretly watched him as he carefully took a sip of his own. The rich aroma of coffee filled the car, and I felt, rather than heard, my stomach launch a low growl of hunger. I'd been too excited to eat the bowl of cereal my mom had poured for me when I woke up, and now the scent of the coffee was waking my appetite up in a big way.

I raised the cup to my lips and took a swallow.

Holy buckets!

Talk about hot! For a second, I thought it was going to burn a hole right through the front of my throat as it went down. So much for making my debut as an experienced birder—I was lucky I didn't scream like a girl when that coffee hit my tongue.

Sorry for the sexist remark. I should know better. I'm a sensitive high school counselor. I guess I could say "scream like a twelve-year-old boy," but it just doesn't have the same ring to it, you know? Girls are expected to scream; prepubescent boys, not so much.

As it was, my mouth popped open to drag in as much cool air as I could and I gasped for breath. I could feel tears in my eyes. I looked over at Nip.

"A fresh pot," he apologized. "A little strong, huh?"

At which point, I finally tasted the coffee itself as my taste buds recovered from being nearly boiled alive. The liquid was bitter, but it felt bright and cleansing on my tongue. I carefully took another small sip and savored the flavor in my mouth.

"It's good," I told Nip, a little surprised that I did, indeed, like the taste. I'd always assumed my parents drank it simply to wake up in the morning. Based on their grimaces over their first cups, it had never occurred to me that coffee could be a pleasure.

"There's nothing better than that first hit of joe when you've got a bird to find," Nip said as he made the turn towards the interstate that would carry us to the Kite, "but a lousy cup of coffee? That'll kill you every time."

After twenty-three years of drinking coffee, I'd have to agree with Nip: bad coffee will kill you, figuratively. What I didn't know, until recently, was that being the person to bring the coffee could get you killed.

Literally.

I'D JUST PICKED UP MY NAME TAG at the registration table for the MOU's Annual Meeting and Paper Session at the Bell Museum in Minneapolis when I heard a familiar voice call my name.

"Bob White!" Nip Kniplinger boomed from across the room.

I peeled off the backing of the nametag and smacked it on my shirt, then turned to greet my old birding buddy.

"Nip, how have you been?"

"Never better," he assured me, energetically shaking my hand. "Retirement's a wonderful thing. I can chase birds at the drop of a hat, and I don't have to ask anyone's permission to leave work early. Except for Mavis. She thinks I retired to become the full-time handyman around the house." His big laugh shook his round belly. "I'm working on re-educating her. So far, I've botched two plumbing repairs and one cabinet re-hanging. The only thing she asked me to do around the house this week was refill our birdfeeders on the back porch, so I think I'm making progress."

His eyes darted past me. "Is that our little Birdchick over there? I've got to go say hi and razz her about that corny commercial she did last week. Talk with you later, Bob."

I watched him scurry back across the entrance hall of the University of Minnesota's Bell Museum to catch Sharon Stiteler, known to birders around the country as the Birdchick. A highly regarded birding blogger and self-professed bird nerd, Sharon had cobbled together a solid career for herself as an avian expert and advocate, a career I occasionally envied, especially when I overdosed on drama queens in my counseling day job at Savage High School. About the same height as Nip, Sharon threw her arms around my friend's rotund shape, and the two of them squawked in delight, stamping their feet in excitement, reminding me of a couple of Greater Prairie-chickens doing their courtship dance during mating season.

"You know, if I were one of those really obsessive birders you run into around here every once in a while, I'd say that behavior looks a lot like Greater Prairie-chickens, wouldn't you, Bob? It's the foot stomping—a dead giveaway."

"Hey, Ron," I replied, turning to shake the strong hand of Ron Windingstad, the former Audubon at Home state coordinator for Minnesota. "Are you trash-talking birders again?"

Now retired, Ron was probably the state's foremost authority on Chimney Swifts, given the fact that he'd coordinated the agency's Chimney Swift Conservation Project for eleven years. On top of that, he's given countless hours to educate the public about Chimney Swifts, and he and his teenage son, Lucas, were experts at sharing their enthusiasm for the birds. I once tried to set up a date for Ron to come out to Savage High School to teach our woodworking class to build Chimney Swift towers, but our assistant principal, Mr. Lenzen, nixed the idea. He was afraid the birds, when they started congregating in large flocks before fall migration, would cause too much excitement around the football field.

If they had, it would have been a first for Savage High, let me assure you. Ask any Savage resident, and they'd tell you that excitement is just about the very last word associated with our football field.

"Bob, I want you to meet Pheej Vang," Ron said, resting his hand on the shoulder of the young Hmong man beside him. "Pheej is presenting a session this morning about the Chimney Swift towers his Boy Scout troop built and installed around the Twin Cities. He's a talented young man, and one of our up-and-coming birders here in Minnesota. Pheej, this is Bob White."

"Hello," Pheej said, shaking my extended hand. "I'm happy to meet you, Mr. White."

"It's a pleasure," I told him. "Where do you go to school, Pheej?"

"Central in St. Paul," he said. "I'm a junior there."

"I'm a counselor at Savage High," I replied. "Central's got a topnotch math team, don't they? In fact, if I'm recalling this right, they won state last year and came in second at nationals."

Pheej looked away and smiled shyly. "We did," he said. "I'm the co-captain of the team."

"Congratulations, then." I nodded at Ron. "You've got to find more Pheejs for us, Ron. The birds of Minnesota are counting on you."

"That would be a switch," Pheej said, catching my eye for a second before he again looked away. "Ron is the one who's usually counting the birds."

"Show Bob the photo you took last summer," Ron urged Pheej. "It's a great shot," he assured me.

Pheej pulled a picture out of the folder he was carrying and handed it to me.

"That's a Chimney Swift on Ron's shoulder," he said. "The bird had been rehabbed at the Wildlife Rehabilitation Center. I took the picture just before we released it back into the wild at a roost site where hundreds of swifts were gathering for the night."

Ron nodded. "We watched it fly off and join the others. I know this is my own interpretation, but those Swift's eyes looked so thankful to be free. It was one of those moments that really hit home when you've spent your life loving birds."

I handed the photo back to Pheej, who slipped it into his file. "Nice shot," I told him. "You do good camera work, Pheej."

"Where's the coffee?" Nip boomed, returned from his public display with the Birdchick. "Birders can't begin an annual meeting without joe."

"Joe who?" Pheej asked Ron.

"He means coffee," Ron explained. "Don't ask," he added when Pheej gave him a confused look. "I don't think anyone knows for sure, though lots of people have their own opinions on it. Some say it was the Secretary of the Navy who banned alcohol from ships in the early 1900s, or that 'joe' sounds like the word 'hot' in French, or that it's from an old song from the 1800s. Whatever you call it, it's the drink of choice of most birders."

"I thought Birdchick was in charge of coffee this year," I said. "Didn't I see her on television last week hawking some local organic coffee shop?"

Sharon—Birdchick—was the promotional queen of the Minnesota Ornithologists' Union. She represented so many products, I figured she probably had a list of company names written in indelible ink along the inside of her arm so she wouldn't forget which product went with which company.

"Yup. That's the one I had to tease her about." Nip looked around my left side and then around my right side to the table behind me. "She said the coffee would be set up next to the registration table, but I don't see any. Sharon!" he bellowed across the room at Birdchick.

I saw her blonde head pop up from a conversation.

"The coffee isn't here!" Nip yelled again.

Sharon waved at us. "I'm coming!" she shouted back.

"I thought birders were quiet people," Pheej softly observed.

"Only when they're birding," Ron replied. "Believe me, some of them can make a whole heck of a lot of noise when they want to."

Sharon bustled up to our little group.

"Hey, Bob," she greeted me. "Where's Luce?"

Luce was my wife and birding partner. She was also an incredible chef for a conference center on the west side of the Twin Cities. This particular morning, she was busy cooking up a gourmet chocolate fantasy brunch for a local food shelf's annual fundraiser at the conference center. While I was waiting for my first cup of plain old joe, Luce was probably brewing five kinds of mocha espressos and icing chocolate biscotti.

I almost salivated just thinking about it.

"She's working a brunch this morning," I told Birdchick. "Nip needs his coffee, Sharon, and he needs it now, or it's going to get ugly."

"Heaven forbid!" Sharon clasped her hands over her plump bosom in mock horror.

I rolled my eyes in exasperation. "Just tell me where the coffee is, Sharon, and I'll go get it."

"Trisha Davis picked it up and is bringing it in for me," she said. "I just got a text from her. She's parked in the lot downstairs and should be bringing it up in the elevator even as we speak."

"In one trip?" I asked.

Last year, there had been four large coffee urns standing on the refreshments table. I couldn't imagine one ride in the elevator would be enough to bring it all in.

"I'll go give her a hand," I said. I turned to Ron's protégé. "I'm looking forward to your talk, Pheej. I'm sure you've got some great information to share with us."

I walked over to the elevator just as the doors slid open, but no one was inside. I stepped in and pushed the button for the underground parking level. A few moments later, I found myself in the dimly lit garage, looking for Trisha Davis, a short blonde woman a little older than I was. I knew Trisha from the last two years of sitting together on the Minnesota Ornithologists' Union Records Committee, or MOURC, as I liked to call it. There were five of us on the committee, and it was our responsibility every six months to evaluate records of birds seen in the state. Using photos and any other documentation offered, we verified sightings of unusual and rare birds for the state-wide birding community.

Most of the time, birders who submitted records respectfully accepted our evaluations since all five of us were extremely experienced birders. Occasionally, though, a birder got upset when we rejected his or her identification of the bird in question and accused us of being prima donnas trying to maintain some kind of elite superiority to the rank-and-file birders in the state. The few times I'd had that experience, I told the upset birder to get a life and find something they were good at, because birding clearly wasn't it.

Just kidding. I didn't really say that.

I'm Mr. Sensitive, remember? I make my living helping young people deal with challenging circumstances, like failing art appreciation class twice, or not making the dance team's first string, or having a dog who continually ate their homework assignments even though the assignments were supposed to be submitted online.

Really—I had a student once who swore his dog ate his online homework assignment. Obviously, he wasn't the class valedictorian.

Or salutorian, either.

Actually, he may have been in the bottom twentieth percentile.

He did manage to graduate, though, even if it was a year later than the average Savage student. Last I heard, he was in Los Angeles and well on his way to making his second million as a record producer.

Go figure.

"Trisha?" I called into the rows of cars parked beneath the Bell Museum. I listened for a response.

Nothing.

Had I missed her when I came down in the elevator?

Not possible. There was only the one elevator in use this morning, and there was no way Trisha had hauled one of those big coffee urns up a flight of stairs.

I closed my eyes and listened again.

I could hear something dripping.

Since the roads had been unseasonably dry for the last week, I knew that the noise wasn't the result of ice melting off someone's car. I walked toward the sound and saw a car door ajar, but the inside light wasn't on.

It was Sharon's car, though. I knew her license plates as well as my own.

BRDCHK1.

As I got closer, I could see a body slumped back in the driver's seat, and what looked like a big cardboard box wedged between the body and the car steering wheel.

I sprinted the rest of the way to the car and jerked the driver's door wide open.

The huge take-out carton of coffee slipped to the cement floor of the parking garage into the growing puddle of joe beside the driver's door. Trisha's motionless eyes stared past me and up at the garage ceiling. Just below her ribcage I saw the handle of a knife protruding from Trisha's wind jacket.

I took a sharp breath in through my teeth.

"Memo to me," I whispered. "Say 'no' if anyone asks you to pick up the coffee."

My eyes returned to the knife handle.

"In fact, say 'hell, no.'"

CHAPTER TWO

"I ASSUME THIS WOULD be properly termed a rarity," Pheej said when I sat down next to him at the table outside the Bell Museum's gift shop. "It's not a common occurrence to have an MOU member found dead at the Annual Meeting, is it?"

"Definitely a rarity," I agreed.

I looked around the entry hallway where about forty birders stood silently, or spoke quietly in small groups. Periodically, police would usher a few people at a time into the adjacent lecture hall for private questioning as they tried to assemble any information that might prove useful for the investigation into Trisha's murder. All the morning sessions and speakers had been cancelled, and it was still up in the air as to whether any afternoon sessions would be held. As the only general membership meeting of the year, the MOU's annual Paper Session was a big event that many Minnesota birders eagerly anticipated and arranged to attend even if it meant several hours of driving to Minneapolis. With the plug suddenly pulled on the day's schedule, no one was quite sure how to proceed.

"Do you think we'll have our MOURC meeting tomorrow afternoon?" Nip asked me.

He and Ron sat at the opposite side of the table from me and Pheej. I noticed he had a paper cup of coffee in front of him.

"The police brought up the other two cartons of coffee that were in the backseat of . . . the car," he explained when he caught the direction of my gaze. He tried an apologetic smile. "They told us to help ourselves, and I figured it was going to be a long day . . ." his voice trailed off.

I lifted one eyebrow at him.

"I didn't want to waste good coffee," he added, taking another sip. "You know me and my joe, Bob."

"What are you going to do about MOURC?" Ron picked up the conversation that had abruptly died. "Especially since there are just the three of you now. Can you meet with only three members?"

Shoot. I'd forgotten that one of the things supposed to happen in the morning session was to ask for a new member for the records committee to take the place of Sonny Delite, a well-known birder who had died suddenly back in October. Now, with Trisha gone, the committee was two members short, and I wasn't sure if the MOU bylaws would allow the committee to function with only three birders in attendance: me, Nip, and Harry Harrison.

"Harry would know," I said. "He's been in the MOU for over fifty years, and sat on the records committee for the last twenty. I'll go find him and ask."

I stood up to go look for Harry and almost tripped over the Birdchick.

"Geez, Bob," Sharon said, "look where you're going. Just because you're a giant doesn't mean you get to step on us little people."

Her voice seemed to lack her usual bright confidence, but I guessed that knowing she'd been under the same roof at the same time as a murder was occurring had shaken her badly. Unfortunately, I had experience when it came to being involved in murder scenes and investigations. Of all the birders at the Bell Museum that morning, I thought I was the calmest and most collected in the course of the morning's ordeal. It wasn't exactly something I'd like to become known for among birders—*yeah, he's the guy who doesn't blink an eye when a body turns up*—but I've always believed that experience can be an educational thing.

Even when it does have to do with dead bodies.

Sharon turned her attention to Nip. "I thought you were going to be hosting our guest speaker, but I haven't seen him yet. Did the great Duck Man duck out on us?"

I detected a little false cheeriness in Sharon's voice. I had the impression that given other, happier, circumstances, there might have been a hint of sarcasm in her question.

"No, he's here," Nip said. "His plane was rerouted because of the blizzard in Denver last night, so he didn't fly in until early this morning. He took a taxi here from the airport and arrived just after the police showed up. You must have missed him in all the commotion around here."

"Who is the great Duck Man?" Pheej asked Ron.

"He's a birding blogger," Sharon said. "Like me. Though he's not as well-known as I am."

"Do you mean Duc Nguyen?" Pheej lit up. "His blog is Duc on Ducks. I read it every day. It's fascinating."

Sharon threw him a blank stare. "Really."

"Yes!" Pheej enthused. "He travels all over the world, and he combines his observations of ducks with interesting insights into the cultures around them. He's Vietnamese, and he's making many people interested in birds."

"That's always a good thing," Sharon said, though her enthusiasm for Duc Nguyen clearly fell short of Pheej's estimation of the man. "I guess I'll have to take another look at his blog sometime."

Again, that odd note in Sharon's voice caught my attention. It almost sounded as if she had something personal against Duc Nguyen.

Then a possible explanation popped into my head. Was the Birdchick feeling competition from the Duck Man?

I knew from past conversations with her that Sharon was very protective of her blog and her following of readers, but not being a regular visitor to the blogosphere myself, I couldn't begin to guess what that might mean professionally. I supposed it somehow translated to income opportunities or popularity, but that was about as far as I could fathom. The intricacies of social networking were still pretty much a mystery to me. At work, I spent my days connecting with living, breathing, and sometimes obnoxious, human beings instead of online avatars. My office budget was devoted to boxes of tissues for crying teenage girls, not high-tech software to land myself a world-wide net of fans.

My phone vibrated in my pocket, and I pulled it out to read a text message.

Text messages, I got.

Social networking? Not even a blip on my radar.

"Whoa," I breathed.

"What?" Sharon asked. "What is 'whoa'?"

"It's an Ivory Gull on the Mississippi," I told my colleagues. "Flaps and Babs Andersen are there right now, not far from the old Schmidt brewery in St. Paul, looking at an Ivory Gull."

"No way," Nip said.

"Flaps and Babs don't lie," Ron pointed out. "They're two of the sharpest birders in the state."

"An Ivory Gull?"

We all turned to see Pete Moss standing behind our little crew.

"And you believe that?" he asked incredulously. His dark eyes peered out from beneath his mop of black hair and heavy beard. "I'd say reporting standards have really taken a nosedive in Minnesota if you people are ready to accept a sighting just because some old couple says it's so."

He held up his hand to stop Ron's next remark.

"I know the Andersens," Pete said. "They're good. But they're also slipping. They've made three incorrect bird IDs in the last six months. Given that recent track record, I don't know how much credit I'd give a sighting of an Ivory Gull. Especially since there have only ever been a few verified occurrences of the species in this part of the state in the winter."

He stroked his thick beard. "Verified. Isn't that the key word? Oh, wait, I'm sorry. You records committee people prefer 'documented,' don't you?"

Nip stepped directly in front of Pete and crossed his arms over his big belly. "Let it go, Pete. How many years ago was that? Three?"

"Three," Pete repeated, "and it's hard to let go when I know what I saw, but thanks to a bunch of better-birder-than-thou types, I was denied both the sighting and a state record. I'd never had a better year with more rarities, but MOURC just couldn't bring itself to give me the credit I deserved. So, no, I can't let it go, Nip."

He crossed his arms over his chest and jutted out his bearded chin. "Not until I feel like justice has been done."

Out of the corner of my eye, I saw Pheej tug gently on Ron's sleeve, and Ron bent down to hear the boy's whisper.

"I'll tell you later," Ron said, his voice muted.

"Well, I don't know about 'justice,' but I know I'm done here," I announced, hoping to move the conversation away from Pete's bitterness and back to the happier prospect of seeing a rare bird. "And I'm willing to give Flaps and Babs the benefit of the doubt, so I'm heading to St. Paul to see if they've got an Ivory Gull or not. Ron and Pheej, you interested? I'm driving."

Ron laughed. "Sure, we'll go check it out with you. But I'll take Pheej in my car, Bob. No offense, but you drive like a maniac, and I'm responsible for Pheej today."

I shrugged. It was true I drove like a madman. Sometimes. Maybe more than sometimes.

"Okay," I said, "but if you miss the gull by minutes, it's not my fault."

I turned back to see that Pete Moss and Nip had ended their tense confrontation, thanks in part to the Birdchick's wedging herself between the two men.

"Show me the Duck Man," Sharon commanded Nip, grabbing the lapels of his coat. "You can have him later, Pete," she threw over her shoulder as she dragged Nip away. "I need to have a few words with our guest speaker, once we find him."

Pete watched them leave, invisible waves of anger rolling off of him, unless I missed my guess. He caught me looking at him, and after shooting me a quick glare, he walked away into the thinning crowds in the Bell Museum's entrance lobby.

"He had a bird identification denied?" Pheej asked Ron.

"Pete Moss is an incredibly talented birder," Ron told him, "but—to put it nicely—he doesn't take criticism well. Three years ago, he reported he saw a Chimney Swift in late November outside the old Hamm's brewery. You know the place, Pheej," he reminded the boy. "You counted swifts there this past summer. But you and I also know the swifts are long gone from Minnesota by that time of year."

"And Pete couldn't offer any kind of evidence to support his sighting," I added. "No photos, no second spotter, nothing. So MOURC tossed it out. It was just too impossible."

We headed out the doors of the museum. For the first time, I noticed that Pheej walked with a slight limp.

"Where did you park?" I asked Ron. I hoped it was nearby, for Pheej's sake. Walking on sidewalks that still held stubborn patches of ice from our last snowstorm was difficult enough when your balance was good, let alone having to manage with a bum leg.

"We're right here," he said, pointing across the street to a handicapped spot. "My parking tag from my knee replacement surgery hasn't expired yet, and I figured Pheej would appreciate a shorter walk this morning."

"I fell off a ladder helping my dad clean out the house gutters this fall," the young Hmong explained to me. "The doctor said I was lucky I didn't break my leg, but I didn't feel lucky, since it ended my soccer season early."

We waited on the curb for a car to pass by.

"But aren't you on MOURC?" Pheej returned to our conversation about Pete's claim. "Why was Mr. Moss so angry at Nip, but not at you, if you're on the committee, too?"

"This is only my third year on the committee," I explained. "I was a new member the year Pete submitted his claim. I wasn't as confident in dismissing it as the other members, because I've found birds that no one else has seen, too. I deferred to their expertise. It's pretty well accepted that, in a questionable case like that, the longer-established committee members have more say."

I pointed in the direction of my parked car and waved goodbye to Ron and Pheej. "I'll see you two in St. Paul."

I did recall, however, hearing that Pete had not taken his sighting's rejection well, and that, for the next six months, he targeted Sonny, Harry Harrison, Trisha, and Nip with nasty emails about our ruling on the bird identification. It reminded me of a few students I'd counseled over the years—the belligerent, angry ones who claimed that certain teachers "made" them fail their courses by not giving them passing grades.

"And why was that?" I'd ask them. "Why do you think you didn't get passing grades?"

"Because they wanted me to fail! They're unfair, and they're lousy teachers."

I'd put on a concerned face and make a steeple out of my fingers. "And you don't think it had anything to do with your missing half of the class sessions? Or failing to turn in homework assignments?"

"That shouldn't count in my grade!" the indignant student would insist. "I was really expecting to pass that class, and they failed me on purpose!"

"Maybe you should lower your expectations," I'd say. "Maybe you should expect to fail, and the only way you might pass is to do the work."

The student would scoff. "Are you kidding? Where did you go to school?"

"On the planet called 'I have to earn my grades.'"

"You are so full of it, Mr. White. There is no planet called that."

"Apparently not in your universe," I'd reply.

But even though he'd acted more like a child having a temper tantrum than a responsible adult birder who accepted the decision of a committee of his peers, Pete Moss was no neophyte when it came to birding. He knew birds and their field marks. He had to have been more than one hundred percent certain of what he'd seen even to consider making such an outrageous claim.

Unless he'd figured he'd already earned his credentials in the Minnesota birding community, and, therefore, no one would question his sighting. He wouldn't be the first birder to prize a state record over total accuracy.

I shook my head as I popped the lock on my car door and got inside. Birding was such a great hobby that connected you to the wonders of the natural world. For me, birding was about expanding horizons, not shrinking them. I always hated it when people turned it into something else, like self-aggrandizement or a political card. I recalled the odd expression on the Birdchick's face when she was asking Nip about the Duck Man—did well-known birders feel territorial about their particular field—or species—of expertise?

Wasn't every birder in it for the birds?

I drove over to Seventh Street in St. Paul and made my way down to the old Schmidt brewery that overlooked the Mississippi River. Flaps and Babs had given me directions to where they had parked, so I pulled in next to their black Ford pickup truck, then headed toward the river. A few minutes later, I saw them standing on the sidewalk, their binoculars up.

"Still there?" I called out as I approached them.

Babs lowered her binos and waved. "We told him to wait for you," she yelled back. "We said we had the Birdman himself coming out to verify our sighting."

I took up my position beside her husband, Flaps, and almost immediately spotted the gull floating on the river. I raised my own binos to my eyes to study the bird. It was just slightly smaller than the Ring-billed Gull common in southern Minnesota throughout most of the year, but the real distinguishing characteristic was the bird's pure white plumage. No other species of gull was white without some amount of darker streaking or splotching. Its bill had a blue cast at its base with a yellow tip.

"Looks like an Ivory Gull to me," I said. "I wonder what brought it this far south."

"It's rare they ever leave the pack ice north of Newfoundland," Flaps commented, his head covered in the signature flap-eared hat that had earned him his nickname. "About once every decade or so, we see a stray one along Lake Superior in northern Minnesota. I've read some articles that speculate the Arctic climate change is disrupting the breeding and migration patterns as food sources are affected, but that's still a long way to fly to find something to eat."

"It's like with the polar bears," Babs commented. "The decline in pack ice makes it harder for them to forage and shortens their breeding window. It makes sense all species might be encountering trouble because of the weather changes."

"At least the gulls can fly to find new ranges," Flaps countered. "The polar bears don't have that luxury."

"I thought we were looking for an Ivory Gull," Ron said as he and Pheej joined us on the sidewalk, "not a polar bear."

I pointed out to the river, where a raft of gulls floated.

"In there," I said. "Look for the all-white bird with black eyes." Ron lifted his binos, as did Pheej.

"Got it," Ron said a moment later. "It's definitely smaller and whiter than the Herring Gulls around it."

"Actually, polar bears and Ivory Gulls have something in common," Pheej informed us as he continued to watch the bird bobbing in the icy water. "The gulls feed primarily on small fish, but they're also known to scavenge carcasses left by polar bears."

I looked at Pheej in amazement.

He lowered his binos and gave me a shy smile. "I looked it up on my Smartphone on the way here," he explained. "I've never seen an Ivory Gull, so I wanted to learn what I could before I saw it."

"You blew it," Babs laughed. "You could've let us all think you were a walking ornithology encyclopedia, the MOU's newest prodigy."

She patted Pheej on the shoulder with her mittened hand. "We love it when young birders show up with all this information already in their heads. It reassures us there'll be avid birders to take our place someday. I'm Babs," she added and nodded toward her husband. "That's Flaps. Glad to meet you."

Ron introduced Pheej to the Andersens and explained how he'd met the young birder. They all talked a few minutes about Chimney Swifts and building towers, and then Ron and Pheej left.

As if he suddenly remembered what day it was, Flaps turned to me and asked, "You're not at the annual MOU meeting at the Bell Museum today?"

"Been there, done that," I told him, then gave him and Babs the condensed version of the morning's events.

"Believe me, I was happy to leave the Bell when you called," I said, "and finding an Ivory Gull has never been easier."

I desperately hoped the police could say the same thing about finding Trisha Davis's murderer, but judging from past experiences, I seriously doubted it.

CHAPTER THREE

FOR THE FIRST MONDAY morning in months, there wasn't a line of students waiting for me outside my office door when I walked into work. I would have liked to attribute that to the fact that all my students this semester were demonstrating exemplary behavior and scholarship, but, unfortunately, I knew that wasn't the case. The more probable reason was that my charges were all still at home, since the heavy snow overnight had convinced our district superintendent that we needed to have a late start for classes. Being the early bird I am, I was already awake when I got the 5:45 a.m. phone call about the late start, so I figured it was my chance to catch some worms: I shoveled out the driveway and fishtailed over to the high school in hopes I could make a good-sized dent in the pile of catch-up work on my desk before the first students straggled in.

What I didn't expect was to find a gift-wrapped package lying on top of that pile of catch-up work.

I dumped my briefcase behind my desk and hung my parka on the hook on the back of my office door. I picked up the package and read the attached gift tag.

Happy holidays from just us chickens!

It was signed *Your Secret Santa.*

Shoot.

I'd forgotten about the high school staff and faculty annual gift exchange. Two weeks ago, we'd drawn names from a hat to select our secret giftee, and today was the first day we were supposed to surprise our colleague with some small token of holiday cheer, along with a clue to our real identity. Amidst a murder, a rare bird sighting, and a snowstorm, the December tradition had completely slipped my mind.

I weighed the present in my hands and guessed it was some kind of picture or enlarged photograph. I tapped on the package's flat surface and was fairly certain I felt glass beneath the gift wrap.

"Are you going to open it or just play with it?"

I looked up to see our school nurse in my doorway.

"Hey, Katy," I said. "What are you doing here so early? The kids won't be in for another two hours." I held up the present. "Is this from you?"

"Yeah, right," she laughed. "Like I'd tell you if it were, which it isn't. There was a present on my desk when I walked in a little while ago, too, so I think there's a ring of Santas with a master key among them. And I'm guessing they made their deliveries last night before the worst of the snow hit, since I drove into the parking lot this morning right behind Elway, and there weren't any other tire tracks."

Elway was one of our school custodians, and in the winter, he attached a monster plow on the front of his pickup truck to clear the parking lot when it snowed. Especially with a deep snow like we'd had overnight, the last thing you'd want to do is get to school before Elway showed up. I high-centered my SUV twice coming in early after heavy snows before I learned that particular bit of wisdom. He also had a master key to the building and offices, of course, so it was conceivable Elway was the Secret Santa who'd delivered my package before I arrived.

Although Elway being my Secret Santa wouldn't explain how Katy's gift had appeared.

"A ring of Santas, huh?" I nodded at Katy. "Not a bad theory. We'll have to watch for any suspicious conspiring among our compatriots to see if we can ferret out the members of a Santa ring."

Katy's eyes dropped to the wrapped gift still in my hands. "So are you going to open it or what?"

In answer, I pulled off the red, green, and white-striped paper to reveal an eight-by-ten photo in a bright-yellow frame.

I recognized it right away and held it up for Katy to see. It was a photo from a school assembly back in October. We'd had a hypnotist come in, but he'd accidentally been knocked out right after hypnotizing a group of students to think they were chickens. Another faculty member and I had ended up corralling the students in the girls' locker room where they'd disappeared to hatch basketballs they thought were eggs.

Typical high school stuff, you know?

"The chickens!" Katy laughed again. "Someone took this right before the students scattered off into the halls. Look," she said, tapping the face of one of the students in the photo. "Here's Bill Madison crowing like a rooster on the school stage. Oh, my gosh, I laughed so hard when you brought those kids back to my office, squawking and shaking their arms like wings."

"Yup. One of our students' finer moments this year," I agreed. "So I wonder who took the photo?"

"Good luck with that, Bob," Katy said as she turned to leave my office. "At least half our students and staff carry cell phones that can take pictures. Heck, it's probably more like ninety-five percent. I think you're going to have to figure out who gave you the photo in order to find the photographer."

She was right. There was no way I could track down my Secret Santa by that process of elimination. Thanks to technology, every person in the building was probably carrying a phone with camera capabilities. Clearly, the identity of my Secret Santa was going to stay a secret at least for today.

Which reminded me I needed to pull together a small something for my own gift exchange recipient . . . who happened to be my brother-in-law/best friend Alan Thunderhawk.

Luckily, that was a no-brainer.

I didn't mean Alan. Alan was brilliant.

The gift idea. I meant the gift idea was a no-brainer.

I laid the chicken picture on my desk and set off for the faculty lounge. Everyone on staff knew Alan was practically addicted to peanut M&Ms. With any luck, I'd find the vending machine in the lounge well stocked with them. I could buy a couple individual packs from the machine and slide them into Alan's mail box in the faculty lounge, and he'd have no clue it was me.

Except that when I walked into the lounge, Alan was there, apparently emptying the vending machine of its entire supply of peanut M&Ms.

"Are you kidding me?" I asked him in exasperation. "You're buying candy at 7:00 in the morning?"

He stuffed the last package into a pocket on the front of his down vest.

"I'm going to need some serious sugar to get through the day, White-man," he said. "Louise is cutting her first tooth, and it isn't pretty. I'd already been up an hour with her when I got the late start phone call, so I figured I might as well come in to work since I was already wide-awake, instead of trying to get back to sleep and then having to wake up again. Louise, the stinker, promptly passed out when I laid her in the bed next to Lily," he added.

He patted his candy-filled pockets. "But I'm good to go, now. By the time those students show up, I'll have my lesson plans finished for the next two months."

He threw me a questioning look. "What are you doing here so early?"

"I thought I'd catch up on work while it was quiet," I said. "I've got about fifteen recommendations to write for seniors' college applications, and you know me," I shrugged, "I've always been an early bird."

Alan folded his arms across his chest. "And I bet you're not sleeping that well anyway since the MOU meeting on Saturday. It was on the 5:00 a.m. newscast this morning," he informed me, "which I happened to catch with my lovely, but drooly, daughter. And you know what I thought as soon as the reporter said there'd been a murder at the Bell Museum?"

"You hoped it wasn't me, right?"

Alan shook his head. "Nope. I told Louise that I was pretty sure her favorite uncle was up to his old tricks again, finding bodies. You did, didn't you? You found the body."

I leaned back against the vending machine and scrubbed my hand over my eyes, before returning his gaze.

"Yes, I did," I said. "The coffee for the meeting was late in arriving, so I offered to go help bring it in from the garage. I found Trisha Davis, who is—*was*—on the records committee with me, dead in her car. She'd been stabbed with a knife."

Alan blew out a low whistle. "Man, Bob, I'm so sorry."

"Yeah, it wasn't fun, that's for sure."

The image of Trisha trapped in her car seat behind the leaking coffee box, a knife in her body, popped back into my head for the hundredth time since Saturday morning. Too bad my Secret Santa hadn't left me some kind of miraculous brain-cleaning fluid. It was going to be a while before that mental snapshot faded.

"On the newscast, they said the police are saying it looks like a random mugging," Alan said.

I shook my head. "A random attack in the Bell Museum's parking garage, in the middle of the University of Minnesota campus, on a morning when you've got hundreds of birders driving into that same parking garage for an annual meeting? I don't think so."

Alan's eyes held mine. "What do you think?"

I crossed my own arms over my chest.

"I think someone wanted to kill Trisha Davis, and he, or she, planned for it to happen at the MOU meeting."

Alan opened his mouth to ask me more, but a chirping tune began calling from my pocket. I held up a finger to ask Alan to wait, and took out my cell phone. I read the caller ID. Nip Kniplinger.

"I've got to take this," I told Alan as I thumbed the phone on. "Nip, thanks for getting back to me."

"I can't believe it," he said, his voice cracking over the connection. "First Trisha, and now Harry."

"Look, Nip, I just wanted to check in with you." I concentrated on making my voice calm and reassuring. "I know all of us are still stunned about Saturday morning, but I just thought . . . well, it wouldn't hurt to keep in closer contact for a little while, you know? Support each other, right? I mean, this is hard on all of us, and I'm sure Harry's passing away has nothing to do with what happened at the MOU meeting, but it's still really . . . upsetting."

Upsetting?

Geez. You'd think I could come up with something smoother than what was fumbling out of my mouth. I was a trained counselor, for crying out loud, and I've had plenty of practice consoling grieving students over the years. If this had been a role-playing assignment in graduate school, I would have just flunked.

Upsetting? More like devastating.

I glanced at Alan. From the look of confusion on his face, he seemed as surprised as I was at my babbling.

But I couldn't seem to stop.

"Really, Nip, I'm sure you're fine," I struggled on. "It's just so coincidental with Trisha . . . I mean, I'm sure Harry's heart attack yesterday was . . . ah . . . not surprising, given his advanced age and health lately. I just wanted to, you know, check in with you."

Alan's eyes got wider as I continued to blather into the phone. I ran my hand through my hair.

"I know you two go way back, Nip. That's why Harry's wife called me yesterday afternoon. She was trying to get hold of you because she didn't want you to hear Harry had died from anyone else, but she was having trouble reaching you."

Nip mumbled something about his lousy mobile phone coverage.

"It was probably the snowstorm moving in and messing with cell phone reception," I told him. "That's all. I wasn't . . . ah . . . worried about you or anything. I just thought I should . . . touch base . . . see how you were doing."

Now Alan was making hand signals at me to wrap up the call: he wanted me to tell him what was going on. Meanwhile, Nip was telling me he was heading over to Harry's home as soon as his road was cleared by the county plows.

"You do that, Nip," I said to my old birding companion. "And let me know about funeral arrangements. I'll want to attend the service."

I slid the phone back into my pocket.

"You want to tell me what that was all about?" Alan asked. "And what has got you so distraught that you could barely get out a coherent sentence?"

"Yeah, I didn't handle that very well, did I?" I pushed off from the vending machine and started for the door.

"Bob," Alan's serious tone stopped me in my tracks. "What's going on?"

I looked up at the lounge's old ceiling tiles and blew out a long breath of air. At the same moment, I realized my fingers were busily jiggling my office keys in my pants pocket, a dead give-away I was feeling stressed.

Extremely stressed.

"Here's the deal," I said to Alan as he seated himself directly in front of me on top of one of the lunch tables in the lounge. "Harry Harrison died of a heart attack within twenty-four hours of Trisha's murder. If you include Sonny Delite's death two months ago, that makes three of the five MOURC members very recently deceased, leaving only Nip and me on the committee. I sort of feel like a contestant on one of those 'reality' shows waiting to see who gets dumped next."

"But Sonny's death was accidental," Alan reminded me. "We know that for a fact. And I just heard you say this Harrison guy's health was bad, anyway."

"I know," I agreed. "And there's no evidence these three deaths are connected."

I sat on the table behind me so I was looking directly into Alan's eyes.

"So why is my gut saying otherwise?" I asked him. "Three birders responsible for documenting claims made by the membership of the MOU—who could be threatened by that? It's a hobby."

Alan raised his eyebrows in mock horror and clutched his chest.

"Okay," I amended, "for *some* of us, it's a lot more than that. It's an obsession, an identity, a reason to get up every morning and go outside."

And for at least one birder I knew, it had become much more: a deeply personal matter of what he considered a blow to his reputation for which he wanted "justice."

Pete Moss had said he wouldn't let his rejected sighting rest.

And now—barely forty-eight hours later—there were two less people alive who had shared responsibility for that decision.

Call me paranoid, but I thought that was a fairly disturbing coincidence.

I pointed at the edge of the M&M bag sticking out of Alan's vest pocket. "At least your obsession doesn't involve other people. It's highly unlikely one of those M&Ms will go psychotically ballistic and come after you."

Alan pulled the small package out of his pocket and tossed it to me. I grabbed it out of the air.

"You know I've got your back, Bob," my brother-in-law said. "But just to be on the safe side, stay away from getting coffee for anyone for a little while. And don't drink tea, either," he added, reminding me of the cause of my old friend Sonny Delite's fatal poisoning.

"In fact, why don't you just stick to M&Ms for a while?" Alan suggested. He stood up. "Seriously, man, I think your imagination is working overtime here. I know it's really hard to lose your birding buddies, but life happens."

He clapped me on the shoulder. "You'll see," he promised. "It's just a crazy coincidence. Not everything works out in the worst possible way you think it could."

Alan left the lounge and I stared at the M&M bag in my hands.

He was right. Not everything turns out badly.

Against all odds, I had today's Secret Santa gift for Alan dropped directly into my hands.

Maybe it wasn't my turn to get voted off the island after all.

CHAPTER FOUR

By THE TIME THE FIRST students arrived for their two-hour late start of classes, I'd completed the counselor's section on four college applications. Two of them hadn't taken much thought, since all I had to do was enter class rankings and cumulative grade point averages. The remaining two were more demanding—I had to rate the students in twenty categories and then compose a paragraph evaluating their college preparedness.

Given that the applicants were facing submission deadlines the next day, I'd say their preparedness could use a little . . . well . . . preparing.

A knock on my open office door ended my consideration of how to word my recommendations to make my students look good despite their obvious lack in the forethought department. I looked up to see Bridget Dandorff, one of my senior softball players, grinning from ear to ear.

"I got in! I got in!" she sang as she danced over to my desk. She slapped an acceptance letter on top of the recommendation I'd been working on. "Stanford, here I come!"

I read the first paragraph of the letter and practically jumped up out of my chair to give her a big hug.

Yes, I know. Counselors aren't supposed to be touching students, and if my boss, Mr. Lenzen, had been walking by, he would have keeled over in anticipation of a sexual harassment suit. But I'd coached and counseled Bridget for three years and through numerous breakups with boyfriends, and known her grandpa, Fritz

Dandorff, for decades, so I didn't think twice about cutting myself some slack so I could celebrate with her.

Bridget hugged me back, hard. "Thank you so much for all your help," she said. "I couldn't have done it without you."

"Aw, shucks, ma'am, that's mighty kind of you to say," I drawled with a bad western accent. "You didn't do too badly yourself."

With a bubbly laugh, she dragged one of my two visitors' chairs close to my desk and dropped into it.

"I'm so glad you talked me into getting on the advanced math team during my junior year," she said. "I'm sure that placing in the top five at the state competition two years in a row looked really good to their engineering department."

"It sure didn't hurt," I agreed with her. "And acing the college boards wasn't a bad idea, either."

Bridget laughed again. "Whoever would have thought that being on a math team was such a great idea? I mean, really, you find nerds on math teams, not ballplayers like me. Except for Cai, of course. He's not a nerd at all. He just happens to be both a baseball player and super smart."

She grinned again. "And wonderful."

I gave her a mock surprised look. "Really? Cai is wonderful?"

"Hey," she said. "I'm just calling it the way I see it."

Cai Xiong was Bridget's current boyfriend. A senior like Bridget, Cai was going to be the first in his immigrant Hmong family to graduate from high school in America and go on to college. He'd joined the high school's advanced math team while still in middle school, and though his parents hadn't initially approved when he'd tried out for the boys' baseball team the following year, they'd changed their opinion as soon as they watched him steal bases to set new school records.

That boy could fly, let me tell you.

He was also going to attend Stanford next fall on a full ride scholarship, but he'd gotten his early acceptance letter two months ago, while Bridget had been left sweating out the decision.

"I assume Cai knows you got in," I said.

"He was the first one I called after I got the letter on Saturday afternoon," Bridget told me. "We were going to go out to celebrate, but his cousins in St. Paul were coming over for a big family dinner that night, so he came over yesterday afternoon instead."

She abruptly stopped smiling.

"Were you at that meeting where they found the dead woman in a pool of coffee?"

It took me a second to follow her quick jump in topic.

"The birding meeting at the university?" she clarified. "You go to those things, I know you do. Cai's cousin Pheej went to it, and he told everyone about the murder when they all had dinner together on Saturday night."

I was still trying to decide how much to share with her, but based on the way she was carrying the conversation all by herself, I'd be lucky to get a single word in at all, let alone a full sentence of information.

Which, I'd learned long ago, was not unusual with teenage girls. Especially verbal ones, like Bridget. I think it was programmed into their hormones.

"Oh, my gosh!" my scholastic star continued. "You were there! That's right! Cai said his cousin asked him if he knew you, because he'd met you at the meeting and you discovered the body and then you went to the brewery to see some bird. Oh, my gosh!" she repeated. "You found a dead person!"

My eyes automatically glanced up at my open doorway, and I fully expected to see my boss, Mr. Lenzen, standing there, struck speechless with fury. Mr. Lenzen, the high school's assistant principal, hated it when I found dead bodies, which I'd unfortunately done a few times in the past few years.

Okay, it had happened five times in less than two years, but at least I hadn't found any dead bodies on school grounds or during the school day. I'd been very careful to limit my body-finding to my personal time.

Not that Mr. Lenzen appreciated my thoughtfulness. He still threatened me with job suspension every time I got pulled into a murder investigation.

The man clearly had no sense of civic duty, let alone a sense of humor.

"Geez, Bridget, keep it down," I said, motioning with my hands to lower her volume.

"So, you met Pheej, right?" she barreled on. "Cai's cousin? He's really smart, too, but I think he's a little weird. I mean, he's a nice guy and all, but he has some kind of creepy ideas about spirits and stuff like that."

"Spirits?"

Bridget stood up and plucked her acceptance letter off my desk. "Like in religion. Pheej believes there are all these spirits around us—like house spirits and the spirits of ancestors. He claims he even had a photo of a ghost from this summer." She folded the letter and neatly slid it back into its envelope. "But he won't show it to anyone because he says he doesn't want to lay a curse on anyone. A *curse*. You know what I think?"

She paused to give me a knowing look.

"I think either he's making it all up, or he was doing something *illegal* when he took it, and that's why he won't show it to anyone."

I thought about the bright young math scholar I'd met at the MOU meeting. Pheej hadn't struck me as the delinquent type, and

I'd worked with enough of those in my career as a high school counselor to know one when I saw one. Delinquents and scholars were not birds of a feather, nor did they flock together. Pheej was as nerdy as I'd been at that age, and believe me, I was nerdy. But I'd always felt at home with birders, and I'd seen that same level of comfort in Pheej on Saturday.

Before I could ask her to elaborate, though, Bridget slipped the envelope into her schoolbag and hoisted it over her shoulder in one quick move. "I have to go meet with the other student government officers in the cafeteria," she said. "We're doing candy cane grams for a fundraiser again this year. See you, Mr. White."

She scurried out the door, leaving me to mull over what she'd said.

Candy cane grams again this year.

That meant I would be finding bits of peppermint ground into the heels of my shoes for the next three months, because last year, candy canes seemed to consistently end up crushed in the hallways. The school janitors were not going to be happy.

Again.

Then I thought about what she'd said about Pheej.

He believed in spirits.

Well, so did a million other people. Nothing weird there, as long as he wasn't involved in public conversations with them. *That* would be a little awkward, not to mention scary.

Besides, I knew for a fact that a belief in spirits was part of the Hmong heritage. Given that we had a small group of Hmong students at Savage High, I'd learned a little from them about their cultural and religious heritage. In fact, many of the students straddled two worlds: the one their parents, or grandparents, knew in Laos and the one that surrounded them in America. When I'd met Pheej on Saturday, he'd impressed me as one of those kids who was quietly making the most of his opportunities by joining activities that suited his talents, like math team and birding. He wasn't afraid to embrace what he found good in the culture even if it was foreign to his family roots.

At the same time, he'd been respectful and polite with everyone he met, which I'd noticed was characteristic of our Hmong students who came from families that continued to practice their cultural traditions. Pheej's modest, but obvious, pride in his photo of Ron and the Chimney Swift also impressed me with his maturity, not to mention his willingness to present a report at the MOU meeting to a room filled with strangers. Based on my solid first impression of the boy, I couldn't imagine the young Hmong lying to Bridget about taking a photo to mask being involved in some kind of criminal activity.

Then again, anyone looking at me would undoubtedly see a respectful, quiet, responsible, honest, law-abiding citizen . . . unless that person happened to be a police officer standing on the other side of my driver-side car door, writing out a speeding ticket for me, which has happened more times than I liked to admit. It wasn't that I willfully broke the law, either.

I just had a bad habit of forgetting that my foot was pressing down on the accelerator when I was trying to catch a bird sighting to add to my life list.

So I guess I could be guilty of misplaced enthusiasm, perhaps, as in "misplaced" on my gas pedal.

Criminal intent? Not a chance.

As for spirits and curses, I knew those things were very real for many traditional Hmong families, and I suspected Pheej's comments about them were grounded in his religious perspective. Besides, while I was no authority on world religions, I was pretty sure a photo alone couldn't curse someone, even if it did have a ghostly image.

The sudden chirping of my cell phone made me forget about Pheej and Bridget when I saw who was calling.

"Hey, Nip," I said. "Are you over at Harry's place?"

"Is this Bob White?" an unfamiliar female voice asked.

I looked at the phone in my hand. I was sure I'd seen Nip's name displayed on my caller ID.

"Yes," I said into the phone's speaker. "Who's this?"

"Mr. White, I'm with the county paramedic crew. We're trying to locate some family for Ken Kniplinger. Since your number was the last one called on his cell phone, we thought we'd start with you."

My mouth wouldn't work to form any words.

"Mr. Kniplinger has had a heart attack," the woman explained, "and we're transporting him to the hospital. He was shoveling snow in his driveway when a neighbor saw him fall down. We're trying to locate next of kin."

"Is he . . . ?" I asked, immediately realizing they wouldn't give me any information because of patient confidentiality. "I'm his nephew," I blurted out. "On his sister's side."

So much for that honesty trait I'd just been claiming.

"I'm so sorry, Mr. White. Your uncle's dead."

I laid the phone on my desk.

Nip was dead.

Harry Harrison was dead.

Trisha Davis was dead.

Sonny Delite was dead.

I was now the only records committee member left.

Coincidence, right?

My thoughts spun back to Pheej, and Bridget's comments about his mystery photo and a curse.

"Yes," I said aloud, finding some comfort in the almost-normal tone of my voice. "It's just a coincidence."

Somehow, talking to myself didn't make me feel a whole lot better.

Worse, I couldn't stop thinking the word *curse*, as in the *Curse of the Records Committee*. Did that make me superstitious, or just suspicious?

Either way, my gut said it wasn't good.

This was not the way to start a new week.

CHAPTER FIVE

LUCE WAS IN THE KITCHEN, stirring a pot of her mouthwatering chili, when I walked into the house after work. God love her, she always knew exactly what I needed, and the only thing that was going to get me through a lousy late-start Monday was a bowl of her chili.

I hung up my parka on the brass wall hooks in our tiny mudroom just as I caught a whiff of her pecan cornmeal muffins baking. If my mouth hadn't already been watering, the scent of the muffins alone would have released a flood of saliva—Pavlov's dogs had nothing on me when it came to conditioned response. After fourteen months of marriage, I could hardly even think of my gastronomic wizard of a wife without experiencing a rush of food-related responses, chief among them being automatic salivation and a rumbling stomach. While those behaviors might not qualify as the most romantic to many women, I'd lucked out with Luce.

She loved it when her cooking brought me to my knees.

Or to the table, as it were.

"I'm so sorry about Nip," she said over her shoulder as she stirred the pot on the stove. "I know he was one of your first birding buddies."

I went to her and slipped my arm around her waist and dropped a kiss on her cheek. Her face was warm from the heat rising up from the chili, and the wisps of her blonde hair that had straggled out of her long ponytail curled slightly along her neck.

She looked like a goddess of domesticity.

Not that I'd ever say that to her, unless I wanted a swift kick in the shins. "Goddess" she would like. "Domesticity," not so much.

I opted for a different compliment that wouldn't get me injured.

"You're an artist in the kitchen," I said.

"I know," she replied, turning to give me a smile. "That's why the conference center pays me the big bucks to create pretty little petits fours for their guests. Edible art is very profitable."

"Thank goodness," I told her. I took her chin in my hand and turned her head so I could plant a real kiss on her lips.

"What was that for?" she asked when I pulled back.

"For being here. For being you." I brushed a strand of loose hair off her cheek. "I can't possibly be cursed, right?"

Luce tapped my forehead with her finger. "Hello?" she said. "Anybody home? What in the world makes you think you're cursed?"

I shook my head to clear it of the nagging feeling I'd had all day that something bad was going to happen to me.

"I know it's silly," I began to explain, "but it's just so weird that Trisha, then Harry, and now Nip . . . I mean, three people whose only shared connection was being on the records committee, and they all die within three days . . . that's one a day," I pointed out.

"Yes, it is," Luce agreed. "You count very well. But Trisha was murdered, and Harry was elderly and in poor health, and Nip— well, every time we have a heavy snow, someone overdoes it with shoveling and has a heart attack. You know that."

"I do," I said. "But it's too coincidental."

"And so you've decided it's a curse? Really, Bobby?"

Luce took the spoon out of the chili and laid it on the stovetop. Of course she was right—the idea of a curse was ridiculous. I knew that.

But I also remembered Pete Maas saying he couldn't let go of his resentment over losing a possible state record until he felt that justice was done. Exactly what he meant by that, I hadn't figured out yet, but the fact remained that four of the five people who had denied his claim were now dead.

If it wasn't a curse, could it just be murder?

That idea was equally ridiculous. Unless Pete Maas had the ability to stop a man's heart from a distance, or could order up a dangerous snowfall to compel Nip to overexert himself into a heart attack, our denied birder could not have been behind their deaths.

This wasn't some harebrained plot created by a cozy mystery author.

This was life.

Weird things happened.

Deal with it.

"Do you still want to go to the Birds and Beers tonight in downtown Minneapolis?" Luce asked. "I'm sure the roads are all fine by now, and I heard that Duc Nguyen is going to be there."

She ladled chili into two bowls and set them on our kitchen island bar. I grabbed some napkins from the cupboard and soup spoons from a drawer while she took the cornmeal muffins out of the oven.

"He's still in town?" I asked. I'd assumed he'd left after the Saturday fiasco of the MOU meeting.

"There was a posting on the MOU network from Birdchick," Luce explained. "She said Duc would be there at the Birds and Beers tonight at the Black Forest Inn, and they're going to have some kind of contest to determine who makes the best tweets."

"Treats?" My wife was sounding like the old Tweety Bird cartoon character, as in *I tawt I taw a puddy tat!* "They're having a cook-off in the Black Forest Inn's kitchen?" I asked her.

45

Luce laughed and smacked me lightly on the arm with an oven mitt.

"No, not treats, you idiot," she said. "Tweets. As in Twitter. Social networking. Since they both write popular birding blogs, I think they're going to pit their tweeting skills against each other."

I wasn't surprised. I'd known Birdchick a long time. If anyone could come up with some off-the-wall event, it would be Sharon. A few years ago, she did a book signing at an enormous local discount store, and after she realized the store had set her books up next to a display of coffins, she offered to sign those as well.

Shoot. I wondered if the news of Nip's heart attack had made the rounds.

A lot of the people in the Minnesota birding community were close friends, and they regularly kept in touch. For all I knew, both Nip's and Harry Harrison's deaths had already been shared on the MOU network. Since I'd spent my snow-shortened school day grinding out college recommendation letters for my students, I hadn't had the time to check my personal email for MOU updates.

"Yeah, I think we should go," I finally answered her question. "In light of the weirdness that's been going on with birders in the last few days, it'd probably make everyone feel better to hang out together for a little while."

"Birds of a feather flock together, right?" Luce smiled.

"If you say so," I replied. "I just think a couple of cold beers sounds pretty good."

WE WERE ON OUR WAY downtown within the hour, and as Luce had predicted, the roads were all plowed and easily traveled. I made a slight detour west so we could circle Lake Calhoun on our way to the Black Forest—a birder had posted seeing a Great Black-backed Gull on the city lake yesterday, and I was curious to see if it was still around in tonight's twilight.

"I think we're too late, Bobby," Luce said when we pulled into a parking area on the north side of Calhoun. Beyond my car windows, the lake shimmered in the frigid cold, ringed with ice and small mountains of snow that plows had piled up. I couldn't see anything on the water, and the sky was already too dark to spot any late flyers.

"This is why birders need another hobby for the winter in Minnesota," I said. "The daylight hours are too short to go chase a bird after work, and by the time it's light enough in the morning to see anything, I'm already in the office."

"You should demand the window office at the high school next year," Luce suggested. "You've been a counselor there—how long now? Can't you pull seniority or something? At least then you might see a bird or two on winter days."

I thought about my cubby-hole of an office that had more in common with a broom closet than a counseling site. One day in the distant future, archaeologists would uncover the ruins of Savage High School and decide my office was a holding cell.

Either that, or one big recycling container filled with drafts of unfinished college recommendation letters.

It hadn't exactly been my most productive day at work between thinking about curses and composing lukewarm evaluations, to put it mildly. In fact, I was seriously considering purchasing a rubber stamp that read "do not return to sender" to use on counselor report areas on applications.

"A window would be wonderful," I agreed with Luce. "But to get that particular office, I'd also have to be the department chairperson, and believe me, I'll take bird-less days over that alternative any day."

A white glide of big wings passed over the hood of my car.

"Was that . . ."

"A Snowy Owl," I finished Luce's sentence, complete disbelief in my voice.

"No," she said, sitting forward in her seat and trying to peer through the windshield.

I hopped out of the car and searched the low-hanging branches around the parking area's perimeter.

"Over there," came Luce's voice from the far side of the car. She'd gotten out of her seat at the same time I had. "On the back of that park bench," she said, pointing to a bench surrounded by mounds of snow. "What in the world is it doing here?"

I walked around the side of the car to join her in staring at the big bird. Snowy Owls were basically diurnal—they did their hunting and feeding in the day when they summer in their Arctic breeding habitat. In the winter, however, they tend to hunt more in the early morning or late evening, and sometimes even into the night. Regardless of their meal times, though, they're usually found near large open spaces, not in the middle of busy cities like Minneapolis.

"Maybe it's the Snowy Owl everyone sees near the airport in the winter," Luce said, "and the storm last night blew it up this way. Although that'd be the opposite direction of the winds we had," she added. "The winds were from the north last night."

I strained to see the owl clearly since its white plumage made it almost disappear against the snowy backdrop. At the same moment, it swept away across the park, low to the ground, then angled up and off into the darkness.

"You saw it, right?" I asked my wife. "I didn't just imagine this?"

Luce nodded. "Yup. I saw it. You've got an eyewitness."

We both climbed back into the SUV.

"No one will believe this," Luce said as she buckled her seat belt.

"I know," I agreed and shrugged. "Well, we know we saw it. That's good enough for me. It's not like I'm trying to get a state record."

I suddenly remembered Pete Moss's comments about his big year of birding and how he'd been denied a state record.

Was it possible he'd actually seen a Chimney Swift in late November?

Would anyone believe we'd just seen a Snowy Owl in the middle of Minneapolis after dark?

That was the tricky thing about birds. Just when you think all the research is done and compiled about a bird's habits and habitats, it shows up where—and when—it doesn't belong.

Take, for instance, the Rufous-Necked Wood-Rail that took American birders by surprise—a HUGE surprise—a summer ago when it walked through a photo being taken of a Little Bittern at the Bosque del Apache National Wildlife Refuge in New Mexico. Normally at home in Mexico's tropical forests and down through Central America to northern Peru, the Wood-Rail caused an impromptu tidal wave of birders to head for the refuge and see the bird, which had never before been sighted in North America. I remember seeing an interview with Matt Daw, the young birder from North Carolina who first saw the Wood-Rail in the eye of his camera. He said he was so stunned, he dropped the camera. The news of the sighting—a U.S. record—flew through birding networks and even made headlines on national television.

Why the bird was walking around in New Mexico was anyone's guess. It could have been a result of unusual weather, strong winds, a change in food sources, faulty GPS, or bad advice from an inexperienced travel agent. No matter the reason, the Wood-Rail made a walk-on appearance that turned it into a national celebrity among birders.

And no one expected it, just like I hadn't expected to see a mature Snowy Owl sitting on a park bench at Lake Calhoun on a December evening.

At some point, out of curiosity, I might check to see if other Snowy Owls had been sighted in the lake's vicinity, but I didn't have any illusions that it might be a state record. The record bird sightings I did have were the results of challenging chases, and that was what appealed the most to me—the challenge of finding a rare bird. I liked my lists as much as the next birder, but competing to have the most state records had never been my priority.

Unlike Pete Moss, apparently.

I carefully guided the SUV back onto Lake Street and headed west to Eat Street and the Black Forest Inn. Despite the road crews' best efforts, some of the corners I navigated were slick with ice, and the end of the SUV swerved more than once. I found a parking space across the street from the restaurant, and Luce and I waited at the corner for the "walk" signal.

"You made it," Birdchick called from the opposite curb. She stood in the cold and rubbed her gloved hands together. "I wasn't sure if you'd risk the drive up here from Savage."

The traffic light changed to green, and the white pedestrian crossing light told us to walk, so we did. At the same moment, car breaks squealed, and out of the corner of my eye, I saw a mass of metal, headlights, and taillights spinning toward us in the cross-walk.

I grabbed both of Luce's shoulders and wrenched her back with me two big strides just in time to avoid getting sideswiped by the out-of-control car. Sharon screamed from the other side of the street as the car finally corrected its spin and shot off around the corner, narrowly missing running up on the curb where she'd been standing a moment before.

"Are you all right?" I asked Luce, turning her to face me.

Her face looked pale under the street lights, but her blue eyes were electrified.

"I'm fine," she said, her voice breathy, her chest rising and falling with a blast of adrenalin. "Did we almost get run down?"

"I'm not sure," I answered. "It must have been a patch of ice on the road, and the driver didn't see it in time to brake enough."

My eyes darted in Sharon's direction. She held herself plastered against the wall of the Black Forest Inn.

"Are you all right?" I called to her.

"I think so," she yelled back. "Am I nuts, or was that guy trying to kill me?"

Her words stopped me cold.

Actually, I was already plenty cold—it was December in Minnesota, after all. And despite the old one-liner "Many are cold, but few are frozen," our winters can still be brutal, even dangerous: traffic fatalities on icy streets, for example, aren't the least of winter-related deaths.

I'd just never imagined it would be the cause of *my* death.

Maybe that was why Sharon's question struck a disturbing chord in me, and my first thought was *curse*, as in *I'd almost become a traffic fatality and that would make five of five Records Committee members dead.*

Sharon, however, had assumed the car had not only been heading in her direction, but that it also had been deliberately aiming for her.

A surprise delivery from a Secret Santa?

Somehow, I didn't think so.

So who was right? Was the almost-accident meant for me by way of a curse I hadn't asked for, or was Sharon expecting some bad luck herself?

As in really bad luck. Like murder.

I took a belated look down the street where the spinning car had roared off.

It was long gone.

I couldn't even have said what color the car had been, let alone which make or model. As a witness of an almost hit-and-run accident, I was worthless.

I was, however, very much alive.

Thank God.

Luce pulled me across the now-empty street, and we peeled Sharon away from the wall and led her into the warm entry of the restaurant.

"Are you okay?" Luce asked Birdchick, who was visibly shaking.

"Yyyyesss," Sharon said.

"Take some deep breaths," I coached her, my counselor training kicking in. I'd seen lots of kids shaken up over the years, and though Sharon wasn't going into shock, she wasn't her usual chipper self, either. I placed my hands on her shoulders and looked down into her face.

"Sharon," I said sternly, "focus on me for a minute."

She tipped her head back and looked into my eyes.

"I want you to take a deep breath and let it out slowly," I told her.

She sucked in her breath like she was about to dive underwater for hours, held it, her eyes enormously wide, and then blew it out like she was trying to empty her lungs down to her kidneys.

"Again."

She repeated the routine, and managed a small smile after exhaling. "Okay, I lied. I really wasn't totally okay. I am now, though. Thanks."

She brushed snow off the back of her hair where she'd jammed her head against the building in her effort to stay out of the path of the sliding car. She smiled again at Luce and me. Clearly, it was going to take more than a near-accident to keep her from making her appearance at Birds and Beer night.

Almost as if she had heard my thoughts, Sharon announced that she needed a beer. "Let's get this show on the road," she said. "There are birds to talk about, and beers to drink."

Luce patted Sharon's arm in reassurance. "I'm sure it was a fluke. I don't expect cars to come spinning at me, either, and I don't even want to think what may have happened if Bobby hadn't pulled me back so fast."

That made two of us. And then I suddenly realized that *if* there were a Records Committee curse, and *if* it was now pursuing me, it might slop over onto Luce, as well.

Crap.

But that train of thought got immediately derailed when Sharon quietly laid her hand on my arm, looked around to see if anyone else was within hearing distance, and said, "I'm so sorry, you guys. I never considered I might endanger anyone else just by being here."

A chill slid down my spine, and it wasn't from the fingers of icy wind that crept in around the edges of the Black Forest's oaken front door.

"What are you talking about?" I asked Birdchick.

"Trisha's murder on Saturday," she whispered, her face ashen. "It was supposed to be me bringing in that coffee, remember? Whoever killed Trisha, was looking for me."

CHAPTER SIX

I HEFTED MY STEIN OF BEER and clinked it against Luce's glass of white wine as all of us in the Black Forest's bar took a drink in memory of good birding with Trisha, Harry, and Nip. I was still trying to decide if Sharon's suspicion held any weight, but I was having a hard time believing someone would mistake Trisha for Sharon, let alone that someone would plot to kill Sharon right there at the annual MOU meeting.

And the idea that the same someone, after realizing his or her mistake in killing Trisha instead of Sharon, would then try to run Birdchick down on a street corner, was absolutely laughable.

Yet . . . crazy killers did crazy things. That's why we called them crazy, right? And based on what Sharon had shared with Luce and me while we had waited for our drinks to arrive at our tiny table, there were several reasons to believe there just might be some kind of crazy person on Sharon's tail.

But he wasn't looking to be her Secret Santa, that was for sure.

"I've been getting weird emails for a while now," Sharon had confided in us after we'd greeted the fifteen or so other birders at the bar and taken the table. "Mostly they were about my new book published last month, about how I was no expert, and the publishers would be sorry they hadn't signed a degreed ornithologist to write the book. Hey, Frank!"

Sharon had interrupted her story to smile brightly and wave at another birder who had just arrived. She even gave him her signature thumbs-up sign.

I had to hand it to her. Nobody in the Twin Cities birding community could network like Birdchick. Not even a near date with an ambulance slowed her down.

"Who's that?" I'd asked, not recognizing the guy. "The man with the hair brushed up in front. It reminds me of a crest of feathers."

"Frank Quinn," she'd answered. "He was on one of the Chimney Swift Sit teams last summer. I think Trisha told me once Frank was heavily involved in preserving historic buildings in St. Paul, and that's how he got hooked on the Chimney Swift programs. He might be a city councilman, too, or he ran for city council once. I can't remember."

Frank Quinn had waved back at Sharon and gone to join some other birders at the bar. A moment later, everyone was raising a glass to our fallen birding comrades.

"I even got one email," Sharon continued after taking a long drink from her beer, "that said the book contract should have gone to another birding blogger who had much better professional and academic credentials than I had."

"And who would that be?" Luce asked.

A burst of noise and loud, called-out greetings rolled across the room. I turned in my chair towards the bar's entrance to see who had arrived.

"Speak of the devil," Sharon said in a low tone.

I'd never met the man in person, but I recognized the newcomer immediately from his photo on his world-wide Internet blog, Duc on Ducks.

"Duc Nguyen?"

Sharon nodded. "My email non-fan said that Duc deserved the contract, and it was only a matter of time before my publishers realized their heinous mistake." She took another drink. "Henious. Really. So, so weird."

"Why would someone care so much about who wrote a certain book on birds?" Luce wondered aloud, watching the wine swirling in her glass as she slowly rotated the stem. "It's not like there isn't a big selection of birds and authors to choose from," she reasoned. She looked at Sharon. "What's so special about this particular book you just had published?"

"Nothing," Birdchick replied. "It's just a general guide to birding. The publishers asked several bloggers to submit sample chapters for their review, and they liked my chapter the best, so they gave me the contract. Of course," she added, "the book signings and media exposure are invaluable for me. With any luck, I can turn them into promotional opportunities to land other lucrative marketing jobs."

"Ah," I commented. "Birding for fame and fortune."

"It's my job," Sharon said, "and I'm lucky to have it. It pays my way so I can bird as a profession."

"Nothing wrong with that," Luce agreed.

No, there was nothing wrong with making your passion pay your bills. I had to admit I felt a fleeting twinge of jealousy.

But just a twinge.

Because despite all my griping about cafeteria duty, my shoebox of an office, and my totally no-sense-of-humor supervisor, Mr. Lenzen, I loved my day job. I liked the students, and I liked being a part of their lives during their high-school years. Sure, teenagers could be frustrating, infuriating, dumb as rocks, and manipulative. But they could also be endearingly vulnerable, surprisingly tough, sharp as tacks, and unwittingly hilarious. Counseling them was in my blood as much as birding.

Plus, they gave me candy cane grams every December. Not that I'm crazy about peppermint sticks, but the warm and fuzzy notes that came with them never failed to make my day.

If Sharon was right, however, her email detractor was clearly feeling something else, and it wasn't warm and fuzzy. It was also very personal, since the complaints had gone not to the publishers about their choice of Sharon as author, but to her inbox on her public blog.

"It's still a big leap to thinking that this unhappy reader was so nuts he or she came to the Bell Museum on Saturday through lousy weather," I reminded her, "let alone was planning to kill you."

"Except that I found a private message waiting for me on my Facebook page on Saturday afternoon," Sharon said grimly, "that read, and I quote, 'It should have been you.'"

"I assume you turned this all over to the police," Luce said.

"Not yet," Sharon answered, but then abruptly changed the subject as Duc Nguyen came to stand by our table.

"Birdchick, are you ready for our Tweet contest?" Duc asked, a big grin spreading across his face. "I'm going to smack you down with my amazing tweeting skills, you know."

"Over my dead body," Sharon shot back.

I couldn't believe she'd just said that.

I looked at Luce in disbelief.

She nodded back at me. *Yup, she did.*

Sharon stood up and curled her hand around Duc's arm and marched him back up to the bar, where she turned them both to face the assembled birders.

"Ladies and gentlemen," she announced, her big beaming smile spreading across her face. "For this evening's entertainment, my esteemed colleague, Duc Nguyen," she said with a nod of her head in his direction, "known to most of you as the blogger Duc on Ducks, has challenged me to a competition for the crown of the most followed birding blogger on Twitter."

A ripple of laughter circled the room along with a chorus of "Tweet-tweet."

As we watched, Birdchick and Duc pulled out their smartphones, and with a theatrical flourish, bowed politely to each other, then climbed up on tall chairs at the bar and faced the assembled birders.

"Let the chase begin!" Sharon called out, "and let the feathers fly!"

The two bloggers bent their heads over their phones and began to furiously type in tweets.

"Whoever would've thought you'd find birders more absorbed in what's in their palms inside than in what's in the trees outside?"

I looked to my left to see Ron Windingham drop a light kiss on Luce's cheek in greeting. In response, my wife patted the chair beside her that Birdchick had vacated.

"Ron! Sit with us," she commanded him. "I haven't seen you in ages."

"Not quite ages, Luce," he corrected her. "Five months, maybe? Mid-July, right? Hi, Bob," he added with a small wave.

"July," Luce agreed. "It was amazing."

Indeed, it was.

Luce and I had joined Ron to count swifts at Aquila Elementary School, an old school still in use in one of the inner ring suburbs of Minneapolis. Several locations around the Twin Cities had been selected for monitoring Chimney Swift populations that weekend in mid-July, and we'd decided to try our luck at the old one-story brick school. The site's most critical feature for the birds was the tall chimney stack that rose from the middle of the structure. Every evening at dusk, a large swirling cloud of Chimney Swifts funneled itself neatly into the narrow chimney to roost inside for the night.

Recalling the brilliant aerial display we'd witnessed there, I closed my eyes and tuned out the noise of the bar and the cheering that was being directed at Birdchick and Duc and replayed the memory of that warm July night last summer.

"THERE'S THE CHIMNEY," Luce said, pointing at the dull-brown chimney that rose almost 100 feet into the air above the sprawling one-level school. "It looks the same after all these years. I can remember coming here to watch my cousins sing in the school's annual Christmas concert, back when the schools still called them Christmas concerts, and not winter concerts."

"Boy, you're old," I teased her. "By the time I was in elementary school, they were always referred to as winter concerts. You really robbed the cradle when you married me."

She turned my way and stuck her tongue out. "I'm nine months older than you. That really makes me an older woman, doesn't it?"

I slipped my hand onto my wife's bare knee and gave it a warm squeeze. "You won't hear me complaining," I assured her.

"Keep your eyes on the road, Bobby," she laughed. "I'd hate to have you pulled over for reckless driving because you were making a pass at your wife."

"I don't get stopped for reckless driving," I informed her, though I did put my hand back on the steering wheel. "I'm the state speed demon."

"As most of the state patrol officers know," she reminded me.

"What can I say? They know me and love me. Over the years, I've helped many a patrol officer make his or her monthly ticket quota, not to mention all the fund-raiser raffle tickets I've bought."

I took a right and slowly drove down the block, looking for an open space to park the SUV. Summer adult league ball games were winding down on the athletic fields that surrounded the school, and I waited for one family to finish loading their trunk with bats and bases so I could take their parking space.

"I wonder if the people who live in this neighborhood are even aware of the swift colony inside the chimney," Luce said. "I don't see crowds of people gathering on the sidewalk to watch the show."

"There's still a little time before sunset," I pointed out. "There's one," I commented as I watched a lone Chimney Swift zip through the air over the school and disappear above the trees beyond the ball fields. "And there's Ron," I added, maneuvering the car smoothly against the curb to park.

We got out of the car and walked down the sidewalk to where Ron was setting up a folding lawn chair.

"You made it," he called out to us. "Another fifteen minutes or so, and the flying cigars should be gathering."

Luce laughed at his term for the Chimney Swifts, because "flying cigars" was exactly what a flock of Chimney Swifts resembled. Thanks to their short, stubby bodies, and slim curved wings, the birds could almost pass for an animated cartoon of flying stogies. What many people didn't realize about those flying cigars, though, was that they had an exceptional aerial talent: in flight, a swift was so incredibly agile that, when it made its impossibly fast turns, it appeared that its two wings beat at different speeds.

In truth, they didn't—wings beating at different speeds would cause so much instability and oscillation along the bird's body that it couldn't stay aloft. Instead, a Chimney Swift's blinding speed in banking creates a natural illusion because the human eye couldn't follow the bird's maneuvers fast enough. Whereas it looks to us, on the ground, like the bird's wings were alternating as it turned, actually the entire body of the bird tilted instantaneously, keeping the wings beating in unison.

That illusion, though, was good for plenty of controversy among birding experts back in the early 1900s.

Some things never changed, I guess—birding experts were always arguing over something, it seemed. Dare I mention the

Ivory-billed Woodpecker? Assumed extinct in the United States in the mid-1900s, there was a report of the bird in eastern Arkansas in 2005. To date, however, it hasn't been seen again despite many attempts and organized searches to find it, leading some experts to believe that the Ivory-billed Woodpecker is a buddy of Bigfoot. Sorry, I didn't mean to offend all the Bigfoot fans out there, but you get the idea.

Back to the swifts.

It wasn't until 1932, when one Myron Westover—yeah, I know, definitely a nerdy birder's name—used motion photography to prove that the Chimney Swifts adhered to aerodynamic laws of nature and always beat their wings in unison. To top it off, Westover showed his film to the members of the Bird Department of the American Museum. They agreed he'd proved the alternate-speed theorists wrong and gave him their unanimous stamp of approval.

Sort of like an elite Records Committee, I guess.

Geez, I wonder how they would have handled our own Pete Moss when they turned down his sighting of a Chimney Swift in December?

"I say, old chap, did you get a photograph? No? Tut-tut. I'm afraid we can't give you the record you desire. Go away."

Tut-tut. Those Chimney Swifts certainly had a track record for causing problems, didn't they?

But man, could they fly!

Seriously, if I could drive with half the control and skill a Chimney Swift was naturally endowed with for flying, I would've taken up professional racecar driving and become a world champion many times over.

But then, I wouldn't have a drawer full of losing raffle tickets, either.

Gee, what a disappointment.

By the time we reached Ron at his lawn chair, the noise level on the street had risen considerably. Beyond where he was setting up, a line of cars was waiting to turn into the parking lot near a concession stand busy with incoming ball players, wives, and girlfriends for a late round of games beneath the field lights. Loud laughter and familiar greetings floated on the warm air over to where we stood, and the sound of honking horns and accelerating engines only added to the festive atmosphere of the evening games.

I thought about Luce's earlier comment about the neighborhood residents—did the people who lived around the old school know that within a few minutes they might be able to watch an aerial ballet of high speed choreography and phenomenal precision? Or were they only focused on the ball games about to begin?

"They're starting to show up," Ron said, pointing at ten, then fifteen, then thirty Chimney Swifts beginning to fly wide circles high overhead.

I watched the birds fly in rapidly shifting patterns as more swifts seemed to appear out of thin air. Any musings I might have had about what people valued, or about what they were missing when they kept their eyes on the ball and not on a bird, vanished, as suddenly there were hundreds of swifts sweeping and spiraling in dense black formations against the dusky sky.

"Here we go," Luce breathed, her chin tilted up, her attention locked on the swirling flock.

The birds circled the fields and the school, weaving and flowing through the evening, making pass after pass around the chimney that now stood silhouetted against the darkening night.

A single swift broke out of the cloud of birds and dived into the chimney.

"One," I counted aloud, keeping my gaze fixed on the top of the chimney. "I can't believe all those field lights don't keep the swifts away from here."

"Two," Ron said as a second bird shot down into the mouth of the tall tower. "Three. Four. It varies by year, Bob," he said. "Some years we've had high counts here, and other years—five, six," he continued to count, "it's been low to non-existent."

"Seven. Ten. Fifteen." Luce was trying to keep up as the birds peeled off from the massive swirling flock and dropped into the chimney with increasing frequency. "Twenty. Thirty. How can they do that?"

Neither Ron nor I attempted to answer her since we were both keeping our own counts as the Chimney Swifts went to roost for the night. Ten minutes later, we compared our counts and decided there had been somewhere between two hundred and two hundred twenty-three birds.

"Not bad," Ron said. "I saw some numbers from last night's count across the state, and Rochester was the winner with 371 swifts at a school with an old brick chimney like that one."

He nodded at the Aquila stack behind us that now reflected a sheen of light from the illuminated ball fields.

"And even though a lot of sites had double digit reports," he continued, "there were also plenty with less than ten, which might be the result of either there being nesting pairs in those chimneys and towers, or just more evidence of the decreasing population we've seen in the last few years."

"State-wide?" Luce asked.

Ron folded up his lawn chair and shook his head. "According to our records, we've got forty percent fewer Chimney Swifts now than we had just a few years ago," he explained. "People don't build chimneys like they used to, and unfortunately, some of the old and best roosting spots for the swifts—like this one right here—have been torn down."

"It's really sad to think that future generations of birders might not be able to see what we watched tonight," Luce said.

"I've seen 2,500 Chimney Swifts congregating at that tower before migrating south in the fall," Ron told us. "The idea that no one will ever see that kind of natural spectacle again is part of the reason I keep so involved in Chimney Swift conservation projects. Like building swift towers with Boy Scout troops, and hoping that preservation groups will keep some of these old brick buildings intact."

A ROUND OF APPLAUSE in the Black Forest Inn's bar area brought me back from my summer memory to see Birdchick climbing up on top of the polished bar counter to raise her cell-phone in victory and take a grand bow before the Birds and Beer crowd.

"Always the show-woman," Ron chuckled. "No wonder so many businesses hire her to do promotions for them. She's got the dramatic flair and talent for it, that's for sure. All the world's a stage, I guess."

I watched Sharon accept a shiny plastic tiara from one of the birders near the bar. Funny, I'd never thought of Sharon as a drama queen, though now that Ron had mentioned it, I could see how mindful Birdchick was about her exuberant public persona. That was probably why she'd regained her composure so quickly after the car-scare outside. She'd had fans to face and wasn't about to disappoint them with a trembling lip and distracted attention. Even a local celebrity had to keep up appearances.

Two birders reached up to help Sharon climb down from the bar, and I noticed one of them was the fellow Sharon had waved at earlier: Frank Quinn.

"That guy," I said to Ron, pointing in Frank's direction, "do you know him? Sharon said he's a Chimney Swift fan and a city councilman."

Ron studied the man in question. "It's Frank Quinn," he confirmed. "He's been doing the Chimney Swift Sit with us for a couple years now. He generally observes at the old Hamm's brewery in St. Paul." He paused and his voice turned soft. "He and Trisha did that site together."

We both fell silent for a moment, as the tragedy of the weekend came home to us again.

"I got the impression Sharon didn't know him that well," Luce said. I followed her gaze to see Sharon and Frank, arms around each other's shoulders as they clinked together fresh steins of beer. "Guess I was wrong."

"Oh, they've known each other a long time," Ron corrected her. "Sharon's been doing commercials for Frank's air conditioning and heating company for years."

He paused again and tapped a finger to his right temple. "In fact, I thought I heard that Frank wasn't happy with all of Sharon's other promotional commitments and was thinking of replacing her."

The rosy color typically highlighting his cheeks suddenly washed out.

"Are you all right, Ron?" Luce asked, placing a hand on his arm in alarm.

Don't even think heart attack, I told myself sternly, staring at Ron. *There is no Records Committee Curse following me around. This is a fluke. Ron is fine.*

Ron didn't answer Luce, his eyes locked on Sharon and Frank across the room.

"Ron, you're all right, right?" I asked, still telling myself *no curse, there is no curse.*

He finally turned his head to look first at Luce, then at me. "I heard that Frank was going to fire Sharon. And hire Trisha in her place," he added.

I remembered Sharon's insistence that whoever had killed Trisha had really meant to kill the Birdchick instead.

"This is not good," I muttered. I glanced again at Sharon and Frank laughing together at the bar.

Somebody was putting on a show, I realized, but I sure couldn't tell who.

More disturbing, though, was the one word that kept repeating in my head: *Why?*

CHAPTER SEVEN

OVER THE RIM OF MY FIRST CUP of morning coffee, I watched through the front window of our townhome as a small group of five Bohemian Waxwings busily devoured what was left of the fall fruit on our crabapple tree. Although the species was a regular winter visitor to Minnesota, it was primarily seen north of Duluth. The fact that I'd seen reports of the birds as far south as Winona this year was unusual, to say the least. Cedar Waxwings, on the other hand, were a familiar sight year-round for us.

In fact, if I'd had a few more beers last night, I might even have missed recognizing the Bohemians in our tree, assuming they were their more common cousins. As it was, though, I'd focused so much on the weird undercurrents I was picking up in the bar that I'd totally forgotten to sample any other of the Black Forest's brews. Then, after we got home, thinking of the odd glances I'd caught flying between Sharon, Frank, and Duc had kept me awake long past my bedtime. As a result, my mind was sharper this morning than it usually was after a Birds and Beers evening.

"Bohemian Waxwings," Luce said as she stopped beside me with her own cup of coffee. "Their black masks always make me think of the Lone Ranger," she said. "Without the horse, though. And those white patches on the wings? That's how you know they're the good guys."

"No," I said. "That's how you know they're Bohemians and not Cedars. Along with their chestnut-colored undertail coverts."

Luce planted a kiss on my cheek. "Ooh, is someone a little grouchy this morning? You didn't sleep well, did you?"

I gave her a kiss back. "Sorry. No, I had trouble falling asleep. I kept trying to make sense of what was going on with Birdchick and Frank and Duc."

Luce took a sip of her coffee. "I think it's all business related. Birdchick beat out Duc for the book, and Frank doesn't like his spokesperson representing so many other companies. He probably feels like he's losing some control over his promotional image if Sharon becomes identified with a lot of other businesses."

"And what do you think of Sharon saying someone's harassing her?"

Luce shrugged. "I'd say it's possible. Thinking that someone wants to kill her, though, that's a bit over the top, I'd say."

"A drama queen?" I asked her.

Luce took another sip of her drink and looked at me over the rim of her cup.

"Maybe. But you're not her high school counselor, Counselor White, nor is she one of your students. Remember, Sharon works in promotions, the business of getting attention. It's her job," she added.

I clinked my coffee mug against hers. "How do you get so smart in the morning?"

Luce shot me a challenging look.

"Are you saying I'm not smart in the afternoon?" she accused. "Or evening?"

"Oh, no," I laughed, "you're not going to get me to answer that one. I may not be the longest-wed husband on the block, but I know a trick question when I hear one."

I put my empty cup down on the side table next to the sofa and wrapped my arms around my wife.

"You are the most brilliant woman I've ever known," I told her. "If you think of the Lone Ranger every time you see a Bohemian Waxwing, I'm happy for you. If you say the Birdchick is just doing her job, I believe you. And if you plan to make your home-made lasagna tonight for dinner, I'll worship the ground you walk on."

Luce smiled. "I don't recall saying anything about lasagna," she pointed out.

"Lasagna!" I said. "What a great idea. I knew there was a reason I married you, besides the fact that you're brilliant all the time, of course."

"And I like birds, too," Luce reminded me.

"Yes, you do," I agreed. I leaned around to whisper in her ear. "And if you want to sneak out of work for a half-hour right after the lunch rush, I heard there's a Pacific Loon out at Lake Waconia. Personally, I doubt the sighting, but if it's there, we could add it to our county lists."

"You're sending shivers down my spine," she whispered back. "Pick me up at one o'clock?"

"I'll be there," I said, giving her a final kiss on the lips before I grabbed my coat and briefcase to head out to the garage. "And in case you're wondering—that's *my* job."

"Picking me up?" she laughed.

"No," I said, giving her a big wink. "Sending shivers down your spine."

"Better you than sub-zero temperatures," she said. "Stay out of trouble, gorgeous."

As I drove to school, I thought more about what Luce had said about Sharon and her promotional career. My own experience with marketing and sales was limited to a job in a bird store the summer after I turned sixteen. All I had to do was ring up purchases and try to keep the owner's parrot from letting loose with a string of expletives while customers browsed through the birdfeeders and wind chimes. By the end of the summer, I was an expert in timing—every time the parrot started to curse, I'd make sure to start ringing the closest set of big chimes to distract any customers and drown out his obscene monologue.

I decided I never wanted to work with a parrot again.

On the upside, the store manager begged me to come back the following summer since she'd never sold so many high-end wind chimes in one season.

Needless to say, I declined the offer, though I did come to appreciate that timing can make or break a sale.

Actually, I've found that success in any endeavor depended partially on timing, but when it came to birding, it was essential. You wouldn't find a hummingbird in December in Minnesota, or a Pacific Loon, like the one I was hoping to see at lunch, in the middle of summer. Like I said a while ago, unless a fluke weather event carried it in, a bird was where and when it typically appeared. Without the right timing, you just couldn't be one hundred percent certain of what you saw.

Or as it had happened to Pete Moss and the Chimney Swift he claimed to find out of season, the wrong timing could rule it out.

Just like my poor timing had ruined my emergency plan yesterday to empty the vending machine in the teachers' lounge in order to supply Alan with his first Secret Santa gift. A minute too late, and he'd beat me to it. That wasn't happening again this morning, though. I patted my parka's deep pocket and felt the shape of another bag of my brother-in-law's favorite candy.

No excuses for Santa today, I thought.

"I've got your back and your stomach, brother," I promised Alan in absentia.

I signaled my turn into the school parking lot and pumped my brakes to be sure I didn't spin out on any invisible ice that might have formed overnight.

The thought immediately caused last night's terrifying moment to replay in my head.

Once again, I thanked God Luce and I hadn't been hurt.

But it made me rethink what had really happened.

From my angle on the street, I didn't think that car had been anywhere near Sharon on the opposite corner. It had passed a lot closer to Luce and me than to the Birdchick, yet she was the one who assumed it had been deliberately aimed at her. She'd explained why she'd had that reaction after we got inside the Black Forest, but now, in the clear light of morning, her response seemed a bit too theatrical to me, and Luce had agreed.

I mean, really, when Sharon confided that *"Whoever killed Trisha, was looking for me,"* someone could have cued a musical *don-don-don-DON*, and we wouldn't have batted an eye.

Not to mention the quick recovery Birdchick made after a supposed attempt on her life. For someone who claimed she'd almost been killed, she hadn't wasted any time regaining her composure.

And the out-of-control car? It had taken the corner with precision and sped neatly away.

Talk about good timing.

It reminded me of all those television commercials that warned "Do not attempt this at home. These are professional drivers on a closed course."

Sharon's comment a moment later, inside the restaurant's foyer, came back to me.

"Let's get this show on the road."

Now, as I pulled my own car into the school's parking lot, I found myself wondering if last night, the show had already started outside on the street. Had Sharon orchestrated a skidding car in front of witnesses to star in a drama of her own making?

And when it came to her story of threatening messages, wasn't that the perfect frosting for her cake of suspense? She said she hadn't shared it with the police, which didn't make any sense to me. If someone was stalking Sharon, and she had proof, she needed to go to the police with it to assist them with their investigation into Trisha's death.

Unless it was all a piece of fabricated drama.

I lifted my briefcase from the seat beside me and suddenly stopped cold.

Last night in the bar, I'd had the distinct feeling that someone was putting on an act.

At the time, though, I'd been watching the camaraderie between Sharon and Frank. If they were at odds over her promotional commitments, it hadn't stopped them from buying each other a round of drinks. To look at them laughing, you'd never suspect they weren't happy coworkers, yet according to Ron, they'd almost severed their business relationship.

Let me restate that.

Frank had almost severed the relationship. He'd wanted to can Sharon and hire Trisha, and, knowing Sharon, I couldn't imagine she'd make that easy for him in any way, especially when she was a local personality, nationally-known blogger, author, and darling of the birding world.

The Birdchick had promotional clout and a legion of fans. I had no doubt that with a few well-worded posts on the Internet, Sharon could make Frank miserable if she chose to do so. If she were in the market for financial vengeance, she might even be able to destroy his business with some strategically placed negative public comments.

You know the old saying, *"Hell hath no fury like a woman scorned."*

Which, when I thought about it that way, might give Frank a reason—or two—to want Sharon out of the comment-making business altogether.

As in permanently.

On the other hand, it could also possibly give Sharon a reason to want Trisha out of the competition for spokesperson employment. It's pretty hard for an employer to replace you with a dead person.

And as she herself had pointed out to me, Sharon had been the one to send Trisha to get the coffee.

Like I already said, timing was everything.

But who was doing the timing?

Frank?

Or Sharon?

If it was Frank, he wasn't very good at it, since Trisha—the woman he wanted to replace Sharon—was the person killed in the parking garage at the Bell Museum.

But if it was Sharon, the consummate performer as Ron had described her, then maybe the guilt she felt over sending Trisha for the coffee was, in truth, an act. And what better way to further convince your audience of your innocence than to stage an attack on your own person?

A bitterly icy gust of wind slapped my cheek as I climbed out of my car and headed for the school doors.

It almost knocked the wind out of me.

Instead, it knocked some badly needed sense back into my head.

What was I thinking?

The Birdchick—an internationally recognized birding expert—plotting to kill another birder? Just so she could continue hawking air conditioners for a small local company?

A business owner orchestrating a murder gone wrong because he didn't want to have to man up and fire his spokeswoman?

Seriously?

Clearly, I'd needed that cold slap more than I'd realized. The shortened days and extended darkness of the winter season must have been getting to me even more than usual. I wasn't suffering from Seasonal Affective Disorder so much as Amateur Sleuth Syndrome—forget being SAD, I was the new poster boy for ASS. And if anyone was being a drama queen, it was me.

Then it dawned on me: I was in birding withdrawal, one of the most insidious dangers of December in Minnesota for devoted birders like me. Good thing I was going to be getting a fix at lunch. As soon as I found that Pacific Loon with Luce, everything in my world would be right again. *Eyes on the prize*, I told myself. Think loon.

Not lunacy.

Bucking the cold wind, I pulled open the building door and stepped inside.

"Mr. White!"

Bridget, my Stanford-bound star, came barreling down the hall towards me.

"Mr. White, you have to do something!" she yelled as she got closer.

The next thing I knew, she latched onto my arm with a death grip.

"Cai is in jail," she cried. "He'll lose his scholarship! You can't let that happen!"

CHAPTER EIGHT

I WALKED INTO MY OFFICE with Bridget still attached to my arm and talking so fast about Cai and Stanford and jail that I couldn't begin to make sense of what was going on.

"Bridget," I interrupted her, "just sit down and tell me what happened, starting from the beginning. Slowly," I added.

She brushed her long brown bangs out of her eyes and took a deep breath.

"I wasn't there, so this is all from his sister Mim. She called me first thing this morning on my cell," she began. "Last night, Cai and Pheej—you know, his cousin you met at the birding meeting?"

I nodded. "Yes."

"They joined up with some of their other cousins in St. Paul who have been daring them—Cai and Pheej—to go—well—*exploring* with them."

"Exploring?"

Bridget hesitated. I could almost see the wheels turning in her head, trying to decide what and how much she could tell me.

"Bridget," I firmly told her, "if you want me to help, I need to know everything."

She frowned in consideration and for a moment refused to meet my gaze, then looked me straight in the eye.

"They went urban exploring at the old Hamm's brewery in St. Paul," she said. "You know what urban exploring is, right?"

I nodded again. I did know what it was, though I'd never met anyone who did it. Illegal and dangerous, urban exploration was a

75

hobby that involved getting into man-made places where you didn't belong, like condemned buildings, or towering rooftops, or city sewer systems, or abandoned factories. Once inside, usually at night, since most of the places were located on private property posted with "No Trespassing" signs, the UEs—urban explorers—would spend hours wandering around the place with flashlights just to see what was there. Some of them were photography buffs who wanted to document what they found, while others claimed they had an historical or artistic interest in exploring the sites. A lot of them, however, were adrenaline junkies who loved the thrill of danger and the challenge of getting into off-limits spaces undetected. Regardless of their motives, though, if police showed up, the UEs made a quick exit to avoid arrest.

"Cai got caught trespassing in the old Hamm's brewery," I said, fitting together what Bridget had told me.

"Yes!" she exclaimed. "And he'll lose his scholarship if you don't help him!"

I leaned back in my desk chair and crossed my arms over my chest. "Bridget." I was about to launch into the short version of my lecture about accepting responsibility and consequences, but she cut me off.

"Mr. White, you have to go to bat for Cai," she begged me. "He can't miss out on this scholarship. It's to Stanford!" she reminded me. "He's worked so hard to get there, and this, this is just a stupid thing he did. One stupid thing!"

If she was expecting an argument from me on that particular point, she sure wasn't going to get one.

Cai had definitely done a stupid thing.

Trespassing was a crime.

Even more than that, though, he could have been seriously injured.

Or killed.

Old buildings, and especially old crumbling ones, had a nasty reputation for falling down unexpectedly when kids were inside them breaking the law. The first time I ever heard about urban exploration, in fact, it was in connection with a news story about a twenty-year-old who fell thirty feet onto a concrete floor inside an abandoned train station in Michigan. It took emergency responders an hour to reach the kid because the building's stairway had collapsed. Fortunately, the basement had recently been drained of ten feet of toxic water, so neither the rescuers nor the injured kid suffered chemical burns or drowned in acid.

Gee, a hobby like that really separated the men from the boys, wouldn't you say?

More like the intelligent from the incredibly stupid, I'd say.

Anyway, given the heavy snowfall we'd already had this winter, and the accompanying stress that placed on any structure, let alone an abandoned brewery, I figured Cai was lucky he was in jail this morning, and not in a morgue.

"Please, Mr. White," Bridget pleaded. "Cai needs that scholarship. Heck, his whole extended family needs that scholarship. His aunts, his uncles, his cousins—they all came to America for a better life, and Cai's showing them the way to do that. Isn't that what education is all about?"

Ouch.

Bridget landed a hard hit below the belt with that one, and she knew it. As one of the staff sponsors of our school diversity club, I spent a lot of counseling time with our students who belonged to minority groups, encouraging them to work hard to succeed at school, so they could set good examples for their communities. Cai was one of my shining examples of that success, and the prospect of losing him as a role model was more than sobering—it was disastrous.

"You fight dirty," I told Bridget.

"Does that mean you'll help Cai?" Hope glowed on her face.

"Where is he being held?" I asked, thinking it odd that my student had actually been arrested. The police in Savage generally didn't keep high school kids overnight in the jail, unless they had prior warnings or an arrest record, neither of which applied in Cai's case. I assumed the St. Paul police had a similar policy. "You said he's still in jail, right?"

"In St. Paul," she said. "I wrote down the address his sister gave me. Their parents don't speak English very well, and she said they were too scared to go to the police station, because Cai had been arrested."

She handed me a notebook on which she'd written the address. I booted up my computer and located the jail, then punched in the number on my office phone.

"Why is there a chocolate duck on your desk?" Bridget asked, momentarily distracted from the Cai crisis by what appeared to be a large sculpted chocolate duck posed in a nest of bright green shavings on my desk.

I noticed the duck for the first time, too. It was actually kind of hard to miss, unless, of course, you were pre-occupied with getting one of your stand-out students out of jail.

"I think it's a surprise from my Secret Santa," I said, mentally noting that once again, someone had accessed my office before my arrival. Elway, our custodian, got another point in my Santa suspect column. He certainly had the opportunity and the means to make early morning deliveries.

Meanwhile, the ringtone continued to sound in my ear.

"I think that's coconut it's sitting in," Bridget observed. "It looks like the coconut my mother dyes at Easter for cupcake frosting."

She gingerly touched the green nest with the tip of a finger. "Yup, that's coconut, all right," she said. "Are you really going to eat it? Or is it like a work of food art? You know, like for display at the State Fair? "

A woman's voice answered on the other end of the phone connection, and I explained what I needed.

"Do you want me to connect you with the officer in charge?" she asked me.

"Yes, please," I said.

Like I wouldn't want to be connected since that was the reason I was calling? Well, duh.

I glanced up at Bridget, who was still studying my candy duck with an expression that landed somewhere between fascination and salivation.

"I'm being connected to the officer in charge," I told her.

Now that I looked more closely at the chocolate duck, it reminded me of something Luce probably would have made for the choco-holic fundraiser last Saturday.

A new voice came on the line, and I again explained why I was calling. After a few more exchanges with the officer, I ended the call and stood up.

"Looks like I'm off to St. Paul," I told Bridget. "Cai's still there."

Bridget's eyes misted over, and she sniffled once. "Thank you so much, Mr. White. You are the best counselor, ever."

I handed her a tissue from the box on my desk.

"Don't thank me yet," I said. "I don't know what I'll be able to do for him until I get there."

"You'll fix it. I know you will."

"Well, that at least makes one of us," I said, heading out my door.

I turned toward Patty Rodale, our (currently blonde) office receptionist, to let her know I was leaving. A single mom of two teenaged sons, Patty was the most colorful person I knew. Literally. I swore the woman spent her weekends planning out her daily hair color changes for the following week and then coordinating her outfits with her hair. Today, she was wearing a bright-yellow fuzzy sweater with her short spiky hair.

Put a beak on her and she could pass for a chicken.

"I've got an emergency in St. Paul with one of our students," I said. "I don't know when I'll be back. Will you reschedule my morning appointments with students?"

"Only if you give me some of that chocolate goose on your desk," Patty replied. "I could really go for some chocolate this morning."

"It's a duck," I told her, "and you can always go for chocolate, Patty. Tell you what—you reschedule my students, you get half the duck."

"Deal," she said. "But I still say it's a goose."

"If you were a birder, you'd know the difference," I said.

She waved me off. "It could be a hippopotamus for all I care, as long as it's chocolate. Go, already."

I stepped out into the hallway and almost collided with Paul Brand, our new art teacher on the high school faculty.

"You have a minute?" Paul asked.

"A minute," I replied. "I've got to drive to St. Paul. What's up?"

Paul casually crossed his arms over his chest and smiled. A one-time high school hockey star, Paul generally looked like he'd stepped right off the set of a men's fashion magazine shoot. This morning was no different: his blue-and-black-plaid flannel shirt, sleeves artfully rolled up to his elbows, hung open over a matching navy-blue turtleneck and navy-blue corduroy trousers. I almost expected his teeth to gleam with a superimposed sparkle.

"Whatever you did to straighten out Sara Schiller, it sure worked," Paul said. "Not only has she had perfect attendance for the last six weeks, but she's turned into an art protégé."

Sara, one of my habitual problem students, had started the semester by rarely attending her classes because she was joy-riding to Wisconsin during school hours. Since late October, though, Sara had demonstrated a dramatic turn-around in her attitude towards school, thanks to the mentoring she was getting from a World War II veteran who'd taken her under his wing.

The only part I'd played in my student's epiphany was shooting a tomato from a bazooka.

But that was a whole other story.

"Good to hear, Paul," I told Mr. GQ, trying to step around him.

He stepped in front of me.

"Seriously, Bob," he said. "I think Sara has real talent. You should come by my classroom and see the mural she's working on for our unit on street art. It's really powerful."

"Street art? You mean graffiti?"

"No. Not at all," he said, sounding slightly offended. "I teach art, not vandalism."

"Sorry," I apologized, though I wasn't exactly sure why I was apologizing, except that it just felt like the right thing to do. Gauging Paul's reaction changing from miffed to mollified, however, I was pretty sure I'd made the right call. The last time I'd talked with Paul, he was raving about scrapbooking and its ethnographic sensibilities.

That conversation hadn't gone especially well, either, as I recalled.

"Street art is post-graffiti," Paul clarified for me, not that I really cared what it was, seeing as I might be the most non-art person on the planet, and not to mention that at the moment, I was trying to get out of the building to go spring Cai from jail.

"Graffiti is with paint spray cans and primarily practiced as vandalism," Paul continued, clearly intent on correcting any misunderstanding on my part. "Street art is also called 'urban art,' or 'guerilla art,' and it's about social issues and existential questioning. It's a way of bringing attention to those issues through the artistic venue of community space. For artists who feel disenfranchised, it's a terrific medium to reach a broader audience than a traditional gallery. Brazil, in fact, legalized graffiti art in 2009 since it's regarded as one of the most outstanding examples of the contemporary urban art movement. It's been highly influential globally."

Right.

I didn't bother to tell him that he lost me at "existential questioning."

"Tell you what, Paul," I said, clapping him on the shoulder. "I'll stop in this afternoon. We can be guerillas questioning our existence together."

I hustled down the hallway and out the door.

Just as I reached my car in the parking lot, though, it dawned on me that Patty had known there was a candy duck on my desk, even though my office had been locked when I'd arrived with Bridget attached to my arm.

That meant that our receptionist must have seen my Secret Santa making the delivery.

Or that Patty was my Secret Santa.

Except that Patty didn't know the difference between a duck and a goose, which she would have known if she'd bought the candy sculpture on my desk. Not to mention it was physically impossible for Patty to handle chocolate without eating it.

I made a mental note to grill our receptionist when I got back. It was a matter of pride for me—every year, I challenged myself to identify my Secret Santa before the final staff banquet that ended the gift exchanging activity.

Okay, so maybe it wasn't the most critical challenge of my school year, but it beat trying to dream up positive-but-noncommittal things to say about slacker students on college applications.

Honestly?

The main reason I got a kick out of the whole Secret Santa thing was because it was a welcome distraction for me. I'm a birder, and winters in Minnesota can put a real damper on birding excursions—not only because the weather can shut everything down, but because we just didn't have the big variety of species in the winter that we got the rest of the year. It was hard to indulge in my addiction when the objects of my desire had literally flown the coop for the season. That was probably one of the biggest reasons we birders got so excited when a rarity showed up in the winter—it was like getting a life-saving fix when you'd been going through serious withdrawal.

And it was totally, completely, absolutely, legal.

Which refocused me on why I was already on my way out of the office when I'd only just arrived.

Cai Xiong was in jail.

I put my hand in my parka pocket to pull out my car keys and grabbed the bag of Alan's M&Ms instead.

Crap.

I hadn't had a chance to put them in his mailbox, and now I didn't know when I'd be back in the building today.

For a Secret Santa, I had to admit that I was pretty lame. As I got in the car to head to St. Paul to rescue Cai, I hoped I was doing a better job as a high school counselor. Driving to a city jail in order to bail out a student didn't seem to quite fit into that category, though. That seemed to be more parole officer, or poorly written sitcom material.

What had Cai been thinking?

I took Highway 13 east to catch Interstate 35E north into St. Paul. As I passed a long line of spruce trees that stood near the road, I automatically scanned the branches for White-winged Crossbills. While the birds lived year-round in boreal forests, mostly north of the United States, they sometimes spent their winters south of the Canadian border, looking for food supplies. The spruce trees were the key to seeing the birds—White-winged Crossbills had heavy bills with crossed tips uniquely suited to extracting the seeds from conifer cones. When the spruces in Canada had a poor year, but further south we had bumper crops of cones, you'd see the birds feasting in the branches because they tracked—and literally followed—the year's cone production.

That meant we needed both a bad year for cones further north and a good year for cones further south if we wanted to see the crossbills in southern Minnesota. In my experience, that translated to seeing the White-winged Crossbills down here about once a decade. I'd last seen the birds along this same stretch of road four years ago, and from what I could see as I drove by, it looked like this would be another winter with no crossbills since cones were few and far between on the trees.

Just as the spruces gave way to some big old oaks, however, I did spot a Northern Shrike perched high atop a tree that provided a clear view of the empty fields stretching away on the other side of the highway. Another winter visitor like the crossbills, the Northern Shrike got my vote for being the closest thing to a bipolar bird, and I didn't mean as in the North and South poles—shrikes were both song-birds and predators.

Talk about a split personality. Imagine Mary Poppins and the Terminator.

With wings. And only about eight inches long.

Actually, I didn't know if the Mary Poppins singing example was the most accurate, since I'd personally never heard the Northern Shrike's song. When it was wintering in Minnesota, all I'd been able to catch were the occasional raspy shrieks the shrike made. But that wasn't the reason I equated it with the Terminator.

Shrikes impaled their prey on barbed wire or thorns.

Definitely not Mary Poppins-like.

The reason the shrikes do that was because they made a habit of killing more rodents, insects, or small birds than they could eat at one time, as a survival strategy for times when food is scarce. The barbed wire, or thorns, or even sharp plant spines, offered a handy place to store surplus prey, kind of like a shrike's own meat locker. To beat this dead horse—or dead rodent, as the case might be—even more, the Northern Shrike's Latin name meant "Butcher Watchman."

Kind of gives a whole new appreciation for those little grayish-brownish birds sitting on telephone wires scoping out the winter fields, doesn't it?

"Oh, look, that vicious little bird is just sitting on a wire. He's probably thinking about pouncing on a cute field mouse and then ramming him onto a sharp stick."

Just the idea of it made my mouth go dry. I automatically reached for the coffee thermos I usually brought with me in the morning when I realized I'd left it at home in the kitchen before I headed out to work.

Shoot. I could have really used a jolt of java with the way my day was already going. One of my best students was sitting in jail, and now I was driving to St. Paul to get him out. By the time I'd get back to the office, I could only imagine how many students I'd have lined up, waiting for me, even with Patty doing the rescheduling.

In fact, if the morning was any indication, I was probably going to need to pick up a whole carton of coffee-to-go to get me through the day.

Then again, maybe not.

A carton of coffee sure hadn't helped Trisha Davis through the day last Saturday.

Trisha Davis, in fact, got a knife in her gut along with her coffee-to-go.

She'd been impaled as precisely as a Northern Shrike would pierce its future snack.

Except that a shrike wouldn't have a box of coffee between it and its victim.

Why was the carton of coffee on Trisha's lap?

I took an off-ramp just north of downtown St. Paul and stopped at a red light. For a second or two, I tried to picture exactly what I'd seen when I'd opened Trisha's car door in the parking garage. She'd been slumped in the driver's seat, her head back against the head rest. As soon as I'd opened her door wide, the coffee carton slid out and fell to the pavement, as if the door had been bracing it in Trisha's lap. Her seatbelt wasn't buckled. Another carton of coffee sat in the passenger seat. Her purse lay in the foot well beneath the passenger seat.

The car behind me honked its horn. The traffic light was green. I drove a few more blocks and turned into the parking lot beside the Ramsey County Law Enforcement Center. I found a slot and parked.

I was still thinking about that carton of coffee and Trisha's unbuckled seat belt.

Trisha would have parked the car and turned off the ignition. She would have unbuckled her seat belt and gotten ready to get out of the car on her driver's side, so she could walk around the car and lift the heavy coffee cartons out of the passenger seat.

But instead, she'd turned in her seat, lifted one of the cartons, and then turned back in her seat with it . . . and been stabbed.

I mimicked the motions, and it was clear to me what had happened.

Trisha had been handing the carton to someone standing beside her open driver's door.

Someone had stepped up as soon as she had parked and offered to help her bring in the coffee. She'd reached for a carton, and as she turned back, that someone had slid the knife into her midsection. The killer immediately shut the door on her—though it didn't shut tight—which braced the coffee carton between Trisha and the steering wheel.

And her purse was left on the floor in front of the passenger seat.

If it had been a random mugging as the police suggested, wouldn't the mugger have gone after Trisha's purse?

I mean, really, worst case—wouldn't a mugger have at least grabbed the coffee carton so he wouldn't run away totally empty-handed after a botched mugging?

That coffee wasn't cheap, you know.

Nor did I believe for a minute that Trisha would have handed over the coffee to a stranger, even if he, or she, had offered help transporting the cartons. When she hadn't been birding, Trisha had been a self-defense instructor at a Twin Cities fitness center. No way would she suddenly forget her own safety rules even if she was lulled into a false sense of security by the heady aroma of a car filled with hot coffee.

Trisha knew the person outside her car, and it wasn't a random, caffeine-deprived mugger.

It was someone who'd come for the MOU meeting.

CHAPTER NINE

I STEPPED INTO THE LAW Enforcement Center and studied the extensive directory listing posted on the wall near the front reception desk. I read half-way down the board before I heard familiar voices coming from down the hall to my left. I turned to see four people heading my way: Cai, his cousin Pheej, Ron Windingstad, and Officer Anna Grieg.

"What's this?" I asked them as they approached, "Birders' day at the St. Paul police station?"

"Mr. White!" Cai called. "I can't believe you came out here."

"Thank your girlfriend," I told him. "She's a stubborn little thing."

"Hey there, Anna," I said, extending my hand to give the officer a warm handshake before I greeted Ron and Pheej as well.

"Don't tell me you were arrested with the boys, Ron," I kidded him. "Anna here's a tough cookie, I've got to tell you. She'll lock you up and throw away the key."

"Yeah, right," Anna said. "So, did you get that American Black Duck I posted last February?"

"No, I missed it," I said. "I'm hoping I get another chance this winter."

A few years ago, I'd met Anna when we served together on the board of the Minnesota Ornithologists Union. At the time, she'd been a traffic cop in Hastings, a town on the southeastern edge of the Twin Cities metro area that bordered Wisconsin. Thanks to her postings on the MOU list serve, I'd been able to chase and add two new birds to my life list in the past year. Sharing sightings was one of her favorite things to do, and she was always generous with details and directions in her posts.

Unlike some birders, who were deliberately vague, or who posted after the bird in question had already moved on, which prevented anyone else from seeing it. As if wild birds were personal property, which they certainly weren't. My philosophy had always been that birds were one of the few things left one could enjoy and share for free.

Not counting the money spent on bird seed for yard feeders . . . or on filling car tanks to drive to birding spots . . . or on cameras . . . or on binoculars.

Come to think of it, "free" might not be the best word there. "Relatively free" might be better.

Which also sort of described what Anna was at the moment explaining to Cai and Pheej before she released them into Ron's custody.

"You guys are lucky the building owners passed on pressing charges," she lectured them. "But you don't want to risk them changing their minds, so stay off property that isn't yours, especially when there's a sign displayed that says 'PRIVATE PROPERTY—TRESPASSERS WILL BE PROSECUTED.' You don't want to start racking up a criminal record just to take photographs."

"Photographs?"

Pheej lifted a camera bag slung over his shoulder. "I was taking pictures, Mr. White, of the old Hamm's Brewery," he answered. "I want to be an architect, and so I take photos of old buildings that interest me."

"You should see some of his pictures, Mr. White," Cai said. "Some of those buildings look like artwork. You should frame them and get them in an art show somewhere, Pheej," he told his cousin. "I bet someone would buy them."

Pheej shrugged off Cai's compliment and became engrossed in readjusting the bag on his shoulder. I thought I detected a hint of red staining his cheeks in embarrassment at his cousin's praise.

"Pheej counted Chimney Swifts at Hamm's this last summer," Ron reminded me and glanced at his birding protégé. "He says he's sure those signs weren't there before, so he didn't think it would be a problem to get some exterior shots last night."

"It really was cool," Cai assured me, "with the full moon last night, and all the snow reflecting light. Pheej took some great shots. He even got—"

I caught Pheej sliding a silencing look at Cai, who immediately dropped his eyes to the floor and suddenly became intensely focused on rummaging for something in the pockets of his down-filled jacket.

Interesting.

Unless I completely misread the eye-conveyed message, I was pretty sure Pheej was hiding something, and Cai had almost let the cat out of the bag. So far, neither Anna nor Ron had said a word about any urban adventuring action, unlike Bridget, who'd confided in me the boys had joined with their cousins to explore the old brewery. Now I wondered what exactly had happened last night under that full moon: a simple, innocent, albeit ill-advised, photo shoot or an illegal foray of urban exploration.

My inquiring mind wanted to know.

My counselor's sense of responsibility needed to know.

I decided I was going to get it out of Cai even if I had to threaten him with suspension.

Mr. Lenzen—my boss—wasn't the only one who could pull that ploy.

I watched Ron shake Anna's hand and thank her for helping him spring the boys from their unanticipated overnight accommodations.

I grabbed the back of Cai's jacket collar and lightly tugged him towards me.

"Ron," I said over Cai's head, "let me take this one off your hands and deliver him back to Savage. That way, you don't have to make the trip, and I know Cai doesn't want to inconvenience you any more than he already has. Right, Cai?"

I gave him my sternest counselor look.

"Absolutely," Cai readily agreed. "My family and I really appreciate your help, Mr. Windingstad. I swear you'll never have to get me out of jail again."

"Amen to that," I said just loudly enough for Cai to hear.

I offered my hand to Anna. "Thanks. He really is a great kid," I said, tipping my head in Cai's direction. "It's probably his counselor's fault that he ended up in jail. I hear the guy's a real dirtball."

Anna laughed. "I hear he's a speed demon, not that I have any first-hand knowledge of that. I hope you see a Black Duck this year, Bob."

"Me, too. See you, Anna."

I turned to go with my stellar student/almost turned criminal.

"Say, Bob?" Anna called.

I looked back at my former fellow MOU board member. "Yes?"

"I'm so sorry about Trisha Davis," she said. "That makes you two members short for the records committee this year, doesn't it?"

"I wish," I sighed. I told her the bad news about Harry Harrison and Nip Kniplinger.

"That is just too weird," Anna commented. "Those two guys were the face of Minnesota birding for decades, and to think they died within a day of each other is . . . unbelievably coincidental. I'm so sorry to hear that, Bob."

"Mr. White," Cai, standing next to me in the hallway, pointed at a men's room sign. "I'll be right back."

I nodded and realized this was my chance to speak privately with Anna, so I closed the distance between us to continue talking.

"Have you heard anything more about Trisha's death?" I asked. "I found her, Anna. I saw the scene of the crime, and I'm willing to bet ten Black Ducks she willingly opened her car door to her killer. And that means she knew who it was. It wasn't a random act of violence."

Anna shot a quick look around her, but no one else stood in the hallway.

"You're not the only one who thinks that way, Bob, but I can't tell you anything more—just that an investigation is underway. And because it happened on the university campus, everyone's trying to keep it out of the news. No one wants that kind of publicity," she added.

I switched topics. "Level with me about Cai and Pheej, Anna. I'm Cai's counselor, and I should know what kind of trouble he's gotten himself into if I'm going to help him get himself back out of it. Who picked them up, and what exactly were they doing at the old brewery?"

She gave me a confused look.

"They were taking pictures of the building," she said. "The night dispatcher got an anonymous call that kids were on the property, so a patrol car went to check it out. He found the boys inside the fence taking photos."

"There wasn't a group of kids?"

Anna shook her head. "Not that I heard. It was just the two of them. The night officer-in-charge locked them up because he wanted to make an impression on them. The boys are eighteen, so he wanted them to know we mean business about staying off private property, and especially old abandoned buildings like the brewery. We've had a couple kids get killed in the last year doing what they call 'urban adventures,'" she said, "so the department's making a concerted effort to put a stop to that. It's one thing to be a thrill-seeker, but when it results in deaths, we have to step in."

That explained why Cai, with no priors, had been treated to the police department's hospitality for the night. I felt a little less concerned that my student was experiencing a sudden personality change. Counselors hate it when that happens.

"I've heard about it—urban exploration," I said. "To be honest with you, Anna, I thought that was what Cai and Pheej were up to. A little bird back in Savage gave me that idea."

"That's not how the arrest report reads," she repeated. "The boys were clearly trespassing, but they got off easy, thanks to the Hamm Heritage Group. They try to stay out of the news, too."

It was my turn to look confused.

"Hamm Heritage Group?" I asked. "Never heard of it. Is that like a bunch of beer drinkers documenting memorable hangovers?"

Anna laughed. "I don't know about that part. It's one of the local building preservation groups in St. Paul. Seems like we've got a boatload of people interested in preservation these days in the city. Suddenly everyone wants to stop developers from tearing down decrepit, death-trap buildings in the name of preserving the past."

The radio on her belt emitted some static, and she keyed it until it fell silent again.

"This one's trying to persuade the city council to keep the Hamm's Brewery intact as an historic site," she continued. "I heard they have plans to restore parts of it as a micro-brewery, but so far, no one's signing any leases, so the building just sits there empty and decaying."

Down the hall I heard the door open from the men's room and saw Cai walk out. I pointed at the main doors. "Meet you right there in a second, Cai," I called to him.

"And attracting would-be architects with cameras," I finished for Anna.

She nodded. "Unfortunately, yes."

"Thanks again for helping with our guys," I said.

"No problem," Anna replied. "These are good kids. Ron told me about his work with Pheej. Sometimes I think if we just had enough adults like Ron, willing to share their interests with kids, we'd have a lot fewer customers in the juvenile system."

She gave me a little salute and then added, "Hey, if you have a few minutes to spare, you should drive down to the entrance of the Bruce Vento Nature Sanctuary, just around the corner from here. I saw an MOU posting about an hour ago of a Trumpeter Swan on the Mississippi River there."

A Trumpeter.

Though I'd seen plenty of the big swans in several Minnesota locations over the years, I'd never taken the time to see one in Ramsey County in December, which meant that I had an empty slot on my Ramsey County bird list just waiting to be filled. In fact, if I was remembering correctly, adding one more species to my Ramsey list might just put me in a tie with the current county record for birds in December.

Of course, then I'd probably be motivated to break the tie, and that would mean some intense birding in the weeks ahead . . . but winter break was right around the corner, and it wasn't like Luce and I had any other plans . . .

But that wasn't right now. Right now, I was working. I was on school time. I had a student to counsel. What kind of example would I be if I played hooky to go look at a bird?

"I'm afraid it'll have to wait," I told Anna.

"Tell that to the Trumpeter," she laughed. "Birds aren't the best at waiting for birders," she reminded me.

"Tell me about it," I agreed. I'd probably put thousands of miles on my car driving to see birds that hadn't waited around for me, not that it ever stopped me from trying. Eternal optimists, birders.

Eternal fools, some might say.

I waved good-bye and met Cai at the building doors. On our way out into the cold, I checked my watch for the time.

It was barely nine o'clock. I'd thought this errand of rescue would take up the whole morning, which was why I'd asked Patty to reschedule my appointments, but now, unexpectedly, I had time on my hands.

I could get that swan, my birding self assured me. *It's waiting for me. Now.*

The reasons I should jump at the chance to see the bird tumbled through my mind. Aside from the fact it would give me a tie with the record, it wasn't like the sanctuary was really out of the way. It was practically around the corner, and it was just a street over from where we would catch the highway back to Savage, so I almost had to go right by it anyway.

And I could use the time to talk with Cai without the usual mayhem going on just outside my office door. I'd be doing my job, counseling. We'd just have a different setting than normal.

Okay, that made two good reasons I should go birding on school time. One more . . . one more . . .

Anna's comment about adults sharing their interests with kids popped into my head.

Bingo! Reason Number Three to go find the Trumpeter: I would be sharing my interest with a student, which Anna said was really important for teens' character development.

I was a high school counselor. I was all for teens' character development.

I opened my passenger car door for my jailbird. "Have you ever seen a Trumpeter Swan, Cai?"

FIVE MINUTES LATER, I grabbed my binoculars from beneath my car seat, and Cai and I climbed out of my SUV in the little parking lot of the Bruce Vento Nature Sanctuary. Big piles of snow ringed the parking lot, but a narrow trail led down the sandstone bluff into the flood plain where several old railroad tracks still serviced the area. The stream that ran through the park was frozen over, along with a pond that I could see, but on the far side of the tracks, I could see the open water of the Mississippi River.

"Bridget thought you'd gone urban exploring," I said over my shoulder as I led the way down the trail. "She said that's what your sister Mim told her. She's terrified you're going to lose your free ride to Stanford."

"Yeah, that'd definitely be bad," he agreed. "But I'm not going to, right? Nobody's pressing charges. I've already got my acceptance."

He paused a moment, then, his voice less sure, he asked me again, "Right?"

I stopped and looked back at him where he stood on the trail. Cai had come a long way from the insecure freshman he'd been three years ago. Like a lot of our Asian students, he'd initially doubted his ability to fit into the mostly white-bread community of Savage, yet here he was, a confident scholar and popular athlete who had embraced the better parts of American culture, while still maintaining his native Hmong values.

I was proud of him, and rightly so.

Which made me wonder what in the world had possessed him last night to commit a crime.

"We didn't mean any harm, Mr. White," Cai insisted when I met his gaze. "Pheej just wanted to take a picture. That's all. It's just an old broken-down building."

"I know," I replied. "But you guys still broke the law."

Cai's chin quivered almost imperceptibly.

I hated it when that happened.

Here I was going to give him a lecture about responsibility, and with one little chin quiver, all my intentions to be the tough-guy counselor scattered like a flock of pigeons. Like I already pointed out, Cai was neither a slacker nor a reprobate, but the exact opposite. He was a great kid, one of the best young men I'd ever had the pleasure to work with. If I could have another ten students just like him, I'd gladly make the trek to St. Paul's holding tank every day.

Well, maybe not every day. I already spent enough money on my gas bill chasing birds.

Bridget was right, though: Cai had made one stupid mistake. And it didn't seem fair he'd lose his entire future because of it. He was still a kid, and by definition, he wasn't always going to make adult decisions.

Heck, I knew plenty of adults who didn't make adult decisions. Some people rationalized whatever they wanted.

Yeah.

Like looking for a Trumpeter Swan on school time.

Ouch.

"Cai, we're going to fix this," I assured him, going into full consoling, righteous, superman counselor mode. My foot slipped on an icy patch, and Cai's hand shot out to catch me from falling.

"See?" I said. "We're in this together, buddy, and I won't let you down. I'll call the Stanford admissions office as soon as we get back and tell them what happened. That way, no one will be blindsided later. You're not losing that scholarship, Cai."

The cloud of concern lingered on his face, but then he took a sharp inhale of the cold morning air, and gave in to a smile. "Thanks, Mr. White."

"You're welcome," I said. "So why did your sister tell Bridget you were going urban exploring?"

Cai shrugged in his jacket. "I guess she heard Pheej talking about it one day, and when I told her I was going to meet Pheej at the old Hamm's Brewery, she just assumed that was why."

"Pheej does the urban adventuring thing?" I tried to visualize the small young man who had left with Ron as a fearless trespasser, along with being a well-mannered birder. I supposed it was possible.

A fifteen-year-old memory came back to me. A Long-tailed Duck had been sighted in LeSueur county, about forty-five minutes west of the Twin Cities. I was home on winter break from college, and since I'd never found a Long-tailed Duck in LeSueur, I hopped in my car and drove out to the water treatment plant where the duck had been identified. As soon as I arrived, though, I was confronted with a dilemma: in order to see the duck, I'd have to climb a fence surrounding the plant, since it was off-limits to the public. I might risk arrest.

On the other hand, I might miss the only chance I'd have to add the duck to my LeSueur county list.

Duck or jail?

For a birder like me, it was no contest.

I climbed the fence.

I also got the Long-tailed Duck…and a lecture from the nice patrol officer who was waiting for me when I climbed back over the fence to my car. Fortunately for me, I hadn't been the first birder to scale the fence that winter.

So yes, I supposed it was very possible—and probably very probable—that Pheej might not be deterred from a goal by a private property sign.

Now that I thought about it, maybe birders had something in common with urban adventurers, after all: the thrill of the hunt. I knew I got an adrenaline rush every time I found a rare bird. I supposed that was the appeal of a lot of hobbies: the sense of accomplishment you got when you achieved a goal.

The satisfaction of risk that was rewarded.

Considering that some of the risks urban adventurers faced included getting crushed under crumbling walls or drowned in ancient sewers, however, I was really glad that the majority of my risks were limited to frostbite or speeding tickets.

Cai and I worked our way down the slippery trail to the bottom of the hill. We stepped over the railroad tracks and noticed another man bundled up in a heavy coat and woolen cap standing a distance off to our right. The stranger had binoculars lifted to his eyes.

"Someone else is looking for your swan," Cai said.

I followed the direction of the man's binoculars and spotted the big white bird in the middle of the Mississippi. After I took a look to verify the Trumpeter Swan, I handed my binoculars to Cai and pointed out the bird.

"It's really big," Cai commented when he focused on the swan. "But its neck looks straight after a little crook at the base. I thought swans had a curved neck. You know, like in pictures, like half a heart-shaped outline."

"That would be a Mute Swan," I explained. "Those are the ones you usually see in parks or movies. They're not native to North America. They were brought here by immigrants. The Trumpeter and the Tundra Swan are the swan species that are indigenous."

Cai lowered the binos. "I never thought about birds being immigrants, too. Seriously?" He put the binoculars back up to his eyes. "I don't know that I've ever thought about birds at all, actually. At least they don't have to learn English to come here."

I was about to explain the difference between migrants and immigrants when Cai's attention swung to something behind me. I reflexively glanced over my shoulder to see that the other birdwatcher we'd noted had closed the distance between us and was heading our way.

"He was there last night," Cai said to me quietly, his breath making little puffs in the cold air. "I recognize his cap. He was standing at the corner, under a streetlight, when the policeman put me and Pheej in his patrol car."

"Well, if it isn't Bob White," the birder said as he approached. His tone was less than welcoming. "I'd ask what brings you to St. Paul, but it's fairly obvious." He waved a hand in the direction of the swan. "But now that you've seen it, feel free to leave anytime. Unless you feel compelled to 'document' it."

"Hey, Pete," I greeted him, blatantly ignoring his sarcastic remark. Instead, I noted his bright-yellow knit hat with the words *Birders Rule* emblazoned across the front. No wonder Cai remembered him. The hat would be hard to miss, even in low light. Under a streetlight, it must have looked like a neon beacon warning of bad road conditions ahead.

With good reason, too, if the man's attitude at the MOU meeting last Saturday morning was any indication.

Pete Moss had an ax to grind, and I really wasn't interested in being the one ground with it.

"Cai," I said, introducing my student to my fellow MOU member, "this is Pete Moss. He's one of the best birders in the state."

And one of the angriest, I mentally added. I remembered more of his tirade during our brief encounter at the Bell Museum. His comment that he wanted "justice" for his denied bird sighting had reminded me of the kind of overly dramatic antics I got from students now and then, but Pete was no high-schooler venting to his counselor.

He was an adult, who also happened to be an angry birder.

For a split-second, my mind pictured a bearded Pete Moss as one of the Angry Birds characters that seemed to be everywhere these days—on iPhones, clothing, kids' toys, lunchboxes. The goofy-looking birds were a cultural phenomenon, not to mention a billion-dollar goldmine for their video-game creator. But in that moment, all I could think of was a round Pete Moss, yellow cap on his head, catapulting through the air at some crazy stack of bricks and planks.

Seriously, some birding group should give the Angry Birds an award for single-handedly raising America's consciousness of birds.

Even if they were goofy.

Pete, on the other hand, was not goofy. Pete was intense— intense and angry. And in all my years of experience in counseling, I'd never found that to be a particularly good combination.

Cai, however, had neither my experience with anger management nor my familiarity with Pete Moss. What he did have, though, was the directness of youth . . . for better or worse.

In this case, I was definitely afraid it was for the worse. Cai took a step towards the older man.

"I'm Cai Xiong. You're the person who called the police," he said. "Last night. At the brewery. We were taking photos," he informed him. "But what were you doing there?"

CHAPTER TEN

*F*UNNY YOU SHOULD ASK, *Cai*, I thought, since I was, at that very moment, wondering the same thing.

I just hadn't planned to be quite so in-your-face about it with Pete.

But Cai didn't have that problem. He stood defiantly in front of the man, his arms crossed over his chest, waiting for an answer. *You go, Cai.*

Pete glared at my student, shifted his eyes to my face, then moved them back to Cai.

"Trying to prove a point," he said, "the point being that I don't make false bird reports, unlike what some people might think."

His eyes returned to my face. "If it's the last thing I do, I'm going to prove I saw a Chimney Swift at that brewery years ago. It happened once. It'll happen again. And then I'm going to make the MOU Records Committee publicly eat crow."

And that would be me, I realized, since I was the only MOURC member still living. It occurred to me that perhaps Pete hadn't heard about Harry's and Nip's deaths, but he anticipated my comment with his next remark.

"And seeing as you're now the only MOURC member left, Bob, I suggest you bring a big appetite when it happens," he sneered at me.

I'm not kidding—he actually sneered at me.

I almost expected him to twirl one side of his beard with his finger like a villain in a melodrama twirling one end of his mustache. I was pretty sure it wouldn't have made the same effect, though—

Pete had so much beard that his finger would have gotten caught in a knot and then he'd be stuck with his finger tied up against his face.

Intimidating?

Not so much.

Amusing?

Definitely.

But I didn't want to find myself trying not to laugh out loud at an already angry Pete Moss, so I tried to move the conversation on with a conciliatory note.

"You know, Pete, I've had sightings rejected, too," I told him. "But I don't take it personally, because it's not. All it means is that people who weren't there aren't convinced about what you saw."

He continued to glower at me.

"Does it really make a difference what other people think?" I asked. "You know what you saw, and you can be happy about that. At the end of the day, the only bird list that matters is the one you keep for yourself."

"Oh, like you don't compete with other birders to score sightings?" Pete pressed. "You're saying that, if you saw more birds than anyone in the state, you wouldn't be annoyed if your name, *BRRDMAN*, wasn't included on the annual MOU report of the states' top bird listers?"

The denial lodged in my throat. I didn't consider myself competitive, but I had to admit I liked having the reputation of being one of the state's most prolific birdwatchers. Ever since I saw my first eagle when I was a little kid, birding had been more than my hobby—it was my passion and part of the way I identified myself. As Pete had just alluded to, even my car's license plate announced me as the "BRRDMAN," for crying out loud.

There's a reason they call special-order license plates "vanity plates," you know.

They should probably just call them "self-involved."

Or maybe just "stupid."

"Aha," Pete gloated. "I thought so. You'd be just as indignant as any other birder to find yourself excluded, so don't give me any of that "it only matters to me" attitude. You know it doesn't."

"Actually, Pete," I said, "that is my attitude."

I could feel my temper warming up in the face of his sarcasm despite the cold morning air, but I was also very aware of Cai's presence and the need to model adult behavior in front of one of my students.

Would I like to punch Pete in the nose?

Yes! I'd love to punch Pete in the nose!

Pete Moss was being a jerk and a self-important son-of-a-gun. (See—even under duress, I can monitor my private thoughts for counselor-appropriate language.) But since I wanted to set a good example for Cai, and I was on school time to boot, I passed on the urge to man-handle Pete. Instead, I aimed at making it a "teachable moment" for my young charge.

"Sure," I told Pete, "I'd feel excluded, but my self-worth isn't dependent on other people recognizing my birding skills. Yes, it's nice to be considered an expert birder, but really, it's what I get out of birding that makes it worthwhile for me—the friendships I've made, the amazing places it's taken me, the pure magic of birds and the natural world—those things feed me, Pete. Without birding and all the experiences it's brought me over the years, I wouldn't be the man I am now."

Pete slowly applauded me with his gloved hands. "Nice speech, Bob. But save it for someone who cares."

And with that parting remark, Pete Moss turned his back on us and walked away toward the river.

Now I really wanted to punch him in the nose.

"He's not a very nice person, is he?" Cai asked. "I thought all birders were like you, Mr. White. Quiet and polite. But this guy— he's a real ass-hole."

So much for trying to keep the language counselor-appropriate.

I gave Cai a disapproving glance.

He held up his hands in surrender. "I'm just calling it the way I see it."

Then he grinned. "Bridget taught me to say that. She says it all the time."

Yes, she did. And I was the one who taught it to her out on the softball field when she was a green sophomore working on her ball skills on my girls' squad. If I'd known how often I'd hear it from her in the next two years, I would have taped my mouth shut.

Or I would have taught her to say something else, like "Mr. White is always right."

That had a nice ring to it . . . even if it wasn't always true.

"Speaking of your girlfriend," I said, suddenly mindful of the time I'd commandeered to see the swan, "we better head back to Savage. I don't want Bridget to decide she needs to come check up on us."

We trudged back along the sanctuary's snowy path to where I'd parked the car. I popped the locks open, we climbed inside, and I put the key in the ignition.

Nothing happened.

I turned the key again.

Nothing. Not even a click.

"Your battery's dead," Cai informed me.

"It can't be," I assured him. "I just put a new battery in last year."

I turned the key again.

Still nothing.

"You got a bad battery, then," Cai said. "Or just bad luck."

Bad luck.

A curse?

I almost got hit by a car the night before, two of my birding colleagues had suddenly died, one was murdered, and now my battery had given up.

Not the best run of luck by a long shot.

But a curse?

I again pictured Pete Moss demanding justice at the MOU meeting, along with his sneering at me down by the river.

"You're saying that if you saw more birds than anyone in the state, you wouldn't be annoyed if your name, BRRDMAN, wasn't included on the annual MOU report of the states' top bird listers?"

Did Pete really think I would care so much about a list?

A bird list, yes—I would certainly care about that.

I did care about that. I'd been keeping lists of birds for more than twenty-five years. I had county lists, state lists, even country lists, of the birds I've seen. It was why I was here at that very moment.

But I've never sneered at someone because of them.

Pete Moss, on the other hand, clearly wanted bragging rights because of his lists. And he cared enough about it to carry a serious grudge.

He hadn't hesitated to remind me that all the other MOURC members who had denied his sighting claim were dead, and since Saturday, I'd been tailed by enough bad luck to wonder if there might really be something to the idea of a curse. Was there a connection?

Connection.

I suddenly had an idea about my dead battery.

"Stay here," I told Cai as I released the interior latch of the front hood of my car. I got out and walked over to look at the battery.

Sure enough, one of the battery cables was unattached. I hooked it back up and got back in the car.

"It was a loose battery cable," I explained to Cai as I fired up the engine. A reassuring low roar filled the silence. "That road down to the lot here was pretty bumpy, so I'm guessing it jolted the cable loose."

I didn't share with him that I'd just had the car serviced last week, nor that I'd never had a loose cable in all my years of bumping over dirt roads to chase birds. I figured my student didn't need to know those things, just like he didn't need to know another thought that had clicked in my head: Pete Moss knew my license plate letters: BRRDMAN.

I glanced at the other two cars parked in the little lot as I backed out. If one car belonged to Pete, who else was here?

I didn't have to wonder about that more than a moment, though.

A gunshot cracked and my back window exploded.

Ah! Question answered.

The other car belonged to someone with a gun.

CHAPTER ELEVEN

I INSTINCTIVELY REACHED OUT and pushed Cai's head down below the dashboard and pressed my accelerator to the floor. The car shot up the slight incline to the main road, and I pulled a fast and furious right. No more shots followed us, but I wasn't taking any chances that someone still had us in a gun's sight, so I drove another block, hung a left, and then another right. I pulled over to the curb in front of a Mexican grocery store, leaned over to the right as low as I could in my seat, whipped out my phone, and called 911.

"Are you all right?" I asked Cai, who was huddling in the foot well on the passenger's side.

He looked up at me, his brown eyes wide and intense, and nodded. "Yeah," he breathed.

I told the emergency dispatcher what had happened and within a moment or two, I heard the sirens.

"Someone shot at your car?" Cai asked in disbelief.

"Yup," I said, reaching for a normal, matter-of-fact tone in order to try to contain the situation and keep us both calm and level-headed.

Actually, we were very level-headed at the moment. Literally. Our faces were only about ten inches apart—mine almost lying on his empty seat and his under the dashboard's glove compartment.

"It doesn't happen that often, really," I assured him. "Just every once in a while."

He began to unfold himself from the foot well, but I put a hand out to stop him. "Give it a minute, Cai."

I wanted him to stay where he was until the police arrived. I was already hyper-aware that I had a student in my car, as it was. The last thing I would risk was exposing him to any additional threat. On the wild outside chance that the shooter had managed to follow us, I knew that the less of Cai visible, the better.

And, oh crap, Mr. Lenzen was going to have my hide for this one.

A knock on my window announced the arrival of the police. I looked up and saw a familiar face.

"Hey, Anna," I said, pulling myself upright. "Gee, I haven't seen you in a long time, then twice in one day."

Anna gave me a half-smile. "I don't know if that's good or bad, Bob." She nodded at the SUV's rear window frame that was now edged with broken glass. "Given the shattered window and the 911 call, I'm hard pressed to say it's a good thing. Are you all right?"

She glanced at Cai, who had remained in the well. "Cai, are you okay?"

"I think we're good, now that you're here," I told her. "Do you think it's okay if Cai gets back in his seat?"

Anna nodded. "We're secure. We've got another two units at Bruce Vento on the scene. Right now, I want you boys to catch a ride with me back there so you can tell us exactly what happened. I'll get another officer over here to bring your car back to the station, Bob. I expect someone's going to want to take a look at that window."

"You got it," I told her, then turned to Cai. "Cai, you get another ride in a patrol car. Aren't you glad I showed up this morning?"

Cai pulled himself out of the foot well. "It's definitely more exciting than selling candy cane grams for the fundraiser," he said. "But Bridget's going to be ticked off I missed my shift."

We got out of the car and climbed into Anna's cruiser. Cai sat in back, and I rode shotgun.

Sorry.

Maybe not the best choice of words, under the circumstances.

Cai must have had a similar thought, because he leaned forward and tapped me on the shoulder.

"Have you really been shot at before, Mr. White?" Cai asked.

I debated how to answer.

I could be truthful and say, "Yes, I have," and leave it at that. Knowing how high school students (and faculty, too, for that matter) thrive on speculation, though—the more sensational, the better—I decided that giving that answer would be like a virtual invitation to Mr. Lenzen to put a listening device in my office to confirm all his worst suspicions of me as a counselor. My history of crime scene association had not particularly endeared me to my public relations-obsessed supervisor, to say the least.

Or I could be evasive, and answer Cai with, "There have been a few times I think I might have been someone's target, but since I never sustained a gunshot wound, I'm only guessing the shots in my vicinity were intended for me."

Talk about non-committal. Like I was just walking around, and gee whiz, bullets just showed up on their own. One of life's little mysteries.

Or I could flat-out lie, and say, "No, I was kidding."

Liar, liar, pants on fire. How could I lie, when I was always telling my students that honesty was the best policy? Don't let anyone fool you—being a role model was hard work.

Instead, I chose to answer a slightly different, but less problematic, question.

"You mean my car, right? Yes, I've had my tires shot out," I told Cai. "I think that counts."

He looked visibly relieved. So was I.

Anna, however, had caught my deflection of the original question. She turned to me briefly while she waited for a car to pass before moving into the street. "Nice catch, Counselor."

"I try," I said.

Anna's radio came on, and she gave her status to the dispatcher.

"So, let me guess," she said as she headed back toward the entrance to the Bruce Vento Nature Sanctuary. "You were looking for the swan. You know, that makes me look a little bad here, since I'm the one who suggested you go to the place where a crime then occurred. A shooting that involved you."

I looked at her incredulously. "Are you kidding me?"

She shrugged, wheeling the patrol car around a corner. "Before we can say it was a random shooting, we have to look at circumstances and see if there are any coincidences that are too coincidental."

"You could be a suspect?" Cai asked her. "But you're a police officer."

"Cops can be criminals, too, Cai," she said, checking her side view mirrors. "We're all human. We all make mistakes. Just look in a history book—some of our biggest crooks have been respected citizens. But like it or not, I have a direct connection to this incident," she pointed out. "Not that I'm worried about it, because I'm not. I was actually talking with the dispatcher when your 911 call came in, Bob, and as soon as you told her where you had pulled over, I ran out to the car and hightailed it over here."

"I appreciate that," I said.

"As soon as you said Bruce Vento, I knew what you were doing there," she continued. "I even told the dispatcher, 'He's after the swan,' and she gave me a funny look. I told her it was a birding thing."

"More like birding gone bad," I corrected her. "Really bad."

I turned in my seat to address Cai. "For your information, guns are not a typical part of a birdwatching experience. Birding is a safe, rewarding pastime. It gets you outside into the natural world and connects you to it in enjoyable, healthy ways."

I threw a glance at Anna. "That's my canned speech," I told her. "Stop grimacing."

"It sounds like a life sentence when you put it that way," she replied, catching Cai's eyes in the rear view mirror. "Birding is a blast, Cai. It's like being an adventurer discovering exotic new places all the time. It's the thrill of the chase. Like being in a secret society with an awesome objective."

"Well, yeah," I conceded, a little miffed that Anna did a much better job describing the allure of birding than I had. "It's like all that, too."

"I think what Bob is trying to say is that there's something else going on here," Anna concluded, "and you guys just happened to stumble into it. Birding isn't a dangerous activity."

"Normally," I couldn't help but add. My SUV had been somebody's moving target practice, after all. As far as I was concerned, it was a miracle that both Cai and I were uninjured. Not only had we survived a shooting, but I'd also managed not to crash the car in our wild escape from the sanctuary.

My car.

With my vanity plates.

I thought again about Pete Moss and the fact that he was so bitter about his rejected claim. He'd been at the sanctuary while we were there. He knew my car.

But unless he could bilocate, there was no way he could have detached my battery cable or taken a shot at us, I realized. Cai and I ran into Pete down by the river. He had clearly been there before we arrived, and when we left, he continued in the opposite direction.

And while he may have been bitter—okay, make that obsessed, since he was a birder—with his rejected sighting, I was pretty sure that was a different level of anger from shooting at people in a car.

Shooting at people required some planning, like bringing a gun to shoot with, and knowing where the people were. My decision to look for the Trumpeter Swan was spur-of-the-moment.

I glanced at Anna beside me in the front seat of her cruiser.

"I know this is a stupid question, but did you tell anyone I was on my way to the sanctuary? I mean, like post something on the MOU list serve?"

"No. Why are you asking?" she countered. She slid me a worried frown. "Please don't tell me you've been getting threatening phone calls . . . from other birders?"

"Not exactly," I hedged. "It's just this crazy feeling I've had since Saturday. Trisha was killed . . . and then Harry died. And Nip."

"You think someone's stalking you?"

"No, not really." I thought about it a moment, trying to put my feeling of impending doom into perspective. "Although I almost got run over last night downtown, and then my battery cables were mysteriously disconnected, and now my SUV needs to have its rear window replaced because it got shot out," I added. "What do you think?"

"I think you need a keeper. You have this knack for trouble, I've noticed." She shook her head. "Your poor wife."

She drove past the two police cars, their lights flashing, which now blocked the entrance to the Bruce Vento Nature Sanctuary. In the small lot, a third police car was parked next to the only remaining car in the lot. Near the car's trunk, Pete Moss was talking with an officer who scribbled notes on a small pad of paper.

"There was another car here when we left," Cai immediately noted. "It was parked on the far side of that car by Mr. Moss."

"He's right," I told Anna. "I was wondering who else was birding this morning, and then my back window blew out."

Anna told Cai to wait in the car while she and I got out of the cruiser and walked over to where the officer was wrapping up his questions with Pete.

"Somebody taking potshots at you again?" Pete asked as I approached.

So much for playing down the human target thing, I thought. Fortunately, Cai was out of listening range inside the cruiser, though why I would've expected any kind of moral support from Pete was beyond me. He'd made his estimation of me totally clear in our earlier discussion.

But that was before someone put a bullet in my car which, at the time, not only contained me, but an innocent high school student for whom I'd taken responsibility. Counselors don't like it when their charges are put—literally—in the line of fire.

Call it professional pride, maybe.

Or simple courtesy.

Not to mention it was really bad for business.

Or that it made us angry.

For the first time that morning, I began to feel my usually solid restraint in the presence of a student begin to slip.

"Is that what you saw?" I asked him back, unable to keep a note of hostility from my voice. "Someone shooting at me? Thanks for the news flash, Pete. I really appreciate it."

He held up his hands to warn me off.

"Hey, I'm just a birder," he said. "Dead bodies aren't my thing, unlike some people I know."

"Oh, that's right," I agreed. "You're the guy who wants 'justice' when other people don't agree with you. What kind of justice are you looking for, Pete?"

"I'll fill you in later about Mr. White's history," Anna told her fellow officer, who was raptly following the exchange between Pete and myself. She grabbed my arm and dragged me away from Pete. "Show us where you parked, Bob."

I gave Pete a final glare and turned to go with Anna. "He's pushing your buttons, Bob," she said in a voice pitched low. "Let it go. Don't forget, Cai's watching."

I nodded and took a deep breath of the cold air. Behind me, I heard a motor growl to life.

"Pete's leaving," Anna reported. "Let's see if we can figure out where the shooter was."

I walked over to where my tire treads had left their mark in the snow, and mimicked backing out and turning towards the entrance. I gave them an estimation of where the rear window would have been when the bullet hit, and Anna and the other officer began to do some rough triangulations of a possible bullet path to help them scour the area for any clues to the mystery attacker.

With Pete gone and my equilibrium restored, I returned to the police cruiser and asked Cai to step outside the car to verify my estimations. To my surprise, he made a beeline to a spot midway between the trail entrance and where the officers were scanning the piles of snow heaped around the edge of the parking area.

"The bullet had to come from this angle," he said. "While you were showing Officer Anna where you drove, I did some calculations in my head taking into account the probable speed of the bullet and the trajectory it would have had to take to damage your rear window in the pattern it made."

Right.

I gave myself a mental head-slap. I'd totally forgotten that Cai was a math wizard. Personally, I never got past the story problem with the speeding train and points A and B. I think it had something to do with Kalamazoo, though I could be mistaken on that.

"Anna," I called to her. "You might want to come over here for a minute and hear what Cai has to say."

"Give me a minute," she called back.

I watched her bend over and pick something off the ground, which she then dropped into a clear plastic evidence bag she pulled from her police jacket. From where I was standing, I couldn't quite make out what it was she'd found, but it looked like some kind of soggy piece of cloth. She said something to her fellow officer, and then they joined Cai and me at the edge of the lot.

Cai explained his location method to Anna and her fellow officer, and they looked suitably impressed. Not only that, but within minutes, they found a shell casing deep inside a narrow hole in the snowbank—the hot shell had clearly plunged into the pile and then melted enough snow where it hit to cover itself with a thin coating of re-freezing ice.

"The shooter used a handgun," Anna said, examining the bullet she held in a pair of tweezers. "Whoever it was, wasn't planning on a very long shot. We see a lot of this type of ammunition with the street gangs in the cities."

She traded a look with the other officer, then turned to Cai.

"Cai, is there anything you want to tell us?"

Cai's face looked pale and drawn. "I think the shooter might have been looking for me."

Chapter Twelve

"Say that again," I said.

Cai stared down at his feet for a moment, clearly grappling with how much to say. After a few moments, he looked up and focused his attention on Anna.

"My cousin Pheej, he's getting pressured by some tough guys at his school to join their gang, but he won't do it," he told her. "Pheej and I made a deal a long time ago that we would make our parents proud and never go that way. We don't have any gang problems in Savage, so I don't think about it anymore, but where Pheej lives, it's a problem. Last night, while I was at Pheej's house, a couple of these guys came and said they'd hunt him down and make him join their gang. I told them we would report them to the police."

I could tell where this story was heading.

"And then you two were caught trespassing, put in a patrol car, and driven to the police station the same night," I said. "So now you're thinking that these gang members heard about your visit to the station and think you reported them to the police. They had you staked out at the station, followed us this morning when we left, and they shot at you as a warning to Pheej."

Cai shrugged. "It's a possibility, right? I mean, it makes a lot more sense than somebody shooting at you, Mr. White, unless you've got a stalker you don't know about."

I blew out a breath into the cold air and didn't answer. Toying with the idea of a curse following me around was one thing, but bullets trespassing in my personal space was an entirely different matter.

Curses didn't shoot guns.

Gang members did.

"We're going to follow up on this," Anna assured us. "We see all kinds of crazy stuff with these gangs, and we don't take any of it lightly." She dropped the shell casing into another plastic bag that her colleague offered her, and led us back to her cruiser.

Once we were inside the car, Anna let out a sigh of frustration. "I hate it when this happens. We'd actually seen a noticeable drop in gang activity lately. We thought we were making progress. And now this."

She shook her head and started the car. "We'll go to the station, you can make your statements, and then you guys should head back to Savage."

"Sounds like a plan," I said. "Cai?"

"Let's do it," he replied. He reached inside his coat and brought out his smartphone to check the time. "Yes!"

"What?"

"My shift for selling candy cane grams is now over," he announced. "I'm off the hook."

I, on the other hand, was undoubtedly going to find myself on a rather sharp one with Mr. Lenzen as soon as he heard about our morning escapade. I had no illusions Cai and I could keep our adventure under wraps—especially since Cai was already busily texting messages to everyone in his phone book. As Anna drove the cruiser towards the station, I tried to imagine how I was going to avoid getting slammed with a suspension from my counseling duties, but I kept coming up empty.

It was going to take a sizable distraction to keep Mr. Lenzen's attention away from me when we got back to Savage, and I was fresh out of ideas.

"I need some coffee," I told Anna when we parked at the St. Paul facility. Maybe a jolt of java would kickstart my brain to come up with some diversionary tactics for the afternoon.

"You don't want our coffee, trust me," she warned me. "On your way to the highway ramp, you'll pass Swede Hollow Café. It's tiny, but it's one of the area's best kept secrets. You can run in and get a great double mocha there."

We all got out of the cruiser, and Anna looked at me over the top of the car. "But promise me that's the only stop you'll make on the way home. I don't want to hear your voice on another 911 call today. We can only take so much excitement around here."

"Scout's honor," I promised her.

"Were you a Boy Scout?" Cai asked me, waiting a few steps away on the curb. "Pheej is really into it, you know. He made all those Chimney Swift towers with his troop last year. That's how he met Mr. Windingstad. You know, the guy who helped us out this morning, and left with Pheej?"

"I know," I said, following Anna into the police station.

Pheej.

Crap.

I grabbed Anna's arm.

"Pheej and Ron," I blurted out. "Are they all right? If gang members were watching us, did they go after Pheej and Ron, too? Does anyone know?"

I had a sudden vision of Ron Windingstad and Pheej Vang sitting in a car with bullet holes in their heads.

I pulled out my own smartphone and found Ron's cell phone number in my contact list.

Punched it in.

It rang three times and went to his voice mail.

"He's not there," I told Anna, cold dread pooling in my stomach. I turned to Cai. "Cai, call Pheej. Right now. See if he's all right."

"I can't do that," Cai said. "He's in class by now. He'll get in trouble if his phone's on."

"Call him!" I ordered. "I'll make it okay later!"

Cai took out his phone and called.

"It's going to voice mail," he reported. "See, I told you. He's got it turned off because he's in class."

Please, God, I silently prayed, *let Pheej be in class with his phone turned off and not sitting somewhere with a hole in his head.*

I looked at Anna in desperation. "What do we do?"

She was already on her own phone. "I'm calling Central High School in St. Paul. I'm going to ask the attendance office if he's there."

I felt a spasm of relief. Of course. The attendance office would know. Anna knew what to do. She was a police officer. Everything was going to be fine.

I felt like I was going to throw up.

"You want to sit down, Mr. White?" Cai asked. "You look kind of . . . white."

I planted the palm of my left hand against the wall of the building and leaned over until I could feel the blood rushing back into my head.

Then my ears started ringing.

"You going to answer that?" Cai asked.

I looked up at Cai who was pointing at my parka where I'd stashed my phone.

Idiot. It's your phone, not your ears.

I thumbed on the call.

"Hi, Bob," Ron said. "Sorry I missed your call a couple minutes ago. What's up?"

I was so relieved to hear his voice, I almost passed out.

"Nothing," I croaked. "Well, no, that's not right. Someone took a shot at me and Cai, and I wanted to be sure you and Pheej were okay."

The connection was silent a moment or two before Ron asked me to repeat what I'd said.

"Someone shot at my car when Cai and I were in it," I said. "We're back at the St. Paul police station, and we think it has something to do with Pheej, so I had to make sure you two were safe."

"I dropped Pheej off at Central right after we left the station," Ron said.

My eyes caught Anna's. She was nodding in confirmation as she finished her own phone call.

"He's there," she affirmed.

"What's going on?" Ron asked.

I gave him the short version of what had happened, along with the information Cai had shared about Pheej's trouble with the gang members.

"I guess I can't say I'm surprised," Ron sighed. "Gang pressure is a problem for a lot of these kids, it seems. They need worthwhile things to do. That's one of the reasons I like working with the Boy Scout troops and getting them involved with the Chimney Swift programs. Some of the most eager Scouts I've worked with are the ones with the least opportunities in their neighborhoods." He paused. "Trisha really enjoyed teaching them to count swifts last summer. I know she and Pheej got to be pretty good friends."

A virtual barrage of warning sirens went off in my head.

Trisha and Pheej were close.

Pheej was being harassed by gang members. He'd been threatened, and last night, he'd been seen with Cai.

This morning, Cai's involved in a shooting, and the police not only suspect gang involvement, but they seem to have been expecting it, judging from their pointed question earlier of Cai.

Is there anything you want to tell us?

I looked at Anna, who was holding the door open for us into the police station.

"You have something that connects this shooting of ours with Trisha's murder, don't you?" I asked, beginning to feel sick again because I knew she was going to say 'yes.'

"Yes," she said.

I was right. I definitely felt sick again.

Anna threw a glance in Cai's direction to see if he was listening, but he was once more engrossed in texting as he walked past her on his way inside. She waited till he was out of earshot. "We now have two matching pieces of evidence, Bob. One was found with Trisha's body, and the other I picked up in the parking lot at Bruce Vento."

Crap.

Sometimes I hate it when I'm right, and this was definitely one of those times.

I was right.

And I hated it.

Pheej Vang was the target of gang violence, and anyone who associated with him was at risk. Trisha Davis had been killed in a parking garage. Cai had been targeted with a bullet.

I immediately thought again about Ron.

"Anna," I said, locking my eyes on hers, "You make sure that Ron stays safe."

"Got it covered, Bob," she nodded. "Ron's going to have some new close personal friends for a while, courtesy of the department. Unless, of course, he'd rather be a snow bird and leave town for a while until we get this gang shut down."

She gave me a tired smile. "I hear Costa Rica is lovely this time of year. Lots of great birds, too."

"Let's go with him," I suggested. "I could really use a change of scene right about now."

"You and me, both," Anna replied.

"You guys coming?" Cai called to us from down the hall.

"Look at that," Anna said. "One visit and he already knows his way around the place."

"He's always been a quick study," I said. "Let's hope your detectives are just as fast, because I really need that coffee."

CHAPTER THIRTEEN

I PARKED THE LOANER Anna had arranged for me against the curb, steps away from the Swede Hollow Café. To be on the safe side, and, frankly, well over the line into paranoia, I wouldn't let Cai get out of the car until I opened his door for him and escorted him into the tiny bistro.

After the insanity of the last few hours, I decided I not only needed a good cup of coffee, but I really deserved one. And even though the last time I took Anna's suggestion, I ended up losing my rear window to a gunshot, I figured I'd chance a coffee stop.

Besides which, Cai had reminded me he was in no rush to get back to Savage High School, since he was taking two courses at our local community college this term in the afternoons, and today was his one class-free afternoon of the week.

"You want a coffee, Cai?" I asked him as we both stared up at the big menu board nailed to the back wall of the café. I glanced at the tall bakery case next to the cash register. It was filled with a variety of fresh-baked goods that set my mouth watering. "Or maybe a scone or a muffin?"

Cai studied the inventory and pointed to a cinnamon roll slathered in cream cheese icing. "One of those," he decided. "And a Mountain Dew."

I cringed.

No doubt about it: Cai Xiong was all American when it came to being a high school boy—he liked sugar with his sugar, and lots of it. I didn't even flinch when I gave his order to the barrista behind the counter. We collected our drinks and rolls and claimed a tiny table next to the window that looked out over the café's outdoor patio with its impressive stone fountain. A small flock of Dark-eyed Juncos lightly hopped in the snow around the fountain, probably finding seeds shed by the surrounding bushes.

"Guess they must turn that off in the winter," Cai observed. "The ice patterns overlaying the stone look pretty cool, though."

His mention of patterns reminded me of his accurate location of the shooter's position at the sanctuary's parking lot.

"You were pretty cool yourself helping Anna and her buddy with finding that shell casing," I said in between sips of my double mocha. "You ever think about going into police work?"

Cai finished chewing the enormous bite of roll in his mouth. "No. I want to do computer aided design for bioengineering companies. Work in nanotechnology and maybe anthropometry, if I can."

I nodded as if I understood what he was talking about. It's a sacred rule for counselors: never let your students know they're smarter than you are.

"But it's amazing what simple triangulation can do in locating sources," he continued, excitement in his eyes. "That's what Pheej and I . . ."

He broke off and stuffed another piece of the cinnamon roll in his mouth, and turned his head to stare back outside. Unless he'd suddenly developed a passion to watch those Juncos foraging around the fountain, I was convinced he was withholding something from me.

I flashed back to earlier in the morning when he and Pheej had exchanged some kind of eye signal in the hall at the police station. I had thought at the time the boys were hiding something, but I'd totally forgotten to pursue it with Cai once we became shooting targets.

Funny how a little-bitty bullet can take up so much of your attention.

I focused on Cai.

"That's what Pheej and you . . . what?"

Cai swung his eyes back to my face. "I can't tell you, Mr. White. I gave him my word."

"Is this about the gang thing?" I pressed him.

Cai wiped a smear of cream cheese frosting off his fingers with a napkin he found on the table.

"No, it's not," he said. He looked me directly in the eye. "It really isn't. I swear."

"Cai," I said, holding his gaze. "Given the circumstances—that someone fired a bullet in your direction the morning after you and Pheej took your law-breaking jaunt onto the Hamm's brewery property—I think maybe you should re-evaluate the necessity of keeping this promise. Especially if it's putting you or Pheej in bodily danger."

"It can't be, Mr. White," he insisted. "We were taking photographs. That's all."

I took another swallow of coffee and set the tall cup down on the tabletop.

"I think you're going to have to trust me here, Cai, and let me be the judge of that."

My future bioengineer folded his arms on the table and dropped his head down, thinking it over. When he looked up again, I could tell he'd made the right call.

"Pheej wants to document ghostly activity in the old brewery so he can send the photos to some parapsychology journal. Either that, or he's trying to land a guest spot on that *Ghost Hunters* reality show on television." He gave me a half-smile. "Pheej is sort of obsessed with the idea of a spiritual dimension."

Okay.

That was totally not what I'd been expecting to hear. To be honest, I wasn't sure what I expected, but that was definitely not it.

Pheej wanted to take a photo of a ghost. I vaguely recalled Bridget saying something, too, about Pheej and being creepy and curses.

Curses.

Why did that word keep following me around lately? I almost expected to see a Raven fly into the patio area and perch on the top of the fountain, except that Ravens in Minnesota generally stayed north of the Twin Cities. Really, the last thing I wanted to see right now was an omen of ill fortune—I'd had my daily allowance of it already, thank you very much. The only good thing I could see coming from this morning's trip to St. Paul was that I was going to get a new rear window in my SUV.

Which I'd needed like a hole in my head.

Then again, I didn't get a hole in my head from the bullet that shattered the window, so I really should have been thanking my lucky stars instead of complaining.

"Do you know anything about the Hamm kidnapping?" Cai abruptly asked, ending my brief dip into a seasonably cool pool of self-pity.

"Hamm kidnapping?"

Cai finished off his Mountain Dew and pushed back in his chair.

"In 1933, William Hamm—he was the company president—was grabbed off the street and kidnapped by members of the Barker-Karpis gang," Cai explained. "They hid Hamm in a house in Illinois and demanded $100,000 in ransom. The Hamm family paid the money, and Mr. Hamm was dumped out of a car about an hour north of St. Paul. He was totally fine. I read somewhere that they even gave him Hamm's brand of beer while he was being held prisoner so he wouldn't be offended."

I smiled at Cai's story. "Ah, for the good old days when kidnappers respected your sensibilities," I commented. "That was class."

"But there's more to the story," Cai informed me. "The kidnappers thought they got away clean, but the FBI had just developed a brand new investigative technique that used silver nitrate to raise fingerprints from places they couldn't dust. The G-men used it to lift fingerprints from the ransom notes the kidnappers sent to the Hamm family, and that's how they tracked down the kidnappers. It was a forensic first."

"Case closed, right?" I asked, beginning to wonder what this had to do with Pheej and his ghosts. "And you just happen to know all this . . . because . . . ?"

"My Minnesota history class at the community college," Cai explained. "We had a field trip last month to downtown St. Paul to tour points of historical interest. A bunch of my classmates made plans to go back later and barhop. I had to say 'no' since I'm not twenty-one."

Oh, good. My high school scholars were getting invited to go barhopping by classmates. Maybe we should put that into the information packet for the program.

"But that didn't close the case," Cai continued. His enthusiasm told me the kicker was just ahead, so I took another sip of my coffee and waited for him to go on.

"The police knew who the kidnappers were," he reported, "but they took awhile to catch them, even though they kidnapped other people, too. What gets kind of sketchy is what was going on with the brewery. There were rumors that Hamm was hooked up with the Keatings mob, who were St. Paul bootleggers—this was during Prohibition, remember, and sales were low for the brewery—legal sales, that is. Hamm crossed the mob in a business deal, so they kidnapped him and made the family pay. And of course, there were also speculations that the police were in on it, too, and got a big cut of the ransom money."

Anna's remark came back to me: *"Cops can be criminals, too. We're all human. We all make mistakes."*

"So you're saying that gangs are nothing new to St. Paul?" I ventured. "I thought you said what you and Pheej were doing had nothing to do with gangs."

"I'm not done," he told me. "This isn't about gangs, but yeah, I guess you're right. Gangs aren't new to St. Paul."

I circled my finger in the air to move him on. "And so . . ."

"Hamm's mother died while he was being held for ransom. Pheej thinks her spirit is hanging around the old brewery, still waiting for Hamm to come home, and that's the ghost he's been trying to photograph." Cai stood up from the table. "You going to bring the rest of your coffee with you?"

I looked up at Cai. "So did he get a picture of her last night?"

Cai shrugged. "I'm not sure. He has to develop the photos today. He has a photography class at Central, and he was going to try to get them done. But based on the triangulations we did, I think we came as close as possible to the spot where he saw her last summer. That's why we had to climb the fence last night, Mr. White—to get the best angle we could at the window."

I sat glued to my seat. "He saw the ghost of Mrs. Hamm last summer?"

"He says he did. He even says he had a picture of her, but he gave it away. Are we going now?"

I pushed myself up from the table and snagged my cup of coffee. "Lead the way."

We threaded our path around two more tables that were occupied, and Cai reached to open the front door just as it opened.

"Uncle Duc!" my student exclaimed. "What are you doing here?"

Duc Nguyen came into the crowded café and brushed some snowflakes off the collar of his jacket.

"I could ask you the same thing, Cai," the duck blogger replied. "I'm hoping to see a Trumpeter Swan near here. Shouldn't you be in school?"

"I'm his school counselor," I said, extending my hand to shake his. "We're . . . on a field trip. I don't think we've been introduced. I'm Bob White."

The birding blogger shook my hand. "Duc Nguyen. You were there last night," he said. "At the Black Forest, with the Birds and the Beers."

"I was," I acknowledged. "You and Birdchick were quite the entertainers, I have to say."

He smiled broadly. "Spoken like a true birder. I doubt that any other audience would find a comic riff on the regurgitation reflexes of vultures to be so funny."

"You've got to be kidding," Cai said. "Eeuuw."

"Suspicions confirmed," Duc laughed. "Look, I don't want to hold up your field trip. Are you going to the wake tonight for Ken Kniplinger? I'll be there, so maybe we could talk more then."

"I'll look forward to it," I said. "Nice to meet you. And, by the way, we saw the Trumpeter Swan at the Bruce Vento Nature Sanctuary ourselves earlier this morning. It seems to be hanging around, so hopefully you'll get a look at it. "

Cai pulled the door open and said good-bye to Duc. I followed him out onto the front step of the café and zipped my parka up to my chin.

My car was gone.

Then I remembered: I didn't have my SUV—Anna Grieg and her buddies had it while they presumably dug a bullet out of the upholstery somewhere. I had a loaner—the old Crown Victoria parked right in front of me.

I hoped the loaner had a good heater, because otherwise, it was going to be a long cold drive back to Savage.

"I didn't know Duc Nguyen was your uncle," I said to Cai as I pulled into the street.

"He's not really my uncle," Cai replied. "He's some kind of distant relative on my mother's side of the family. Maybe he's a third or fourth cousin, I don't know. I've always called him Uncle Duc."

"But Pheej knows him, right? When he was talking about Duc on Saturday at the MOU meeting, he never said he was related to him." I took the exit for 94 west and stepped on the accelerator to merge with the highway traffic.

Or at least I tried to. The loaner wasn't exactly responding to a gentle tap, so I pushed the pedal harder.

Whoa! Up a whole two miles per hour.

In my rear view mirror, I could see the driver behind me was about to land in my back seat. That would be the icing on the cake this morning: a rear-end collision in St. Paul in a police loaner. With a student in the car. I'd never work again as a high school counselor.

On the bright side, I'd have all the time I wanted to go birding.

I floored it.

Yes! The loaner roared up to what was apparently its top speed of fifty-five miles per hour. I made a mental note to accuse Anna of trying to guarantee I wouldn't exceed any posted speed limits by giving me the slowest car in St. Paul.

"He's not," Cai said, not missing a beat in our conversation. "Duc is on my mother's side. Pheej is on my father's side. I think they met for the first time on Saturday night when Pheej's family came over for dinner and Duc was visiting us. He's here from California for a few days. He told my dad he had some unfinished business with a woman here."

I threw him a quick look as my speed-challenged loaner settled in behind a truck on the interstate.

Business with a woman?

Duc had been scheduled as our guest speaker at the MOU meeting. Unless George Janssen, our programming chairman, had experienced a very recent sex-change of which I was unaware, I didn't see how Duc's speaking engagement could fit that description. Besides, until I saw him last night at the Black Forest, I had just assumed that Duc had returned home in the wake of the MOU paper session cancellation. The unfinished business Cai referred to must have been the blogger's reason he was still in town.

"I think he's getting a wife," Cai speculated. "He was really nervous at the house on Saturday night. He kept jumping every time the doorbell rang, like he was afraid to see who was going to walk in next. Pheej said he figured Duc was just spooked from what happened at your bird meeting, but I don't buy it. I think he's shopping for a wife."

"Shopping? You mean as in having to give money to the wife's family? Like a reverse dowry?"

"Sort of," Cai agreed. "Instead of the woman's family paying property or money to the groom like in some cultures, a Vietnamese man is expected to demonstrate the wealth he's bringing to the bride's family. But I heard Pheej say that Duc doesn't make much money as a blogger, so I don't know what kind of wife he can get."

The truck ahead of me took the next off-ramp, leaving the loaner with an open lane. I pressed the accelerator in hopes of making up even a little time on the road since my errand of mercy to spring Cai had turned into a half-day in St. Paul.

Fortunately, I'd had the chance to call Luce the second time we were at the police station to tell her I had to cancel our after-lunch date to see the Pacific Loon at Lake Waconia. I'd have to hope the bird hung around at least another day or two if I was going to have a chance to see it.

Thinking about Luce reminded me of what she'd said this morning while we were talking about the interactions I'd watched between Birdchick, Frank Quinn, and Duc the night before. Luce thought that business concerns was the underlying cause, and now Cai had said that Duc's reason for his trip to Minnesota was unfinished business with a woman.

Could that woman be Sharon, our little Birdchick?

If it was, Duc's reason for lingering in Minnesota had nothing to do with shopping for a wife, as Cai had surmised. Sharon was already married. The only business Duc and Sharon had in common was birds—bird blogging, to be exact. Of course, there was also the "business" of authoring the bird book, a plum, and possibly profitable, assignment, which Duc had lost to the Birdchick. I'd noted a competitive edge to Sharon's comments about Duc on Saturday before he'd appeared at the MOU meeting, but last night at the bar, the two birders seemed as comfortable with each other as two chicks in a nest.

As long as they're not eagle chicks we're talking about. Eaglets are not good nest buddies. In fact, they can be fatal. Bald Eagles lay their eggs on consecutive days, so the first-hatching chick virtually lays claim to the nest, attacking any later-hatching sibling and hogging the food the parents bring to the nest. As a result, it's not uncommon that only one eaglet survives.

Golden Eagle hatchlings are even worse, though. Females lay their eggs three to five days apart, resulting in what can be drastic differences in size. Sometimes, the older one may deliberately push the younger one out of the nest, which has led researchers to dub it "cainism" in a nod to the Cain and Abel story in the Bible.

Talk about sibling rivalry. I used to go crazy with the way my sister, Lily, teased me, but at least she didn't force me to starve to death, or peck me to pieces, or push me out a fourth-story window.

Last night, Birdchick and Duck Man had companionably shared the spotlight in a friendly competition at Birds and Beers. But if "unfinished business" hung between the two over the book contract, I didn't want to be around if they suddenly turned into eaglets and attacked each other.

Attack.

The vision of a car spinning toward me in a crosswalk filled my head. I'd assumed it was a winter night's accident about to happen, but Birdchick had seen it differently—she'd been sure she was the deliberate target of a vehicle attack.

And then Duc had conveniently arrived at the Black Forest shortly thereafter . . . but late enough, I now realized, to have parked an out-of-control car a block or two away and walked back to the bar.

At least, what had appeared as an out-of-control car.

"Besides," Cai mused, "Duc's pretty old. He might be just as happy with any wife, as long as she's alive and kicking."

"Excuse me," I said. "I'm about as old as Duc. Aren't you being a little age-biased here?"

Cai laughed. "No offense, Mr. White. I'm just calling it—"

"The way I see it," I finished for him. "Tell you what—maybe I'll just corner your Uncle Duc at the wake tonight and see what I can get out of him in regards to some hush-hush bride shopping."

Along with a few other items of concern, which I was not sharing with Cai, like 1) did Duc have car-driving skills no one suspected; and 2) exactly why was the Duck Man still in town?

The jangle of a ringtone ended our conversation.

"Hey, cuz," Cai said into his phone. "What's up?"

I glanced at Cai and mouthed "Pheej?"

He nodded, apparently listening to his cousin's voice at the other end of the connection.

"Mr. White asked me to check up on you," Cai explained. "We think some gang members followed us from the police station this morning and shot out Mr. White's rear window, and we wanted to be sure you were okay."

He listened some more, then said, "At a nature sanctuary near the police station. No, we're fine. I told them about the gang, Pheej. When somebody starts shooting, that's serious business. You've got to let the police know."

A few moments later, Cai finished the call, only to have his phone ring again.

"Hey, Bridget," he said. "What's up?"

I shot him another glance, and he met my eyes.

"Really? Wow. I'll tell Mr. White. We're on our way back right now. Okay, I will."

I waited for Cai to tell me what Bridget had said.

"Don't worry about us getting back to Savage too soon, Mr. White," he told me. "The high school is in lockdown for a bomb threat, so we won't be able to get in for a while, anyway."

"Bridget called you during a lockdown?" All my emergency procedures training kicked in with a vengeance. "No one's supposed to use any electronic devices in case it triggers a bomb!"

"There's no bomb, Mr. White. Some slacker just didn't want to have to go to class, so they called in a bomb threat."

"You don't know that," I said, an unintended sharp edge on my words. "Crazy stuff happens all the time these days, and we have those rules in effect for a reason—like to keep everyone as safe—and alive—as possible. Bomb threats aren't a joke."

"I know that," Cai responded. "I'm not the one who called it in, Mr. White. Hey, is that another one of those swans we saw in St. Paul?"

I followed the direction of his finger pointing out his side window to see a Trumpeter Swan dropping down towards the Minnesota River as we crossed over the I-35 bridge.

"Good eye, Cai," I complimented him. "It's a Trumpeter, all right."

Nice to know at least one good thing had come out of the morning—Cai had scored his first Trumpeter Swan for his life-list.

Not that Cai had a life-list, although maybe he'd be inspired to start one now.

You're never too young, or too old, to start birding, you know. Just calling it the way I see it.

"Sorry if I snapped at you, Cai," I apologized as we turned west towards Savage. "Bomb threats tend to make me a little edgy."

"That's okay, Mr. White," he allowed. "I guess it's been kind of a stressful morning for you, huh?"

I nodded. "Yup. I guess you could say that."

Students in jail, car shootings, nasty birders, gangs, bomb threats.

The day could only get better.

I hoped.

Then I thought of one really good reason to be glad I'd been in St. Paul ducking bullets this morning: if I'd been in the high school, I'd be on the staff task team looking through lockers for bombs right now.

Gee, I guess I didn't have to come up with a distraction this afternoon for Mr. Lenzen after all.

Somebody already did.

CHAPTER FOURTEEN

BY THE TIME I GOT to the turn into the high school, the flashing lights on a whole fleet of emergency vehicles had all been turned off, and their crews were getting ready to leave. I parked in the nearest empty slot and walked over to the closest fire truck.

"No bombs, I take it," I said to the fireman who was about to climb up into his engine's driver's seat.

"False alarm, thankfully," he said. "I hope I never see a real one."

"You and me both," I agreed.

Cai and I passed by two police cruisers pulled up near the school's front doors. Rick Cook, our school police officer and my close personal friend, was standing with three other officers on the far side of the car.

"You missed the excitement, Bob," he called to me. "We had the canine patrol here, but the only suspicious thing they found was a pile of green coconut on your desk."

"What about the duck?" I asked.

"What duck?"

I had the undeniable feeling that Rick was feigning ignorance, along with innocence.

"When I left this morning, there was a chocolate duck on the coconut nest," I said.

I noticed that Rick's fellow officers were all trying to hide smiles.

"Did you guys eat my duck?"

Rick burst out laughing. "If only!" he said. "Unfortunately, one of the German Shepherds—Wanda, the Wonder Dog—got to it first and practically inhaled it."

The other officers were laughing out loud.

"And since chocolate is toxic for dogs, she threw it back up again," one of Rick's buddies informed me. "Right outside your office."

"Euwww," Cai said.

"Crap," I said.

"Not crap," Rick pointed out. "Vomit."

"Thank you for the clarification," I told him. "I feel so much better now."

"But you must have the nicest receptionist in the whole world," the buddy continued. "She cleaned it up as soon as we gave the all-clear on the bomb threat."

Oh, man. I was going to owe Patty big-time for that. A year's supply of chocolate might be a good place to start, which, I had to admit, would be a small price to pay in exchange for this particular gesture of hers that went above and beyond her job description. I'd already thought she was a gem for rearranging my calendar this morning, but this put her up in the crown jewel department.

Definitely chocolate, and lots of it.

"See you jokers later," I said, waving goodbye to the still-chortling policemen.

Cai peeled off in the direction of the cafeteria to wait for Bridget to finish classes for the day. I stepped into the counseling suite, only to be met with the strong smell of a pine-scented cleaner.

"I heard, and am forever in your debt," I said to Patty, who was sitting behind her desk, trying to hide the fact that she was touching up her nail polish. "I'm going to shower you with chocolate for the next year."

Patty grimaced. "You know, I think I'm off chocolate for a while." She pointed to the newly-mopped space in front of my office door. "It just doesn't have that usual appeal to me right now, if you get my drift."

I nodded. "I get it."

"But the pine scent is really nice, don't you think? Very Christmasy," she commented.

She put her bottle of nail polish back in her top desk drawer. "Oh, and Alan wanted you to call him when you got in, by the way. No one else, including you-know-who," she said, clearly referring to my supervisor Mr. Lenzen, "has even asked where you were."

"Thanks, Patty. For everything," I added, turning towards my office. I stood on my pine-scented threshold and unlocked my office door. Tiny shreds of green coconut scattered across the floor as I stepped inside. Patty was right. If I closed my eyes, I could almost imagine I was standing in the middle of a pine forest on a snowy Christmas day.

Actually, the pine scent was so strong, it was more like I was inside a pine tree on a snowy Christmas day. Combined with the cold air blowing in through my window—I assumed Patty must have left it open to help air out the place—it had to be a balmy forty-five degrees in my office.

"This must be what a Pine Siskin feels like when it's sitting on pine branches in the winter," I muttered. "A pine-sicle."

To be completely accurate, though, Pine Siskins don't sit on pine branches so much as hang upside down from them while they eat seeds on the branches below. Luckily, I didn't have to perform similar acrobatic feats to eat my lunch. All I had to do was walk down the hall and open the refrigerator in the teachers' lounge.

I closed my window and called Alan. He picked up on the first ring, and I told him I was going to go eat a late lunch in the lounge. He said he'd be down in a few minutes.

I took a quick look at some phone messages Patty had left on my desk and finally took my parka off to hang on the back of my office door. As I reached to hang it up, I remembered that the bag of M&Ms I'd brought for Alan's Secret Santa delivery was still in the pocket. I grabbed it and hustled to the teachers' lounge to stuff the candy bag in Alan's mailbox before he arrived.

He was already there, pouring himself a cup of coffee.

So much for keeping the identity of Alan's gift-giver secret.

"I give up," I announced, handing him the candy. "Here you go. I'm your Secret Santa."

He studied me over the rim of his coffee mug. "Yeah, right."

He took the bag I offered him.

"Very clever, I have to admit," my brother-in-law said. "Tell my Secret Santa I'm not so easily fooled, however. I know you're just trying to mislead me. Nice try, White-man."

"No, Alan, I really am your Secret Santa," I argued with him. "With everything else going on right now, I just can't get it together this year to be any more creative with gifts or concealing my Santa identity. What you see is what you get."

"Yeah, right," he said again. "So, did you spring Cai? Bridget told me," he explained before I could ask him how he knew about my little jail-bird.

"He was already sprung by the time I got there," I reported, "thanks to his cousin Pheej and a mutual birding colleague."

"So . . . what? You took the scenic route home via Wisconsin? It's only a half-hour drive from St. Paul to Savage," he reminded me. "You, my speed-demon brother-in-law, can probably drive it in twenty-two minutes flat."

"Give me some credit here, Alan," I protested. "Twenty-one minutes, on a good day."

I took my lunch out of the refrigerator and sat down at one of the long tables in the room.

"So what did the lovely Luce prepare for you this week?" Alan asked as I snapped open the plastic container of food I hadn't finished off yesterday. He sat down across the table from me and peered into the bowl. "Chicken salad?"

"Not just any chicken salad," I said. "Luce's tropical chicken salad. A taste of summer in the midst of winter."

I put a forkful of pineapple, grapes, pecans, chicken, and mango in my mouth. "What do you know about the Hamm Heritage Group?"

"Never heard of them," Alan replied. "Do they have something to do with the Hormel company in Austin?"

"Hamm as in beer, Alan, not ham as in dinner time," I clarified. "Like in St. Paul. The brewing company. 'From the land of sky blue waters,'" I said, echoing part of the old commercial jingle that my dad loved to sing when I was a kid.

"I've still never heard of them," Alan insisted. "Is it like a micro-brewery drinking club?"

I'd had almost the same thought when Anna had first mentioned them. Since Alan was Savage's best-informed news and politics junkie, I was hoping he might be able to shed a little light on the publicity-shy conservation group, but it looked like I was going to strike out on that ball.

"They're one of these citizen historic preservation groups," I told Alan. "Apparently they want to keep the old Hamm brewery standing, so they can turn it into one of those micro-breweries you just mentioned. But so far, no one's stepping up to the plate to undertake developing the site. I'm sure it would amount to a hefty price-tag to bring the building up to code, not to mention spiffing it up enough to attract a new tenant."

"They pulled it off in downtown St. Paul," Alan reminded me. "The old Schmidt brewery on the Mississippi is now an apartment and art studio complex thanks to a $120-million, fifteen-acre redevelopment project. They kept a lot of the original architecture, like brick walls and wood-slat ceilings. I read that they had almost 150 different floor plans in the 260 units they built, because they designed the apartments to fit into the existing structure. The payoff is the economic impact new residents are having on the area. It took a decade for the city to make it happen, but it's a success story now."

He snatched a grape from my bowl and popped it into his mouth.

"Why the sudden interest in a building preservation group?" Alan asked.

"They're the folks who helped keep Cai's police record clean," I said. "The police got a tip that kids were trespassing on private property—the old Hamm brewery near Swede Hollow—and it was Cai and his cousin Pheej, taking photos of the building. After they were brought to the station, though, the property owners—the Hamm Heritage Group—dismissed all charges."

"That was nice of the group," Alan noted. "They could have made an example of the boys and thrown the book at them, hoping it would discourage other trespassers."

"Exactly my thoughts," I told him. "Especially if the site is attracting urban explorers, which apparently it does on occasion."

"Lawsuits in the making," Alan said. "Preservation groups generally don't have a lot of money, and they sure don't want to have to spend it settling claims to families whose kids have gotten hurt in crumbling buildings that might be ruled criminally negligent."

"So why wouldn't the Hamm-sters be forcing the issue?" I wondered.

"They don't want to bring attention to the building?" Alan guessed. "Maybe they hope everyone will just forget about it and leave it alone if they stay out of the public eye."

"But they do a Chimney Swift sit there every summer," I pointed out.

"A what?"

I'd momentarily forgotten that while my brother-in-law was well-versed in current events and politics, he was barely a hatchling when it came to birding affairs.

"A Chimney Swift sit is when birders gather and count the number of Chimney Swifts that go to roost at night in a particular location," I explained. "Chimney Swifts roost in old tall smokestacks or towers. Right around sunset, they flock together and stream into the chimneys to roost. Counting the birds helps monitor populations, which have decreased by about half in the last forty years."

I took a last bite of my chicken salad and snapped the lid back on the container.

"And this Hamm's brewery is one of the places they Chimney Swift sit?" Alan asked.

I nodded. "Pheej counted swifts there last summer, and he said there weren't any 'NO TRESPASSING' signs."

"So maybe the Hamm-sters decided they don't like Chimney Swifts in their chimneys," Alan suggested, "because they're trying to preserve the building, and I can't imagine the birds are cleaning up after themselves. I know you love birds, Bob, but let's face it, they're messy."

"But they roost there, Alan. They come back every year. You can't decide you don't want them there and send them a court order by certified mail forbidding them to make their homes in the chimneys."

Alan tore open his bag of M&Ms and tossed a handful into his mouth. "How do they do that, anyway? Make nests in chimneys, I mean. It's not like there are a bunch of little interior ledges to put nests on."

"The nests literally hang on the walls," I told him. "The birds use their saliva as glue and use it to attach twigs to the inside wall of the smokestack." I pushed back from the table and stood up. "Chimney Swifts can't perch like other birds, Alan, so you'll never see them sitting on a tree branch. Heck, they can't even walk. They can only cling to vertical surfaces with their long claws, and the only time they don't spend flying is when they roost at night or when they're nesting. Vertically."

Alan stood up, too. "So that's why they like the chimneys," he said. "And that's why the number of the swifts has dropped so much—people don't build those kinds of chimneys anymore."

"Right."

I picked up my empty plastic bowl and lid and went over to the sink to rinse them out.

"You and Luce want to come over tonight?" Alan asked. "Baby Lou is cutting a new tooth. She'd be happy to share some of her saliva with you. You could make a nest with it if you want."

"Wow, that's a really hard offer to refuse, Alan. But we can't make it," I said. "We're going to the wake for Nip Kniplinger tonight."

"Man, I'm sorry, Bob. This has been a rough week for you, I know."

"I've certainly had better."

Alan twisted the top of his candy bag shut and held the faculty lounge door open for me as I followed him out into the hallway. "We'll do it another night, then. I think we'll be swimming in saliva for the next few years, anyway. See you later, White-man."

As I watched his broad back retreat down the hall, I realized I hadn't said a word to him about the morning's shooting in St. Paul.

"Just as well," I told myself. With the run of bad luck I'd had since I'd found Trisha Davis dead over coffee on Saturday morning, Alan would probably forbid me to get anywhere near Baby Lou if he heard about my most recent escapade in St. Paul with Cai.

I walked back to my office and looked at the clock on my desk.

It was almost three o'clock in the afternoon. The school day was just about over.

Thank God.

I threw my rinsed container and lid into my briefcase and sat down to read through my phone messages more carefully. I figured I could probably get two more college recommendations written before I left in an hour to go collect Luce and head to Nip's wake.

But I didn't.

Instead, I just sat in my chair, staring at what was left of a green coconut nest on my desk.

A horizontal nest. No Chimney Swifts in this office.

No chocolate ducks, either. I briefly imagined Wanda, the WonderDog, snarfing down my Secret Santa surprise, only to surprise her handlers with its speedy return.

I couldn't help it. I smiled. It was funny—a moment of sheer goofiness in a very bleak day.

I had to hand it to my Secret Santa, though, whoever it was— he or she was certainly clued into my interest in birds, albeit with a creative twist: a picture of student chickens yesterday and an edible duck today. I wondered what bird would be involved in tomorrow's delivery. As to the identity of my gift-giver, I was no closer to an answer this afternoon than I'd been this morning, which was no surprise since I'd been out of the office almost all day. I hadn't even remembered to question my crown jewel Patty to see if I could extract any clues before she left her desk for home.

My Santa sleuthing would have to wait for another day.

Alan, on the other hand, was done with the game. Or he should be, since I'd admitted I was his Secret Santa. The idea that he thought I was covering for someone else made me smile again. It never would have occurred to me that the best disguise was no disguise at all.

Sort of like hiding in plain sight.

I collected the coconut that remained on my desk and dumped it into my trashcan, grabbed my parka and briefcase, and headed out to the parking lot and my speed-challenged loaner.

I had a wake to attend, and, if the opportunity presented itself, a Duc to grill.

Unfinished business, indeed.

CHAPTER FIFTEEN

Bertram's Funeral Home was packed. I had to drive around the block twice before I found an open parking space between a fire hydrant and the end of someone's driveway. The moment Luce and I climbed out of her car, we heard a rush of twittering and saw flashes of yellow as a tight flock of little brown birds erupted from a stand of pines in the front yard of the house.

"Pine Siskins," Luce said.

"So they are," I agreed, watching the birds' distinctive undulating flight pattern, their fluttering wings the source of the yellow flashes. Luce joined me on the sidewalk after skirting a mound of dirty snow piled on the curb.

"I assume you'd prefer I not go heavy on pine-scented décor in the house this holiday season," Luce commented, a smile in her voice. I'd given her the full report of the day, and while she wasn't happy about the St. Paul episode, she'd definitely laughed with me about Wanda the Wonder Dog's contribution to my counseling career at Savage.

I wrapped my arm around her waist and dropped a kiss on her cheek. "Good assumption. I think I'd prefer cinnamon spice scent, if possible. Pine is not my go-to aroma right now."

We hustled down the block to Bertram's, holding each other erect when icy patches on the sidewalk threatened to land us on our rumps. I pulled open the heavy oak door and got slapped in the face with a blast of heat that felt like it had come from a sauna.

"Lots of hot air in here tonight," I commented to Luce.

"Lots of birders," she countered, already nodding and waving to several birding acquaintances in the narrow entrance vestibule.

"Same thing," I responded.

My wife lightly smacked my shoulder and gave me a stern look. "This is a wake, Bobby. Be nice."

"I love it when you're mean to me," I whispered.

Luce shook her head and walked away, but not before I saw the smile on her lips.

"Mr. White."

I turned and found Pheej Vang standing next to me.

"Have you met Duc Nguyen?" he asked. His voice was filled with admiration, and I recalled how he'd praised Duc's work to the Birdchick at the MOU meeting. "He's here," he added. "I can introduce you."

"Actually, I met him earlier today," I told Pheej. "In St. Paul. Cai and I ran into him before we headed back to Savage."

A small cloud of disappointment dimmed the boy's smile. He'd clearly wanted to introduce me to his bird-blogging hero.

"But I didn't have much chance to speak with him," I added. "Why don't you lead the way and I'll follow you?"

Pheej's face immediately brightened back up. "Okay. He's over by the refreshment table. Come this way."

I slowly followed Pheej through the crowd of Nip's mourners, stopping briefly several times to greet and shake hands with the people I knew well. Once or twice, I looked over the room of faces and saw Luce likewise moving through clutches of people, embracing birders she hadn't seen for some time or politely shaking hands with other visitors. As she'd noted when we arrived, there were plenty of birders at the wake, and I wondered how many of them had made it a habit to drink coffee with Nip on birding mornings.

Whether or not I was the first birder Nip introduced to hot joe, I had no idea, but it was a memory of the man that would remain with me the rest of my life. That and chasing a Mississippi Kite with him on my first trip as an independent birder.

"Hello again, Mr. White," Duc Nguyen said, extending his hand to me as I edged around the last person standing between us.

"Please, call me Bob," I said.

"And I'm Duc," he responded. "So your field trip went well, I take it?"

Pheej threw me a confused look. "Field trip?"

"Cai and I went to see the Trumpeter Swan on our way back to Savage," I told Pheej. "Didn't he tell you about it?"

"I saw it, too," Duc said. "Shortly after we met at the café. It was a beauty. Have you seen one, Pheej?"

"Not yet," the young birder replied. "I have school, and I don't have a way to go see it before my classes start, or when the school day is over, either."

"That was always the worst part for me when I was in high school, too," I agreed. "I'd see postings of birds in my email from other MOU members the first thing in the morning, but I'd have to go to school, so I couldn't go and try to see the bird. I was always envious of older people who could drop everything and take off to chase a rare bird that had been reported."

"But I understand you've more than made up for that youthful lack," Duc said. "You hold a Big Year record for Minnesota, isn't that correct?"

"I do," I nodded. "Thanks to a lot of other birders who shared sightings, I was able to set a new record for the state. I don't know I could do it again, though. I don't think my wife would be too happy with me running off at all hours of the day and night to chase birds, even though she's a birder herself. Are you married, Duc?"

Woo-hoo! I mentally congratulated myself. I couldn't have asked for a smoother segue than that into what I really wanted to quiz him about even if I'd planned out the whole conversation ahead of time.

Which I hadn't.

I was, however, a birder. And thanks to years of birding, I'd learned how to make the most of an opportunity when it unexpectedly presented itself. Improvisation isn't just for stand-up comics, you know. Give me a bird and a general idea where it is, and I'll improvise a way to find it.

Like climbing a fence to find a Long-tailed Duck fifteen years ago.

"No," Duc admitted, "there is no Mrs. Nguyen."

I thought I detected a note of sadness in his voice, but that could have been simple wishful thinking on my part, hoping Cai was right about his distant relative's reason for still being in the Twin Cities.

Because the alternative reason—the one I was afraid might be the real one—wasn't simple at all: Duc's "unfinished business" was looking for payback over the book contract he'd lost to his bird blogging colleague. And if he'd been the man behind the wheel of the spinning car last night that had so shaken Birdchick, I was even more afraid his business was not just payback, but payback with deadly intent.

"But you have a lovely wife, Bob," Duc added. "She seemed to enjoy our silly tweeting competition at the bar last night very much. I hope you'll introduce me. Perhaps she has a sister who also likes birding."

He gave me a polite smile, then excused himself to go give his condolences to Nip's grown children on the far side of the room.

Pheej gave me a similar smile, then turned away, trailing after Duc with all the intensity of a star-struck teenager following his celebrity idol.

Okay, so that went well. I now knew nothing more about Duc Nguyen than I'd known when I'd arrived at Bertram's, except that he was a single guy who thought my wife was lovely.

No surprise there. I couldn't remember the last time I met a guy who didn't think Luce was attractive.

So much for my talents of improvisation and investigation. Good thing it worked so well for my birding career because, as a detective, I sure wasn't batting a thousand.

I wasn't batting at all.

I took a paper cup of hot cider from the refreshments table and looked around the room for familiar faces. Birdchick was holding court with a circle of MOU birders not far from the door that led back into the small entry vestibule. Between her and the end of the receiving line that wound towards a group of Nip's family members, I spotted Ron Windingstad, and standing next to him, Anna Grieg. I caught Anna's attention with a small wave, and she raised a thumbs-up in my direction.

I briefly wondered if she was on Ron detail for the evening, and if she was packing a gun beneath her stylish green woolen jacket. It occurred to me that the police might have their guarding eyes on Pheej, too, but if so, the guards were indistinguishable from the guests who milled around the room. I reached for a lemon bar and almost knocked a hot cup of coffee out of the hand of another mourner.

It was Frank Quinn, Sharon's employer.

"Sorry," I apologized. "I didn't see you there."

"No problem." He nodded in the direction Duc had taken. "You know, I just can't get a read on that guy."

He reached out to shake my hand, but since both of my hands were otherwise occupied with refreshments, he dropped his hand back to his side. "I'm Frank Quinn. I know who you are, but we've never been introduced. It's a pleasure to meet you, Bob."

"Thanks, Frank," I responded. "I understand you and Sharon work together. An air-conditioning company, right?"

"And heating," Frank said. "You live in Minnesota, it's all about heating in the winter."

He smiled and lifted his steaming mug of coffee to emphasize his point.

"And yes, Sharon's done some commercials for me," he added. "A few radio spots, a couple television ads. Local talent is a lot more affordable than movie stars when you're a small business owner like me."

I swallowed my last bite of lemon bar. "I'm sure that's true," I replied. "So how long have you been birding? We haven't crossed paths before."

Frank blew on his coffee to help it cool. "About three years. My brother-in-law was on this historic building committee, and as a favor, he asked me to take a look at the old Hamm's Brewery in St. Paul to see what it might cost to bring the place up to code. I ran into Ron Windingstad there, and he was studying Chimney Swifts, and, well, you probably know the rest of the story. I got interested in the birds, and before I knew it, Ron had me counting Chimney Swifts, too."

I laughed. Ron had that effect on people. He was so passionate and knowledgeable about the swifts, I seriously doubted there was a person alive who could walk away from him and not be interested in learning more about the birds.

"That's how I met Trisha Davis," Frank continued. He absently stroked the crest of hair that stood up on his head and which I'd first noticed at the Birds and Beers night. "She was almost as dedicated to Chimney Swifts as Ron is." He shook his head sadly. "What a loss. It's been a rough few days for the Minnesota birding community."

"It has," I agreed.

"But that guy," he motioned again in Duc's direction, "like I said, I can't get a read on him." He lowered his voice to a whisper. "He was at the St. Paul police station this morning. He was being questioned in connection with Trisha's death."

I looked at Frank in confusion.

Duc was linked to Trisha's death?

"How do you know that?" I asked. "I mean, how do you know he was being questioned? I can't imagine that kind of information is publicly available."

Frank shook his head. "It's not. My brother-in-law is a desk sergeant at the station. He knows I knew Trisha. He told me about it."

My eyes involuntarily sought out Duc, who was still conversing with Nip's family. He must have been at the station before Cai and I ran into him at the Swede Hollow Café this morning. He told us he'd come looking for the Trumpeter Swan, but hadn't shared with us that he'd made an additional stop at the police station.

For questioning in a murder case.

Not that he would necessarily want to share that with a distant relative like Cai and a stranger like me. It wasn't the kind of thing one typically opened conversations with: "Nice to meet you. I just finished a Q&A with the local police because they think I might know something about a murder. What's on your calendar for today?"

What had the police found that could possibly link bird-blogging Duc Nguyen to Trisha Davis?

Aside from Trisha's friendship with Sharon, that is.

Trisha's friendship with the Duck Man's rival, who had admitted to me and Luce last night that she'd received threatening emails.

Yikes.

Then I remembered what Sharon, the Birdchick, had said last night about the near-accident: she'd thought the car was heading for her. She'd also maintained she was the intended target in Trisha's parking garage murder. Last night, I'd wondered if Frank Quinn—or someone working with him—had confused Trisha with Sharon and mistakenly killed her to rid Frank of the commercial spokeswoman he no longer wanted. Now I wondered if I had the right idea—a mistaken identity—but the wrong motive and the wrong killer.

Had Duc Nguyen killed Trisha Davis, thinking it was his blogging and book-writing rival Sharon Stiteler, the Birdchick? Who else would have the license plate BRDCHK1?

My mind spun back to Saturday morning.

Though he'd been expected to attend, Duc arrived late for the MOU meeting because of a delayed flight through Denver, according to Nip. Yet the bulk of the storm that would have caused Duc's delayed plane had gone well south of the Twin Cities, leaving the air space in Minnesota clear. I even recalled seeing planes coming in for landings on my way to the Bell Museum that morning as I drove up Interstate 35W. To my knowledge, no one had seen the Duck Man until after the police arrived to secure the crime scene. Not only that, but I got the impression from Sharon she'd never met Duc face-to-face when Pheej had gushed about his birding blog to her, so Duc wouldn't have known Sharon from Trisha.

So Duc just happened to arrive as Trisha pulled in with the coffee, saw the Birdchick's license plate and an opportunity to exact vengeance, offered to help her with the cartons so she'd open the car door, and stabbed her so strategically that she'd died from one knife wound?

I don't think so.

Successful birders have to be great at timing, but nobody's that great.

Or lucky.

There had to be another connection between Duc and Trisha that had attracted the attention of the police, but I couldn't begin to guess what it was.

And this is why, I reminded myself, *we have detectives who are trained to ferret out the truth.*

But it was also true detectives could only ferret using what they had, and sometimes the most important clues went unnoticed because of their seeming insignificance.

Fortunately for our local detectives, I was a master of insignificance, especially when it came to birds and birders.

I don't think that came out right.

I meant to say I might see connections that don't otherwise exist to someone outside the birding loop. Thanks to my very focused perspective, I'd been able to help the police solve murders involving birders before, and I refused to believe this time would be any different.

It was the same as my determination to figure out my Secret Santa every year before it was revealed: I couldn't ignore the challenge to solve the mystery.

Although Secret Santa mysteries generally involved much lower stakes than life or death.

More on the order of little gifts, or favorite candies, or the occasional fruitcake.

Strike the fruitcake. Against my will and better judgment, I've eaten fruitcakes I was sure came close to killing me.

"I was at the police station myself this morning," I confided in Frank. "One of my students was—ah—getting a tour of the facilities."

Frank laughed and lifted his hand to shield his words from prying ears. "I heard about that, too. Sounds like the station was a popular place this morning, especially for birders. I saw that posting for the Trumpeter myself, and considered a run over there during the lunch hour, but couldn't get away from my desk. Like I said, it's heating season."

"What else did your brother-in-law tell you?" I asked, not even trying to hide the fact I was fishing for information. "I'm sure the police are rolling over every stone to try to find who killed Trisha."

"Apparently, they're focusing now on the Hmong gangs in the area," Frank reported.

I got the feeling he was one of those folks who really liked being "in the know," as if it conferred some kind of favored status on an individual. In my experience, though, people "in the know" generally turned out to be people in the "maybe they know," if not the downright "clueless" category. Seriously, I gave up on people "in the know" when nothing catastrophic happened to me at the turn of the millennium. It took me years to eat the canned beans I'd stockpiled in my apartment closet.

"There was another incident this morning," Frank was saying, "the police think was gang-related. Who knows?" he shrugged. "Maybe Mr. Nguyen has some gang ties. Stranger things have happened."

I assumed he was referring to the incident that involved my car's loss of its back window, and it galled me he was claiming some kind of inside tip, especially when I'd been the one who'd been there.

"Mr. Nguyen's a well-respected Vietnamese birder, and he doesn't live here," I reminded Frank, a bit more sharply than I had intended. Besides his 'in the know' attitude, he'd also hit a sore spot with me with his careless innuendo. As Savage High School's diversity officer, I'd learned a lot about how hurtful people could be when they voiced unfounded assumptions about others based on their ethnicity.

Frank might be annoying, but he didn't have to be insulting, too.

Out of respect for the other mourners in the room, I decided not to smack Frank Quinn on the side of his head. Instead, I drew a calming breath and attempted to end our conversation politely.

"The gangs are Hmong teenagers," I added a bit more matter-of-factly. "I doubt Duc is in cahoots with them."

"Like I said, stranger things have happened," Frank repeated, and finally changed the subject. "I've got to catch Sharon to discuss some upcoming Birdchick events, so I'll move along." He gave me a tiny salute and headed in Birdchick's direction.

"You're a jerk," I wanted to shout after him, but didn't.

I looked around for Luce and found her talking with Ron and Anna at the far end of the refreshments table. I started towards her, only to be shoved aside by a small man barreling through the crowd, clutching some kind of package to his chest. Before I could react, two men went hurdling after him just as he ripped the wrapper away from the package and threw it directly at Birdchick's face.

CHAPTER SIXTEEN

Everyone in the room froze in shock while the two men tackled the assailant to the floor.

Sharon, seemingly unfazed, slowly lifted a finger toward her face and then dragged it down her cheek, which was now thickly frosted with white meringue and yellow filling. She stuck her finger in her mouth and then pulled it back out.

"Yup," she announced. "It's definitely lemon. And, I have to say, it's always been one of my favorite flavors."

She took another swipe of the goo off her face and ate it off her finger. "Still is."

Then, with the regal bearing and dignity of a state fair dairy queen, Sharon turned to the funeral home employee who had rushed to her side with a pile of napkins and asked, "Where's the ladies' room?"

Meanwhile, the men on the floor cuffed and hoisted up the attacker.

Ah-ha. I was right. The police were here, keeping an eye on Ron while he attended Nip's wake.

Either that, or the newest item in men's wear this season was a pair of handcuffs, and I'd missed the memo.

Then again, I've never been a trend-setter when it came to fashion . . . unless you counted the hooded bug-shirt I wore when I was birding near mosquito-infested swamps.

I looked for Anna, but she had slipped out of the room with Ron. Straining against the plain-clothes policemen who held him, Sharon's pie-tosser yelled after his target.

"You'll get your just desserts, Birdchick!" the man shouted.

He looked to be in his late fifties, and the crazed expression on his face had everyone backing away from him and his two captors.

"You're a fraud!" he ranted. "You know nothing about birds! Go back to the bad egg that hatched you, Birdchick! Long live the Duck Man!"

Sharon froze and turned back to face the man, her face partly wiped clean, her hands filled with paper towels now soaked in pie filling. Her voice dropped an octave.

"Are you insulting my mother?"

The funeral home assistant laid his hand on Sharon's shoulder. "Of course he's not," he assured her. "He's a lunatic. Please, Ms. Stiteler, let's get you cleaned up."

Sharon brusquely shook him off and marched back to the cuffed man. Drawing herself up to her full height of barely over five feet, her very presence seemed to expand like a bird fluffing its feathers in winter to trap more air for heat. But the heat gathering in Sharon's face had nothing to do with the weather and everything to do with the pie-thrower.

"You want a piece of me, buddy?" she snarled in his face.

The man flinched, his earlier bravado gone. He even tried to take a step back, but his captors held him in place. He clearly hadn't anticipated the Birdchick might display talons in retaliation.

"A pie in the face? Really?" Sharon questioned him. "Ooh, I'm so scared," she mocked, then raised both of her hands filled with paper towels and pie filling, aiming for her attacker's face.

Except that, at that instant, one of the two plain-clothes policemen stepped between Birdchick and the cuffed man and attempted to break up the confrontation.

He was a split-second too late, though. The filling was already airborne.

Now there were two people getting unexpected lemon meringue facials at Bertram's Funeral Home. I knew that Bertram's advertised itself as a full-service funeral home, but this was ridiculous. I almost expected someone else to show up with a tray of nail polish.

General shouting and squawking and scuffling followed, until finally a rather bedraggled and deflated Birdchick was escorted out of the room by both the funeral home assistant and the pie-faced policeman. The other policeman had a death-grip on the collar of the pie-man and made a quick exit out into the front foyer of the funeral home, but not before his prisoner shouted one more time, "Duc rules!"

"With fans like that, who needs enemies?"

"Who needs a blog?" I answered Luce, who had made her way over to me during the brawl. "And just desserts, indeed. Judging from the fact that Sharon is currently cleaning herself up from what's left of a lemon meringue pie, I think she might be the first to say she already got her desserts."

Luce smiled and kissed my cheek. "Very funny. I doubt Sharon is feeling quite that charitable at the moment. It couldn't have been a good feeling to see someone rushing right for her with something aimed at her face, especially given her paranoia of the last few days that someone was trying to kill her."

"The good news is Sharon can rest easy now," I said. "No more pies in the face waiting in ambush."

"Assuming this guy was the one who sent her the awful emails," Luce added.

"He was obviously a big fan of Duc's," I pointed out. "That certainly dovetails with what Sharon said about the threatening messages she'd been getting. Her stalker never hid his admiration for Duc."

Luce wound a hand into the crook of my elbow and pulled me closer, her voice lowered to keep our conversation private as we finally took our place in the receiving line to give our condolences to Nip's family.

"But a pie in the face is harmless, Bobby. That's slap-stick," she insisted. "Trying to hit someone with a car or stabbing someone—that's murder. Criminals escalate their attacks over time, not tone them down." She gravely poked her finger into my chest. "You haven't been watching enough television lately, or you'd know that."

Like I really needed to watch murders played out on television. Believe me, once you've seen the aftermath of the real thing, you'd never go back.

And I didn't mean to a television show. There was nothing like a real live dead body to convince you murder wasn't entertainment.

My wife had a good point, though. The man—whom I had already forever dubbed Birdchick's Pie Man in my head—had tried to retreat from Sharon when she'd approached him with her fistfuls of pie. Nor did he exude scary murderous intent as the policeman hustled him out of Bertram's Funeral Home. He wasn't wild-eyed, or spitting in anyone's face, or creepily composed.

He just looked like he had one too many sets of nuts and bolts rolling around upstairs.

Yes, he was guilty of lobbing a pie in Sharon's face, but after thinking about what Luce said, I had to admit I seriously doubted Pie Man had it in him to try to run anyone down with a car, let alone murder Trisha Davis by mistake.

And after watching his direct path to assault Birdchick in the midst of a room of people, at least that part of any murder theory involving Pie Man as a suspect was resolved: the Duck Man's rabid fan could plainly pick the Birdchick out of a crowd, which meant there was no way he would've mistaken Trisha Davis for Birdchick in the parking garage at the Bell Museum.

That still left a question about who was behind the wheel of the skidding car last night, but then again, there was no positive proof the near-accident had been anything other than that: a near-accident caused by icy roads. If I'd been in Sharon's shoes—or boots, as the case was—and had been the recipient of threatening emails, I probably would have assumed a car heading my way was meant for me, too.

As it was, I chalked it up to . . . a curse.

Birdchick wasn't the only paranoid person in town.

As we moved forward in the line of mourners to speak with Nip's family, I reminded myself that Anna Grieg had confided in me the police now had evidence linking Trisha's death with the morning's bullet that hit my car at the nature sanctuary. That meant, I hoped, the investigation into Trisha's death was likewise moving forward, and the police were able to narrow their search for her killer.

Not that it made me feel any better about Trisha's murder case, because it didn't.

It made me feel worse.

Big surprise.

Because, as I saw it, I was getting drawn closer to Trisha's killer, too. If a gang was targeting Pheej and his friends, I had probably moved into the outer rings around the bull's-eye thanks to my public appearance with Cai this morning at the Bruce Vento sanctuary.

Crap. All I'd wanted to do was protect Cai and his scholarship. Now I was on some street gang's list of people they most wanted to hurt.

I wondered if I should talk to Mr. Lenzen about combat pay.

A soft touch on my elbow caught my attention, and I realized that Anna Grieg was standing next to me.

"Can I talk to you in private for a moment?" she asked.

I told Luce to hold my place in line and walked with Anna back to the refreshment table, which was now cleared of food and drink and void of any lingering mourners.

"You're going to tell me to be careful, aren't you?" I said as soon as we stopped walking and I faced her. "I was just thinking about it myself. I might be a target now for this gang."

Anna made a *pfft* noise.

"You've been watching too much television lately," she scolded me. "I highly doubt you're in any danger from a gang member."

"But my car—"

She held up a hand to stop me. "Bob. Hear me out. That's what I wanted to talk to you about."

I looked her in the eyes. Seeing the calmness there, I relaxed. "Okay. I'm listening."

She glanced around to be sure no one else was within hearing range.

"This is between you and me, because I don't want you thinking you have to watch your back constantly," Anna said. "So here's what's going on: we had a little talk with Pheej this afternoon when school let out. Yes, he's being harassed by a gang, but like the majority of the Asian American gangs we deal with, this gang's into burglary, not shootings or murder."

"Lower profile crime?" I asked.

"Yes," Ann said, "and they typically choose Asian families or businesses to rob, because the chances are very good these won't report the crime. Many of these immigrants came from countries where the police themselves were corrupt, so they don't trust our police personnel. Plus, it's a cultural thing—the publicity those crimes generate would bring shame to their community, and they can't bring themselves to do that."

"Which means police hands are tied when it comes to helping the families," I finished for her, nodding in understanding. I'd had to find ways around ingrained cultural attitudes with my students, too.

"So," Anna continued, "the thing I wanted to tell you is that, after we talked with Pheej, we became convinced the gang giving him grief isn't the same gang we connected to Trisha's murder scene and the Bruce Vento shooting."

"You mean there are two gangs involved?" My stomach clenched in uneasy anticipation. "Please don't tell me Pheej is at the center of a turf war between rival gangs."

"Well, see, that's the crazy thing here," Anna explained. "The evidence we found at both places—bandanas, if you're wondering—weren't the colors of any gangs we have in St. Paul. So we checked with other police departments around the country and finally got the bandanas identified as belonging to a small gang in Fresno, California."

"What does a gang in Fresno have to do with Pheej?"

"Nothing," Anna replied. "Especially since that particular gang fell apart five years ago."

I looked at her blankly.

"There's no gang involved in Trisha's death, Bob. We're almost one hundred percent certain."

I put two and two together—two ruled-out gangs and two obsolete bandanas—and came up with an even more disturbing conclusion.

I looked at Anna as I did the math.

"Someone's trying to blame—or frame—a local street gang for Trisha's murder."

CHAPTER SEVENTEEN

I COULD SEE IT IN ANNA'S EYES: I was right.

Whoever had killed Trisha had deliberately left "evidence" to derail the investigation into gang territory.

"Don't share this with anyone," Anna instructed me. "We want the real killer to think he's got us fooled. I can't tell you anything more, but Bob, you're not in danger."

Good to know. I guessed I could take the butcher knife and machine gun out from beneath my pillow tonight after all.

"And my car?" I asked. "Do you guys have a theory for why this mystery murderer picked my car to shoot up as more 'evidence' for framing an Asian American street gang?"

Anna shook her head. "Not yet. We think you might just have been available, Bob. You and Cai. A deserted nature sanctuary is a better—and probably easier—spot to plant evidence."

"Are you saying I'm easy?"

I pretended to be offended, but in truth, I desperately needed to lighten the mood of our conversation before the seriousness of what was happening bowled me over. Rather than a random spontaneous act of violence, Trisha's murder had been carefully planned and executed—I cringed at the aptness of the word—by someone for a very specific reason.

"Why Trisha?" I whispered to Anna.

"We don't know," my birding colleague answered. "But we're going to find out. And that's the favor I need to ask of you. Bob, I need your help."

"Wait a minute." I held up my hands to ward her off. "I'm always getting my wrists slapped—by just about everybody in the vicinity, it seems—whenever I try to give any assistance to the police in solving cases. And now you're asking me to help?"

"Yes," Anna answered.

"Is this going to include getting my car shot again, or, even worse, me shot?"

"I don't think so," she said. "I hope not."

"Wow." I glared at her. "I can't tell you how much that reassures me . . . because it doesn't. At all."

"All I need you to do is find out from Pheej why he's so fixated on the old Hamm's brewery. It's a conversation, Bob. That's all I'm asking you to do—talk to him," she emphasized. "I just don't buy his explanation about photographing architecture. He could photograph architecture all over St. Paul. Instead he chooses to break the law to take pictures of a crumbling brewery? He's a smart boy. He's not the type to knowingly break the law, but for some reason, he thought it was worth the risk."

"And you want to know his reason."

Anna put her hands on her hips. "Yes."

Her move pulled her jacket tightly against her body, and I could see the outline of a gun holster beneath her jacket.

I was right again: she was carrying a gun.

At a funeral.

I must have missed that particular detail on the wake notice.

"Why do I get the feeling there's something you're not telling me?" I pointed to the outline of her holster.

Anna immediately moved her hands off her hips and straightened her jacket. "I'm keeping an eye on Ron, remember? You asked me to do that. I was planning on being here tonight anyway because I knew Nip, so I was the logical one to accompany Ron."

"And you brought two plain-clothesmen along with you. Or were they here for Pheej?"

I could tell my question hit the mark, because once again, Anna glanced around to be sure no one was listening in on our discussion.

"We think Pheej is in danger," she finally admitted. "Not from any gang, but very possibly from Trisha's killer. The only unique link we can identify between Pheej and Trisha is that they were at Hamm's brewery together last summer, counting Chimney Swifts."

"Frank Quinn was there, too," I told her. "Do you know Frank?"

The information seemed to surprise her, but she nodded in recognition.

"He owns a heating and air conditioning company. I'd heard he'd gotten involved with the Chimney Swifts conservation program," she said.

"He counted swifts with Trisha and Pheej this year at the brewery," I told her. "If you think Trisha's murder has to do with their watching swifts, then maybe you should talk to Frank. Maybe he knows something."

Anna's eyes widened in alarm, and her expression went grim. "Or maybe he's a target, too, and we just don't know it yet."

Crap.

I was beginning to feel like I was trapped in the middle of a whack-a-mole game on a carnival midway. Every time I turned around, another potential victim popped up, just waiting to get whacked.

"I've got to go," Anna said, spinning on her heel.

I grabbed her arm and pulled it back towards me.

"I don't need to talk to Pheej to learn why he's fixated on the brewery," I told her quietly. "Cai told me. Pheej thinks the brewery is haunted by the mother of William Hamm. She died while he was kidnapped."

"He thinks it's haunted?" she said, her urgency to find Frank momentarily forgotten.

"He thinks he saw her ghost," I clarified. "That's why they ignored the signs and trespassed on the property. Cai was trying to help Pheej get a picture of the ghost."

I suddenly remembered my conversation with Bridget on Monday morning. She'd said Pheej had a picture he claimed was cursed, and that he'd taken it this summer.

"Wait a minute," I said again. "If I'm recalling this correctly, Cai actually said Pheej already had one photo of the ghost, but that he'd given it away. They were trying to get another picture last night."

"Of a ghost," Anna said.

"Yes," I confirmed.

"I've got to think about this," she said. "Too many things aren't making sense. First, I'm going to find Frank Quinn, make sure he's alive and kicking, and then ask him some questions."

Out of the corner of my eye, I could see Luce waving me over. Only three people were ahead of her speaking with Nip's relatives.

"Frank's a member of that Hamm Heritage Group I was telling you about, Bob," Anna added. "You know—the group trying to preserve the brewery?"

She let out a sigh of frustration and momentarily closed her eyes. Then she lifted both her hands to rub her fingers against her temples near her close-cropped cap of brown hair.

"Please don't tell me this is another ugly turf war between building preservationists and commercial developers," she muttered. "I'm so sick of nasty jurisdiction disputes and local politics. So help me, if I find out it is and Trisha Davis got caught in the middle of it, I'm going to kill someone. And don't you dare ever repeat what I just said," she warned me, looking me sternly in the eye.

I pretended to zip my lips, lock them, and toss the key over my shoulder.

"I have to go find Frank," she said again and turned away.

I joined Luce in the receiving line.

"Frank Quinn's a Hammster," I managed to whisper in her ear just before we greeted Nip's grieving children. She turned to say something, but I was already extending my hand towards Nip's oldest daughter.

"I'm so sorry about your dad," I told the woman, who was probably about fifteen years older than I was. "He was a great mentor to me when I first started birding."

She looked at me closely a moment, then said, "You're Bob White, aren't you?"

I nodded.

"Dad used to talk about you a lot," she reminisced. "He said you were the sharpest young birder he'd ever met. But I think his favorite story about you was about how he gave you your first cup of coffee. He said he almost burst out laughing when you took that first gulp—you were trying so hard to be nonchalant, like you drank coffee all the time. But he could tell," she assured me, "and you won a spot in his heart forever, I think."

I smiled in acknowledgment. "Just about every time I'm up early to bird, I think about that first cup of coffee with him. I figure it was an important part of my initiation into the real birding community," I laughed.

Nip's daughter returned the smile. "He used to say, 'That little Bob White's a birder down to the bone.' Of course, none of us kids had the slightest interest in birds, so we were so grateful he had someone else's kid to talk about birds with."

She gave me a warm hug. "Thanks for coming, Bob. You meant a lot to him."

I wiped a touch of wetness from the corner of my eye. "You're welcome. I'm going to miss him."

I shook hands with Nip's other grown kids, and then Luce and I were outside the reception hall and standing in the entryway of Bertram's.

"Mr. White!" Pheej called to us, poking his head around the open outer door. "You've got to come out here and see this!"

He immediately disappeared back outside.

Luce and I went out the door to find a cluster of mourners whispering excitedly on the sidewalk just outside the funeral home.

Quite a few of them had binoculars up to their eyes.

Birders, obviously. Who else brought binoculars to a funeral home?

I followed the line of sight of the viewers and located the object of their observation half a block away and up about thirty feet.

"What a beauty!" exclaimed one of the watchers in hushed tones.

It was a Great Horned Owl sitting in the bare branches of a huge oak tree, hardly visible in the darkness thanks to its gray-brown feathers that blended almost perfectly with the bark around it. Thanks to the low lighting that surrounded Bertram's adjacent parking lot, though, the owl's yellow eyes caught enough light to glow balefully at the admiring crowd, giving away its silent presence.

I put my arm around Luce's waist and gave her a little squeeze.

"Nice tufts," I commented in a low voice.

She gave me a swat on my parka-covered chest.

"Hey, I'm just saying," I protested. "The owl's got nice ear tufts. The Snowy Owl we saw last night didn't have any tufts. I'm just appreciating natural beauty where I find it."

Luce turned her lovely blue eyes on mine. "Right. You are such a . . . guy."

I dropped a kiss on her lips. "Yes, I am."

Out of the corner of my eye, I saw Frank Quinn climb into his car in the parking lot. A moment later, the Great Horned Owl swooped off its perch and glided soundlessly away into the night. I wondered what prey it was hunting in the middle of the city. As one of the most common owls in America, the Great Horned Owl could be found in just about any habitat, which convinced me that, at heart, it was a thriving and creative opportunist.

And a killer.

It was a predator, after all. Hunting prey was what it did to survive.

Humans didn't have that instinctual drive, as far as I knew. Murder wasn't a survival skill.

Unless it was to protect your own life . . . or something you valued just as much.

I glanced back at Bertram's Funeral Home and realized it was going to be a long week of attending wakes. Tonight was Nip's. In another two days, it would be Harry Harrison's night. No one had heard anything yet about the funeral arrangements for Trisha Davis. I expected her service might be delayed given the circumstances of her death.

Her murder, to be completely accurate.

Someone had killed Trisha and tried to make it look like it was gang-related by leaving material clues. Literally material, as in bandanas. But whoever had chosen the particular bandana had neglected to verify that it was in use by a local gang. Did the killer think he or she could derail the investigation and escape arrest by planting evidence to point to California?

California.

Why did that ring a bell in my head?

Then I knew: Duc Nguyen was from California.

And Duc Nguyen had been in St. Paul this morning, getting grilled by the investigators about Trisha's death.

I suddenly really wanted to know when Duc had been at the station answering questions for the police. Because if he'd been there before I picked up Cai, he would have had some time on his hands before we ran into him at Swede Hollow Café, when he said he was looking for the Trumpeter. Knowing how fast bad news could travel among relatives (and their friends), Duc might even have known Pheej and Cai were there.

Time on his hands.

Could that be time enough for him to follow us from the station to Bruce Vento Nature Sanctuary to take a shot at my car? Duc Nguyen's arrival at the MOU meeting on Saturday morning had been late, after all, long after I found Trisha dead in her car. Who was to say he hadn't been waiting in the garage for her return to carry out a gang-authorized contract?

At a birding meeting?

I gave myself a mental head slap.

Get a grip, idiot, I told myself. Unless Duc Nguyen led a secret life as a gang enforcer imported by Pheej's tormenters, the whole Duc-as-killer theory was all wet.

And if by some bizarre twist of fate (not to mention an enormous stretch of the imagination), Duc was indeed a skilled assassin, the man should win some kind of creativity award for combining a livelihood as a duck blogger with a sideline in hired-gun violent retribution.

Gee, where would that fit on one of those career interest inventories we're always pushing on our students? Let's see . . . *Hired-gun* would probably fall between *Helicopter pilot* and *Historian.* I expect checking that particular box might also get a student a visit or two with a mental health counselor.

Or, at the very least, a shooting range instructor.

Besides, if a gang wanted vengeance on Pheej, you'd think an attack on someone closer to him—a family member, perhaps—

would fit better with what Anna had told me about the Hmong gangs' typical method of operation.

And yet the police had questioned Duc. They knew something I didn't.

Wow. I was a regular Sherlock Holmes.

Not.

Actually, normally, I was an excellent observer. In fact, as an expert birder, observation was one of my fortes. For example, I could spot the difference between a Chipping Sparrow and a Clay-colored Sparrow from fifty feet away, even without binoculars. I could identify a flying hawk by its flight pattern alone. Case in point: a Cooper's Hawk had a slower wingbeat than a Sharp-shinned Hawk. So far, though, my birding skills were turning out to be useless when it came to identifying who had killed Trisha Davis and why.

I could come up with several possible suspects, but in every case, the closer I looked, the less I was convinced I even had a clue, let alone a killer.

Duc Nguyen as a gang goon?

About as likely as finding a Chimney Swift in December, I realized.

As we returned to Luce's car to drive home to Savage, I thought more about what Anna had said about a possible battle of interests between historic preservationists and developers concerning the Hamm's brewery. A turf war, she had called it. I'd always associated that term with gangs, but now Anna had confided in me that the gang theory had been discounted because of the territorially incorrect bandana.

Or rather, that the Hmong gang theory had been discounted by the investigators.

The preservationists-vs-commercial developer gang theory was now on the table instead.

The Hammsters and the Moneymen.

It sounded like a garage band from the late 1960s. I'd never been a fan of that genre of music, but my mom had been crazy about the song "Wild Thing" when I was a kid. She used to put this album by the Troggs on the old record player we had and sing along with it, except "thing" always sounded like "thang" to me, and I couldn't for the life of me figure out what a wild thang was.

But back to the Hammsters and the Moneymen and their turf war.

As Alan had pointed out to me earlier in the day, urban renewal was not a cheap proposition. The old Schmidt brewery's price tag for joining the twenty-first century of commerce had totaled $120 million. That was a lot of money to pour into a local economy, and I'd never yet heard of a developer who'd sink that kind of money into a project just for the sake of nostalgia. Profits drove renewal efforts as much as, if not more than, civic concerns.

So why would preservationists not want the developers to work with them on the old Hamm's brewery? I had no doubt talented architects could easily re-purpose parts of the building's physical structure while preserving its historic significance, which was what preservationists typically demanded. In lieu of tearing the whole thing down, key features could be salvaged and restored, making the property once again a viable, and probably profitable, part of the community.

So what was the big roadblock keeping the Hammsters and Moneymen from working together? Was it a question of historical integrity, or was it all about money, and who would reap the distribution of future financial rewards?

For all I knew, maybe this was St. Paul politics as usual. Perhaps the Hammsters and Moneymen were descended from the old gangs that operated in St. Paul during the time of Prohibition, when

William Hamm had been politely kidnapped, perhaps as payback for double-crossing the local booze lord. A lot of trades ran in families, and criminal trades were no different. Dare I say "Mafia"?

These people weren't dealing in drugs or laundered money in a high stakes hand of criminal activity, though. They were battling over renovating an old, decaying building. And if somehow Trisha had become a victim of an urban renewal struggle, since when did the fate of an old, decaying building justify a murder?

"What would you think about a quick detour on the way home?" I asked Luce as we settled into her car's plush seats. "I'm suddenly sentimental about beer."

CHAPTER EIGHTEEN

I CRUISED TO A STOP in the middle of the big empty parking lot across the street from the abandoned Hamm's Brewery and shut off the car lights. The old brick building was silent, dark, and rather forbidding with its random broken windows and boarded up doorways. Around us, the parking lot was poorly lit by a few lampposts, though some of the light was reflected by the piles of dirty snow that rimmed the parking spaces. On the far west side of the lot was a low, long, two-story building that now housed the offices of the Minnesota Conservation Corps, along with a few small businesses. Since its exterior was a match for the big vacant building, my guess was that it used to be a part of the company complex, too.

To be completely accurate, the building we were facing wasn't the brewery, but only one of the warehouses for the facility. In its heyday, the Hamm's Brewery consisted of fifty-four buildings, occupied thirty-three acres, employed 1,300 people, and produced 3.3 million barrels of beer a year in St. Paul.

That little bit of Minnesota history, by the way, was courtesy of one of the nights Alan and I won a trivia contest at a local bar in Savage shortly after he came to work at the high school. Seeing as neither of us were married at the time, we made it a habit to go to Trivia Nights at all the bars in the area. Between Alan's obsession with Minnesota history and my store of bird information, we must have won fifty free pitchers of beer in under two years. I don't, however, cite that accomplishment as a compelling reason to pursue a degree in history when I counseled my college-bound students, though it did prove a degree in history had at least one practical application.

To finish the brewery story, the plant changed hands several times, and in 1997, it finally closed. Since then, the site had seen some demolition, a few fires, redevelopment projects, vandalism, and age. The warehouse standing across the street from the parking lot was one of the more intact buildings, though it sported lots of graffiti and was surrounded by a tall chain-link fence topped with barbed wire. Some distance behind it, the tall chimney of the powerhouse towered over the remaining abandoned Hamm's buildings.

Other than the Chimney Swifts that returned to that chimney each spring, no one seemed to have any use for this section of the former brewery.

Except for Pheej, who was hunting ghosts, and the Hammsters, who wanted to preserve it as an iconic piece of St. Paul history.

While Luce and I sat in the car, a city police car slowly rolled past the structure. I checked my watch: it was 9:15 at night.

"That's probably who spotted the boys trespassing last night," Luce said. "Didn't you say it wasn't that late when they were picked up?"

"That's what Cai said," I told her. "But Anna mentioned the dispatcher got an anonymous phone call that tipped the police about the boys being there. So it must not have been the patrol officer, because the dispatcher would have known it was him calling it in."

The expression on Cai's face when he'd first seen Pete Moss at the sanctuary that morning came back to me. My newly-released jailbird had readily recognized the birder from the night before and had assumed Pete was the one to alert the police to the boys' illegal adventure.

But Pete hadn't confirmed, or denied, that assumption. Instead, he'd just offered his own explanation for being there in the night.

He wanted to find a Chimney Swift.

In December.

I started to shake my head in disbelief at Pete's stubborn search when I caught a movement in the darkness across the street. I leaned forward and let my eyes adjust to the mix of shadows and night around the warehouse.

"Do you see that?" I asked Luce.

Her silence assured me she was likewise trying to focus on the shape I could now see gliding along the fence.

"That's definitely a person," she quietly reported, "a person who looks very suspicious, given that he's all in black and wearing a balaclava covering his face."

"Not to mention the backpack and the tool belt he's wearing," I added. "A bit unusual for an evening walk in December, I'd say."

I studied the figure's movement as he continued to move along the sidewalk by the fence. It occurred to me the timing was perfect for an attempt to enter the fenced-off property—the patrol car had just made its pass, meaning that this stretch of the old brewery compound would probably be free of surveillance for the next few hours.

Balaclava Man knew exactly what he was doing.

And I suddenly had a good idea what it was.

"Unless Uncle Sam has secretly shipped in a Special Ops group to train around the old brewery," I told my wife, "I'm guessing Balaclava Man has something illegal in mind, like trespassing. And given that the buildings are abandoned, I'm also guessing he's here for some urban exploration."

We watched the shadowy figure edge steadily towards the corner of the high fence.

"He must not have seen us," Luce noted.

"Or he thinks we're a couple of kids necking in the empty parking lot," I said. I glanced at my wife. "Hey, you want to make out?"

Luce swatted me with her gloved hand.

"I take it that's a 'no,'" I said.

"Look," she commanded, pointing towards the shadow.

He was inside the fence.

"How did he do that?" I asked. "He was just on our side, and now he's inside."

"You missed it," Luce said. "It was like he peeled back the fence. It must have been cut right there, and he knew exactly where to open it. It's an access through the fence."

Pheej must have known about it, I realized. He must have seen someone else use it. That would explain how he and Cai had managed to climb over that fence with the barbed wire on the top of it.

They didn't go over the fence.

They went through it.

Or they really were into urban exploration as Bridget had suspected, and Pheej had learned of the entrance from others in the sub-culture community of UE.

Luce opened her car door and stepped out.

"What are you doing?" I asked her. I ducked my head to see her standing outside the car, pulling up the fur-lined hood of her coat to protect her ears from the cold night air.

"I'm going to go see where he's going," she replied. "With so many people obviously interested in this building, there must be something special about it. I'm going to find out what that is."

"You'll be trespassing."

"And your point is . . . ?"

I gave myself a mental head-smack. Luce was every bit as much a birder as I was. She'd climbed plenty of fences in her birding career, too.

I reached over and popped open the door to the glove compartment in Luce's car and took out the flashlight she kept there for emergencies. A moment later, I got out of the car and walked over to my wife.

"Lead the way," I said.

She threw her arms around my shoulders and laid a big kiss on my lips.

Nice. I'd have to remember to say that to her more often.

"I thought you didn't want to neck," I said when she finally broke the kiss.

She brought her lips back to mine and whispered against them.

"Don't look now, but there's another ninja sliding through the break in the fence."

I looked into her face, dimly lit by the distant lampposts. "Another one?"

"I caught the motion out of the corner of my eye just as you got close to me," she continued to whisper. "I didn't want the ninja to know I saw him and get scared off."

"And you still want to follow him?"

She lightly brushed her lips against my cheek. Her breath was faintly scented of the cinnamon-spiced cider she'd drunk at Nip's wake. "Don't you?"

I briefly wondered if this was a trick question, sort of like when a wife asks her husband, "Does this dress make me look fat?"

If you say "no," she can respond, "Oh, so you think I look fat without it?" Believe me, you don't want to go there. Clearly, only a fool answers "no" to the original question, and only a self-destructive fool would dare tell his wife that, yes, the dress makes her look fat.

Thankfully, I didn't have to come up with any answer at all. Luce took the flashlight from my hand and stuffed it into her coat pocket.

"Good thinking," she said. "A light might be really helpful once we get inside that warehouse. Let's go."

She turned toward the building, and I took a final glance around the parking lot to see if any other people were lurking around.

Nope. It was only us two, for a grand count tonight of four idiots willing to trespass on private property in the dark of night to find who knew what in what was probably a death-trap of an old brewery plant building.

Oh, and if we were really lucky, maybe we'd even make the acquaintance of a rumored ghost wandering the rooms of the death-trap building, waiting and pining for her kidnapped son to be returned home.

Gee, it just didn't get any better than this, did it?

We headed for the warehouse.

CHAPTER NINETEEN

"THE BREAK IN THE FENCE should be right around here," Luce whispered, tentatively patting the chain link where it connected to a post.

Sure enough, the fence gave way to her probing, and we quickly peeled the section back to slip through to the other side. I pushed the fence back to its original position to restore the illusion that it was an unbreached barrier, then turned to follow Luce, who was already standing in the shadows by the warehouse door.

A small pressure of my palm, and the door swung open to deep darkness. Luce took the flashlight from her pocket and flicked it on, aiming it at the cracked concrete floor. We stepped inside, closed the door behind us and waited for our eyes to get accustomed to the minimal light shed by the flashlight.

I took Luce's other hand and began to move forward slowly around scattered metal debris and steel support beams. "Keep it aimed down till we get a little further inside," I whispered. "I doubt anyone out on the street could see this little bit of light through those boarded-up windows, but you never know."

"I don't see any light source ahead of us, either," Luce noted. "The ninjas must be a lot further into the plant."

Empty pop cans rattled together on the floor as I caught the edge of a pile of trash with my shoe. In the silence of the old warehouse, it echoed like a doorbell's jangling.

I stopped and listened, but no other noises followed.

"They must know this place pretty well to be able to navigate it in the dark," Luce said.

"Or they have night-vision glasses," I suggested. "If you're into urban exploration, I'd think they might be really handy to have."

I recalled seeing the tool belt and backpack on the first ninja we'd spotted slinking along the fence. Night-vision goggles would easily fit in the pack, along with a camera and other small items. Like any hobby, there had to be equipment especially suited for the endeavor.

For basic birding, all you needed were your eyes or ears, and not necessarily both—I'd met quite a few blind or deaf birders over the years, and their identification skills were phenomenal, proving once again that birding was absolutely a hobby anyone could enjoy. More advanced birders used spotting scopes and nifty software on their smartphones to record videos and organize data. Now that I thought about it, I also knew several birders who loved their night-vision goggles for owl-hunting.

Night-vision glasses weren't just for commandoes and peeking Toms anymore.

I felt Luce give my hand a squeeze and a tug. I turned to face her, my eyes adjusted to the inky blackness inside the decaying building. She was pointing ahead of us and upwards. She lifted the light in that direction.

A metal catwalk circled the vacant room, probably twenty feet above us and five feet below the line of windows that almost reached to the ceiling. In places, the metal had rusted through and left gaps in the walk. At the far end of the room, a sagging ladder that was missing rungs led up to the catwalk.

I didn't see any ninjas.

"There's a passageway behind the ladder," Luce said. "The explorers must have gone that way."

I walked across the room to the hall opening, which Luce illuminated with her flashlight. Sketches of colorful cartoonish figures intermixed with fat, bright letters, numbers, and symbols covered the walls of the short hallway.

"More graffiti," I said.

"Some of it looks more like art," Luce corrected me. "I think the term is 'urban art.'"

"Really?" I asked her. I studied the areas on the wall lit by the flashlight. A few of the cartoons were intricately detailed, but as far as their making a social comment as Paul had explained to me, I couldn't see it.

"I just happened to get a free mini-lecture about urban art this morning from Paul Brand at school," I told Luce. "He said it's also called guerilla art because it's . . . it's . . . I can't remember the words he used. Something about environmental issues and existential questions."

Luce swung her light up at my face, and I squinted in reflex. "Hey!" I protested.

She moved the light away. "I was just checking to see if you were serious, or if you were making it up. It sounds like something you'd make up as a joke."

"I know," I agreed. "It does sound like a joke: two guerillas walk into an art store . . . But I didn't. Paul was telling me how Sara has become this art genius, and—"

"Look at this one," Luce interrupted, focusing the beam of the flashlight on a small sketch of a girl's face. Incredibly life-like, it was marred by black lines running down from the eyes and across the cheeks.

"She's crying," Luce said.

"She's Latina," I replied. Her thick black hair, large dark eyes, and fine cheekbones reminded me of several of my students at the high school whose families originally came from Mexico or Latin America. "Whoever painted this had a real knack for drawing faces, I'd say."

"I wonder if it's a self-portrait?" Luce mused. "It's sort of haunting, in a beautiful way, don't you think?"

A long low whistle drifted through the room. A slice of ice went down my spine, and I shivered.

"Speaking of haunting—did I tell you Pheej thinks the brewery itself is haunted?" I asked. "I have to admit, I think I can see where he gets the idea. Communication from the dead will do that. "

"That was a whistle of wind," Luce assured me. "An old building complex like this must have a hundred cracks the wind can slide through." She aimed the light beam ahead of us on the floor and held it steady. "Not to mention caves."

I looked at the end of the hallway, where one set of stairs led up, and the other set led down. Old stones lined the wall going down. In the far distance, I could hear the slow drip of water.

Caves.

"They're man-made," Luce said, reading my mind as she seemed to have a habit of doing. "The company dug caves into the sandstone for beer storage. I suppose it was the most economical way of keeping all that beer cold before refrigeration was available."

"Do you think that's one of the big draws here for urban explorers?" I asked. "Caves?"

"Maybe," she replied. "But I'm not an urban explorer, so don't quote me. From what I've read, I think UE is more about old structures than natural formations."

"That's right."

Luce and I both nearly jumped out of our skins at the female voice that came out of the darkness ahead of us. A ninja appeared just beyond the circle of illumination thrown by our flashlight and stepped into the puddle of light on the floor.

"Please keep your light down," the explorer said as soon as Luce started to bring up the beam, "or I won't be able to see for a

185

while. And that's a really bad thing when you're exploring a place like this with rotted timbers and rusted metal. I'm assuming this is your first time," she added. "I mean, you're not really dressed for it or properly equipped at all."

"We brought a flashlight," I offered in defense.

The lady explorer laughed. "Yeah, like that's going to help when you fall through a floor or get lost in the maze of steam tunnels."

"Steam tunnels?" Luce and I asked in unison.

Our ninja sighed. "That's what I thought: you *are* rookies. Really, you should turn around right now and go back. Get out of here. This isn't a shopping mall."

Another ninja appeared.

"What are you doing?"

This time, the voice—deep and raspy—belonged to a man.

"I'm trying to keep these folks from doing something stupid," the woman told her companion.

"Good luck with that," I informed her. "I have a history of doing stupid things."

I could see them both turn towards me in the dimness.

"Just sayin'," I explained. I extended my hand, and after a moment's hesitation, the man took it and we shook. "I'm Bob White. Normally, I'm a high school counselor and a birder, but tonight I'm playing amateur detective and doing a fairly poor job of it."

"I'm his wife," Luce added. "My name's Luce."

Silence filled the hallway.

"I'm Prince Charles, and this is Camilla," the man said.

He paused, waiting for their names to register with me.

Charles and Camilla.

The Prince of Wales and the Duchess of Cornwall.

"Somehow, I don't think those are your real names," I commented, recalling that I'd read few urban explorers used their given names in order to safeguard their privacy, as well as their illegal adventures.

Charles chuckled in a low growl. "Can't fool you, can I?"

"So why are you here, again?" Camilla asked.

My eyes strained to make out her facial features in the darkness. Her eyes were almost black, but her skin reflected the ambient glow from our flashlight, giving her features a soft waif-like quality. I guessed that her hair was quite dark, since it seemed to blend into the darkness around her, and I estimated she was probably about ten years younger than I was.

"The short version," I said in reply to her question, "is that Luce and I wanted to see what was in here, because this brewery seems to be tied to some weird things that have been happening lately."

"Such as?" Charles prompted.

I turned in his direction, though his features were mostly hidden by a black balaclava. It was a little unnerving, I found, to be talking with a masked man in near-total darkness. I immediately ruled out any aspirations I might have harbored of becoming a superhero's sidekick in the near future.

"For one thing," I said, "a student of mine was arrested here last night with his cousin for trespassing, and today someone shot at my car while he was in it with me. An acquaintance of the cousin was killed last weekend, and the police think it's connected to the development battle over this site. Both the cousin and the acquaintance spent time here this summer counting Chimney Swifts."

"I've seen the swifts here," Camilla said, "but there were a lot fewer this summer than other years."

"That's why people come to count them," I explained. "The species is in trouble. Volunteers try to monitor populations in hopes we can learn more about their nesting and breeding behavior so we can take measures to help them survive. The biggest problem is loss of habitat since chimneys aren't as common as they were a century ago."

"Chimneys like the one here," Camilla said.

"Right."

"You want to see the big smokestack here at Hamm's?" Charles asked, his voice sounding not quite so deep. "There's nothing in there at this time of year, but you can look up the chimney if you want, though I can't imagine someone was killed because they watched Chimney Swifts dive into it."

"I know. It sounds crazy," I agreed, although "crazy" was a pretty accurate description of the way my life had been going in the past few days.

"Come on," Charles said. "We'll take you there. It's in the powerhouse of the brewery. It's not far."

I again noticed that the rasp in his voice was becoming increasingly inconsistent. It occurred to me the Prince was either trying to disguise his real voice or he was going through delayed puberty. Since he had the filled-out form of an adult male, though, I decided he must have thought a vocal disguise would protect his identity. Why he was worried about our recognizing his voice, I had no idea. He moved off to the left, and suddenly, a wash of soft light appeared in front of Charles, followed by another wash of light that spread across his back, courtesy of Camilla.

"Headlamps," Luce said approvingly. "Smart. That way you can see where you're going and still have two hands free." She fell into step behind Camilla.

"No wonder they could tell we were new at urban exploring," I commented to my wife's back. "We only had a flashlight. And here I thought it was your high heeled boots that gave us away."

"Duck your heads," Charles called from the front of our line. There are some low ceilings up here."

Obediently, I lowered my head. Within seconds, I could sense the decreased space above my head. Led by the lights that bobbed along in front of me, I trailed after Luce through a room that once housed a lab. Long tables filled the middle of the room, with cabinets mounted along the sides. A few broken beakers and vials littered the floor, and I caught a spot of silver reflection from a set of tall, arced faucets near a boarded-up window.

"This was the quality assurance lab," Camilla announced, almost as if she were leading a tour through the abandoned building. "You'll notice the deeper we go into the facility, the less damage you'll find. That's because there's minimal traffic into the less-accessible areas of the brewery. People who come in to vandalize, or just out of curiosity, rarely go beyond the outer ring of buildings. Thank goodness."

"So this is fairly undisturbed territory," Luce said.

"Yes," Camilla replied, "and that's part of the allure of urban exploration: you get to see places where no one else goes, like an uncharted country or a virgin forest. Let's face it—there aren't too many untouched places my generation can go anymore. But right here in a city, there's a whole world of abandoned structures—a unique landscape, if you will—to explore. Sometimes it's totally underground, like a forgotten sewer system or the steam tunnels here at Hamm's. We're going down steps here—be careful," she warned. "There's no handrail anymore."

I reached out to feel the tiles on the wall as I walked down the stairs. They were cool to the touch, but not icy cold. The building's insulation must still have been intact, I reasoned.

"A year or so ago, I read an article about UE-ers in Europe climbing to the top of enormous construction cranes in the dead of night," Luce said. "They took pictures of each other with the whole of Paris in the background to prove it. The photos were amazing."

"I think you're talking about Bradley Garrett," Charles called back, his theatrically deep voice entirely abandoned now. "He got a Ph.D. in ethnography by studying and participating in urban exploration, but since he published under his real name, a lot of UE-ers began to resent that the press was treating him like the poster-boy for UE. It's like any hobby—the people who do it have different reasons, different perspectives, and different experiences, and they don't necessarily agree with the way it's presented by one person."

"Your voice just changed," I informed the Prince. "Don't worry, though. I still don't know who you are."

He didn't bother to answer me, but I thought I heard Camilla snicker.

We descended another set of steps, and I felt the temperature warm. I unzipped my parka.

"It happens in the birding community, too," I told Charles, picking up his conversational thread. I thought about Pete's criticism of MOURC, along with various angry email debates between specific birders I had read over the years on the MOU list serve. "People take a proprietary attitude toward an activity they love, and when someone disagrees with them about a part of that activity, you get conflict."

"But it shouldn't actually change the enjoyment you get from your hobby," Camilla objected. "It's not like there are hobby police who make you conform to one way of doing it."

We came to a stop in front of a yawning mouth of warm air.

"No, wait," Camilla amended. "When it comes to UE, I guess we do have hobby police. But they don't tell us how to do our hobby. They just want us to stop altogether."

"That's not a problem for us birders," Luce said, "except when we break the law. Which isn't often," she quickly added.

I assumed she was thinking about our current resort to trespassing, though she could just as easily have been referring to my collection of speeding tickets earned while in pursuit of adding birds to my life list. What could I say? When you've got birds to chase, you've got to fly, even if it is on four wheels instead of two wings.

Charles pointed to the tunnel in front of us. "The steam tunnels are the underground skyway. We can get to just about any of the buildings left standing without anyone seeing us. As long as you know your way around them, you can explore for hours in relative peace."

"Hours?" I said. "Can we get the short tour? I have a faculty meeting at seven in the morning, and I don't want to be late."

"No problem," Charles said. "This way to the chimney."

I motioned to Luce to go ahead of me and after Charles. Camilla insisted in bringing up the rear, so I went in after Luce. Within a minute, we came to a crossroads in the tunnel and Charles took a left. Behind me, I heard something squeaking.

When I turned to look, I saw that Camilla was attaching a small sticky-note to the wall of the tunnel we'd just vacated. She wrote the date on it with a magic marker.

She completed her task and faced me. I could barely make out her face beneath the bright light of her headlamp.

"Insurance," she explained. "In underground mazes like these tunnels, it doesn't hurt to leave a trail of crumbs. Except that rats eat crumbs, so I leave sticky-notes instead."

She pointed to Luce's back already disappearing into the darkness ahead. "Shall we?"

CHAPTER TWENTY

FIVE TURNS AND TEN MINUTES LATER, we ascended steps to the building where the big chimney was located. A half-century ago, the building had been a humming center of activity for the brewery. Tonight, its glazed-brick walls enclosed only an eerie silence.

Charles led our little group over to the base of the smokestack where an opening almost the height of a man led to the chimney's interior.

"You can step inside and look up, if you want," Charles said. "Though I don't know if you'd ever want to wear those shoes again."

He aimed his headlamp at the floor inside the chimney.

It was covered with piles of dirt and debris.

"Bat guano and bird droppings," he said. "Urban exploration isn't always as glamorous as it might appear."

I walked closer to the opening and braced my hand against the bricks that lined the outer curve of the chimney. I wasn't keen on stepping inside, but I wanted to look up that tall stack—I wanted to see what a Chimney Swift saw every time it left its roost: a small, distant, circle of light, a portal to another world filled with endless sky.

Gripping the side of the opening with both hands, I leaned in as far as I could without losing my balance and craned my neck to look upward.

A tiny circle of night sky was there, dim, but a degree lighter than the chimney tower's interior. It was a long way up.

As my eyes adjusted to the deep darkness, I began to make out a few tiny bumps on the chimney walls.

Nests.

The nests of the Chimney Swifts who had bred in the smoke-stack.

"Can I have the flashlight for a minute?" I asked Luce, who immediately nudged it into my hand.

I pointed the beam up and marveled at the tiny homes constructed of twigs and glued to the chimney walls with only the saliva of the parents. From my vantage point, they looked like tiny cups sprouting out of the bricks. Even knowing Chimney Swifts had strong long claws specially adapted to clinging vertically, I still found it hard to imagine the perfect balancing act the birds had to continually perform as they raised their young in those tiny nests.

"Can you get a good look?" Luce asked from behind me.

"Good enough," I answered her. "There are only a few left hanging, but it's still an architectural wonder."

I pulled myself out and offered her the flashlight. "Want to look?"

She took my place braced in the edge of the chimney and lifted the flashlight to see the nests. Her balance teetered for a second, so I reached out and wrapped my hands securely around her waist to help steady her position while she looked at the nests.

Unlike Chimney Swifts, humans didn't always have impeccable balance.

Even on solid ground.

A moment later, Luce pulled back out of the chimney just as a scratching noise filtered down from above us in the tower.

"Bats," Camilla said. "They hibernate in the tower in the winter. Your light probably disturbed them, so they're moving around a little. Either that, or a couple of them are waking up to go find some water to rehydrate. They generally do that a few times in the season."

"You like bats?" Luce asked her.

"Not really," she replied, "but if you're into urbex, you're going to run into them fairly frequently. My biggest fear used to be that they'd fly into my hair. That's a myth, though."

"But they love to cling to coat hoods," Charles added. "Especially the ones lined with fur."

Luce immediately twisted her head to each side to check her hood.

"He's lying," Camilla said. "Bats want as much to hang out with you as you do with them. They just get a bad reputation from vampire movies, which is kind of crazy when you realize bats are the ones that get rid of the worst of Minnesota's blood-suckers: mosquitoes."

I wandered over to the cracked window on the east side of the powerhouse and tried to look through the grimy glass.

"Nothing's out there," Charles said. "Actually, we're not far from the lip of the ravine that goes down towards the Bruce Vento Nature Sanctuary. The city tore down the fermentation and bottling building that used to stand between here and the ravine a few years ago to accommodate a development project floated by some local real estate group, but it never got past the discussion phase."

"So nobody accesses the powerhouse from this side of the property?" I asked.

"Not anyone we know," Camilla answered. "All the UE-ers come in through the tunnels. There's no thrill in walking through an open field when you can be exploring subterranean passageways."

I peered through the glass again.

Standing like a lone sentinel on the lip of the ravine was a man, or, at least, I assumed it was a man, because I don't know too many women who say "Hey, I'm going to go walking alone in a deserted area by an abandoned brewery late at night."

Okay, I admit it. I'm being sexist. Women have every right to go walking alone at night in isolated and run-down neighborhoods.

194

Why they would want to do that, I had no idea, but rights are rights.

Right?

Whatever the gender, the person I spotted was wearing a dark heavy coat and what looked like a snug knit cap. Then, as I watched, he lifted a pair of binoculars to his eyes and trained them in my direction.

"I need you to douse your lights," I said to Charles, Camilla, and Luce. "Now."

The room behind me went dark.

"What do you see?" Luce asked.

"Is someone patrolling the plant?" Charles said at the same moment. "We can be back in the tunnels in no time, and he'll never find us."

"I don't think he's a policeman," I slowly said. "He's got binoculars and from the angle he's using them, I think he's looking up at the smokestack."

"For what?" Camilla said.

"Use this," Charles said as I felt him slide a cold metal barrel into my hand.

A metal barrel?

"It's a scope," he added. "It's got infrared."

I knew that.

I lifted the spotting scope to my eye and easily found my target.

He was wearing a bright yellow cap that read *Birders Rule.*

"It's Pete Moss," I said. "He must be looking for Chimney Swifts. In December. The man is obsessed."

"There aren't any here now," Camilla reminded us. "They're all gone."

"Actually, they're not," Luce said from across the room, near the opening to the smokestack.

I lowered the scope and turned around to see her kneeling on the floor, aiming the beam of the flashlight in her hand at the edge of a pile of debris. She pointed at something small and gray and cigar-shaped.

"It's a Chimney Swift," she said. "It's dead, but it's definitely a Chimney Swift."

The sharp blast of a gun outside had me turning back to the window. Even without the aid of the scope, I could see that a second man had appeared over the lip of the ravine.

"He's shooting at your friend!" Camilla yelled, her face pressed to the dirty window.

"We've got to get out of here!" Charles shouted at us.

I smashed out the window with the barrel of the scope.

"Pete!" I bellowed, hoping my voice would carry across the torn-up ground to where he was huddling behind a rusted dumpster. "Pete!"

"What are you doing?" Charles hissed, panic filling his voice.

"I'm trying to save his life!" I snapped back. "I'm hoping that if the gunman knows there are other people around—witnesses—he'll take off."

I caught a flash of fire from Pete's location as another gunshot rattled the night.

No.

Another flash. Another shot.

Crap.

Pete Moss was armed, and he was returning fire.

"The other guy's gone!" Camilla said as Charles dragged her away from the window.

"We need to go!" he hissed at her.

His eyes flew to me and then Luce. "All of us!"

"We're not in any danger," I told Charles. "I know this guy. He's a birder."

A bullet blew in through what was left of the window and smashed into another wall.

"On second thought . . ."

I dashed across the room, grabbed Luce's hand, and ran after Charles and Camilla, who had already disappeared down the stairs to the steam tunnels. Ahead of us, their headlights cast small glows of light that I used as a homing beacon until we caught up to them at the first turn of the passageway back towards our entrance point beyond the quality assurance labs.

"I can't believe I had a bullet go by me," Camilla said, panting. "I didn't know we could move that fast through the tunnels, either."

"Who was that guy?" Charles asked. "If he's a friend of yours, I'd hate to meet your enemies."

"He's a birder," I said. "I've known him a long time. But I didn't know he carried a gun."

"You guys see dangerous birds, or what?" Charles asked, his own breathing returning to normal.

"Not generally," I said. "I don't know any birders who carry guns."

"You do now," Charles pointed out.

Yes, I did. And he happened to be a birder with anger issues, too, along with a conviction that he had been unfairly treated by the MOU Records Committee. Seriously, if I had known he was going to shoot at us when I thought I was throwing him a life-line, I don't know I would have called out of the powerhouse to scare off the other guy.

I lied.

I still would have called out to Pete. I just would have added some qualifiers, like "Don't shoot at us. We're on your side."

Although, come to think of it, I realized I really didn't know what side Pete was on.

Hell, I didn't even know there *were* sides.

What in the world was going on here?

Chapter Twenty-One

W<small>E PLODDED ALONG IN SILENCE</small>, single file, and I tried to piece together what had just happened.

Pete Moss had taken a shot at us.

No, at me. I was the only one who'd called to Pete. No way he'd known there were others with me in the powerhouse.

And I was the only surviving member of MOURC, which he believed had humiliated him. Geez, could I have done a better job of setting myself up for a kill, letting an angry and armed man know I was a sitting duck in an abandoned building?

Except that I wasn't sitting at the moment. I was putting distance between us, passing through aged steam tunnels, praying I didn't hear shots roar out behind me.

"This doesn't make any sense," Luce called back to me over her shoulder. "Why would Pete Moss shoot at us?"

"At me, Luce," I corrected her. "He heard me. He shot at me."

"He shot at the other guy first, though. After the other guy shot at him." She slowed down and I almost bumped into her in the darkness. "I really doubt Pete took the time to identify your voice, Bobby. Seriously, if someone was shooting at me, I wouldn't assume a voice calling my name in the night was an especially good thing. I'd probably think it was a trap."

I gave her a little push in the small of her back. "Keep moving. I'm not completely sure we're not in a trap."

"You think Charles and Camilla are in this with Pete Moss? Are you kidding me?"

The incredulous tone in her voice cut through the growing knot in my gut. What was I thinking? As soon as Charles thought there was someone outside the powerhouse, he'd been ready to beat a hasty retreat. He'd been as startled as I was when the bullet came through the window.

Besides, if Pete Moss had wanted to kill me with a bullet . . . he could have done that at the sanctuary.

As I pulled out of the parking lot.

Crap.

Had Pete been the gunman who shot at my SUV?

But then there was the bandana left in the snow, which tied the parking lot incident to Trisha's death, which Officer Anna said was a red herring to misdirect the police investigation.

The police were focusing on a turf war between the developers and the Hammsters.

And we'd just witnessed an exchange of gunfire that involved Pete Moss, who was armed—armed?—while birding around the Hamm's brewery.

At least, I thought he was birding.

But his quick response to return fire made me question that assumption.

Charles, on the other hand, had been sure anyone outside the powerhouse was associated with patrolling the property, and he certainly had more experience with the site than I had.

So what was Pete Moss doing there, at night, on the far, abandoned, side of the property with a gun in his hand?

"Do you know what Pete Moss does for a living?" Luce asked, apparently following the same train of thought that had me occupied. "I mean, for all we know, he could be a security guard here. That would explain the gun, wouldn't it?"

"And his shooting at the other guy," I agreed. "Camilla! What do you know about the security here at the brewery?"

I could hear Camilla's steps stop, and a moment later, I could see her face dimly illuminated as she turned to answer me.

"The police make their last patrol at 10:20 every night," she said. "But a couple of other UEs I know think there's been increased security since this summer, particularly on the ravine side, by the powerhouse. Judging from our experience tonight, I think my friends are right. I can't imagine there were two random guys wandering around in that same area tonight who decided to start shooting at each other."

Charles's ghostly-lit face emerged from the darkness behind Camilla.

"Okay, here's what I'd heard," he said. "There's some criminal activity going on in the brewery, but nobody's sure what it is."

He paused, then let out a sigh.

"That's one of the reasons I wanted to explore tonight. Check it out, you know? Do the secret detective thing. Be the big hero." His voice lowered in embarrassment. "I didn't think there'd be guns."

In the close confines of the tunnel, I could almost feel Camilla's disbelief radiating from her ninja-costumed body.

"Are you telling me you knew there was a chance we might run into real trouble here tonight, and you didn't think I should know?"

"Let's just get out of here," he said, cutting off the conversation. He focused on Camilla. "I should have told you. I'm sorry. Can we go now?"

She nodded, and we all fell back into single file, continuing to trace our way back through the tunnels. Charles made steady progress in the lead position, never hesitating when he came to intersections of the passageways, but I was still relieved to see Camilla's little sticky notes attached to the walls. I noticed she peeled each one off as she passed it and then stuffed it in one of the pockets that seemed to cover her black jacket.

"You always do that, Camilla?" I asked her as she peeled off the last one when we headed into the homestretch. "Take down your marks?"

"Absolutely," she responded. "It's part of the urbex code of ethics—don't disturb a thing you find, and respect the integrity of the work."

"Sounds a lot like birding," Luce commented. "Do no harm and value nature."

"Excuse me while I throw up," Charles said as we climbed the stairs out of the tunnels. "C'mon, Camilla. You do urbex because it's a blast. It's always an adventure. It's illegal. It's unpredictable and cool. It's an adrenaline rush."

"It's dangerous," I said.

"But that's part of the rush," Charles said. "We go where others don't dare. It's the same thrill that sent Columbus across the ocean, or man into space. You never know what you might discover."

"Like a guy shooting at you," Camilla responded testily.

"I said I was sorry," he reminded her.

My foot brushed a pile that rustled as we walked back through the abandoned lab room. Luce was just ahead of me and I reached out to catch her arm.

"Give me the flashlight for a minute," I said.

She handed it to me and I pointed it at the rustling pile. In the small spot of light, I found the edge of the pile: a collection of candy bar wrappers, empty pop cans, and magazines.

"Not all urban explorers follow your code, Camilla," I called out to her, "unless this is an archaeological trove of evidence from the brewers of fifty years ago."

I studied the cover of the topmost magazine. "Make that six months ago. There's a *People* magazine here from last summer."

I did a double-take as I realized the words on the magazine's cover were all in Spanish. I guess that's what branding in marketing did for you—you know what you're looking at even if it was in another language. Sort of like going birding in a foreign country, where you all see the same bird, but everyone has a different name for it. An owl was still an owl no matter what language you spoke.

Camilla walked over to inspect our find.

"Sometimes homeless people live in these places for a while," she said, "until the police come by and kick them out. That's what I've heard, at least."

She poked at the pile of refuse with the toe of her boot. A tube of lipstick and a small tray of dried paints fell out of the pile and into the beam of my flashlight.

"Looks like this homeless person was a woman and an artist, then," I said. The image of the crying girl Luce and I had seen earlier on the brewery's wall came to mind.

"Would a homeless person take the time to paint a picture here?" I wondered aloud.

Luce sat down on her heels to take a closer look at the trashed items.

"I'd guess it'd depend on how long the person was a resident here and how motivated he or she was," she said. She rifled through the stack of magazines. "They're all from this past July."

"Are we getting out of here, or are we doing an archaeological dig?" Charles asked from the doorway that led out of the old laboratory. "We want to avoid the 10:20 police patrol car."

Without warning, Charles's reminder about the patrol timing set off a chain reaction of ideas inside my head. Timing was always important. For birders, it was the key to seeing birds—you looked for migrant songbirds in the spring and cold-weather ducks and geese in the winter.

And Chimney Swifts after they raised their young.

At the end of summer.

"Do the police patrol here year-round?" I asked Camilla.

"Yes." Her voice trailed back to me as she crossed the lab to join Charles.

"So people who want to explore the brewery would know the times they could access it unseen, right?"

"Right," Charles answered. "Urban explorers prefer to avoid the police since it generally puts a damper on your night. Or lands you in jail," he added.

"Then other people could figure out the patrol times, too, if they wanted to use the brewery for a place to crash," I went on, "or to make a business transaction."

Luce stood up from studying the little trove of refuse.

"I know what you're thinking," she said quietly. "But if the criminal activity going on in here was about drug dealing, I would've expected to find some kind of paraphernalia—used needles, baggies, smoke butts—in that pile. Which I didn't," she pointed out.

I wrapped my arm around her waist and steered her towards Camilla and Charles.

"Drugs aren't the only things that get smuggled," I reminded her. "Animals, reptiles, art, artifacts, documents, secrets. Birds. A huge plant like this could harbor all kinds of contraband. Think about it."

I pointed my thumb over my shoulder back towards where we had emerged from the network of tunnels.

"This place has its own maze, not to mention plenty of abandoned buildings," I reminded my wife. "Some historians—according to Alan—have suggested the brewery might even have been at the center of a liquor smuggling operation back in the days of Prohibition, and that was while the plant was in use and filled with employees. Imagine what an enterprising smuggler could do with it these days."

Luce preceded me out of the lab as we followed the bobbing lights ahead of our new urbex buddies.

"Again, no evidence of any of those things," Luce said. "No animal parts, picture frames, pottery shards or shredded documents. No dead birds."

I heard the intake of her breath in the semi-darkness.

"There was a dead Chimney Swift," she said.

"Yes, there was," I agreed. I paused, because this was the part of my newly forming theory that really nagged at me. "But I've never heard of anyone smuggling Chimney Swifts."

Luce stopped moving and turned to face me, her features somewhat distorted by the shadows thrown by the flashlight I held pointing downwards. Pale and unsmiling, her face could have almost passed for an apparition in the night.

Or like the ghost of a grieving mother of a kidnapped son.

A ghost.

Pheej's ghost. I suddenly knew why Pheej believed that the brewery was haunted.

"What are you saying?" Luce asked at the same instant.

"Pheej!" I said, my thoughts already spinning away from trying to connect smuggling and Chimney Swifts. "Pheej didn't see a ghost at that second-story window in the warehouse this last summer," I said. "He saw a real live woman. Come on. I want to take a look at that catwalk."

I grabbed her hand with my free one and picked up the pace to overtake Charles and Camilla, who were heading for our entry point into the brewery. Instead of heading for the door, though, I moved across the space to stand directly under the sagging catwalk that circled the second story of the warehouse. I pointed up at the grimy window that partially looked out towards the parking lot where we'd left Luce's car.

"Right there," I said, aiming the flashlight's narrow beam up into the darkness. The rusted metal catwalk reflected just enough light to allow us to see it suspended above us.

"It's missing a section," Luce noted, "right beneath the window."

"The metal rusted through," I guessed. "And when someone stood on it, trying to open that window, she fell to the concrete floor, and it killed her."

"Killed who?"

I turned to find Camilla right behind me.

"The woman who left her paints behind in the lab," I said. "Or maybe I should say the girl who left the paints behind."

"The face on the wall," Luce said, excitement catching in her voice. "You think it was a self-portrait?"

"It was a heck of a lot better than anything else on that wall," I reminded her. "According to Paul, there's a whole school of street art in Brazil that heavily influences its artists. You put that face together with the Spanish-language magazines, and I'd bet my bottom dollar a Latina girl was camping out in the brewery this summer."

"And why would she do that?" Charles asked. "It isn't exactly the Ritz."

"Illegal immigrant?" Camilla suggested.

I nodded. "Maybe."

"But why would she risk walking on that treacherous catwalk just to see out a window?" Luce probed.

"To see what was outside?" Charles guessed.

"If she were here illegally, yes, that makes sense," I said. "She'd want to see if anyone was around who might arrest her. She must have known there was a regular patrol schedule."

"Why not exit the plant somewhere else?" Camilla asked. "Like the powerhouse, or through some other building with windows on the ground floor? Why risk it here?"

"I doubt she had a map of the tunnels," Charles pointed out. "She got in here, and maybe this was the only way out she could find."

I looked up at the broken catwalk. Pheej must have seen her face just before she fell through the rusted metal. She'd been trapped.

Another dark possibility took shape in my head

"What if she'd been kidnapped," I said, "and was searching for a way out?"

I could feel Luce grow tense beside me.

"The contraband," she said.

"Could be people," I finished for her. "As in human trafficking."

From just behind me, I heard Charles softly curse a string of obscenities. A moment later, he was making a beeline for the warehouse door, his headlamp almost swallowed by the darkness of the cavernous structure.

Camilla took off after him.

"I think we're done here," I told Luce, who was standing silently next to me. "We don't want to lose our tour guides."

I turned to follow Camilla when a big megaphone voice rang out as Charles cracked open the warehouse door.

"Drop your weapons if you have them!" the amplified voice commanded. "And put your hands up in the air where we can see them!"

Intense bright lights gushed into the warehouse.

"How about that?" I said to Luce, shielding my eyes from the unexpected glare. "We've got a welcoming committee waiting for us. I feel so special, don't you?"

CHAPTER TWENTY-TWO

W E WALKED INTO THE BLINDING LIGHT, our hands held high over our heads.

"You can put them down," a familiar voice greeted us.

The lights were extinguished, and I blinked to focus in the moderate lighting afforded by about a dozen flashlights held in the hands of police officers.

"Hey, Anna," I said. "Fancy meeting you here."

Officer Anna Grieg shook her head and directed her comment to Luce.

"You just can't keep this guy out of trouble, can you?" she said.

I noticed she was still out of uniform, wearing the same green jacket she'd worn at Nip's wake.

"Well, at least it's not a speeding violation this time," Luce replied. "I've been telling him he needs to mix it up a little: auto theft, or jaywalking, or impersonating a police officer."

"Very funny," I said. "I assume you have the royals in custody already?"

"Royals?"

"Also known as Charles and Camilla," I told Anna. "Our fellow trespassers."

"He said his name was Charles?" Anna sounded amused. "I'll have to remember that. He generally goes by Andrew. Andrew Royce."

When Luce and I didn't respond, Anna grinned. "Andrew Royce is our newest, youngest, most vocal, assistant district attorney in Ramsey County."

"Oh, my," Luce said.

"That's why he thought he needed to disguise his voice," I told Luce. "He's a public figure here in St. Paul."

"'Oh, my,' is right," Anna said. "I can't imagine he's too thrilled at the prospect of appearing before the judge as the defendant instead of the prosecutor. I'd heard it wasn't unusual for urban explorers to be young successful professionals by day, but having our own assistant DA in the ranks is a new one on me."

"If he wants a hobby, he should take up birding," I said. "At least it's legal."

Anna laughed. "Said the birder who was trespassing along with him."

She dropped our banter then and got serious.

"Andrew says you have an interesting theory about something going on at Hamm's, Bob," she said. "You feel like taking another trip over to the police station to give us a report? I'll forget I found you trespassing," she generously added. "You help us break up a trafficking ring, and we're going to love you at the station."

I blinked. "I can't believe it. I'm asked twice in one night to help the police. I want this on film to show to every officer who has ever told me to keep out of crime-solving."

"Do you want to see what we found?" Luce asked. "We think it might be evidence."

Anna shook her head again. "Andrew can show us. Believe me, he's going to need the brownie points to save himself from a thorough tongue-lashing at the office tomorrow. Let's get out of here."

We walked to the parking lot across the street, which was no longer empty. Several police cruisers, along with two unmarked cars, were clustered near Luce's car. A few officers were standing nearby talking with Charles and Camilla.

Make that Andrew and Camilla.

"Wait a minute," I said. "Isn't there a Prince Andrew in the royal family?"

Luce gave me a smack on the arm. "Are you ever serious?"

"Only about you," I said. I leaned over and gave her a kiss on her cold cheek.

"Can you two follow me in Luce's car?" Anna asked. "You can pick up your SUV, too, Bob, while we're at the station," she added. "We're done with it."

"Does it have a new rear window?"

"Yup," Anna said. "No worries about too much air conditioning on a winter's night. It's good to go. Though you might want to replace that back seat bench you've got, since it's missing part of the top half now."

As I opened the passenger side door, it occurred to me Luce's car sitting unattended in the big lot must have tipped off the police to our trespassing.

"Hey, Anna," I called to her as she headed for her own car. "Did one of your patrol officers call in a suspicious empty car in the lot tonight? Because I'm pretty sure Prince Andrew over there didn't expect an escort to be waiting for him when he finished up his illegal jaunt this evening."

Anna stopped and walked back to me. "It was a 911 call, Bob. Seems there was some gunfire near the ravine and the old powerhouse."

"Pete Moss!" I said. "It was Pete Moss and someone else, Anna! You've got to get some police over there—Pete or the other guy might be hurt, or worse."

The sound of the guns rang in my head, and I remembered Pete running toward the powerhouse, gun in hand, but I suddenly was unsure that he was the one who had fired at us.

Had Pete sent a shot in our direction after I called to him?

Or did the bullet that tore into the powerhouse come from the other gunman in an attempt to kill Pete?

"I yelled at him," I told Anna, "The other guy was shooting, and I yelled at Pete. I wanted him to know where he could find cover."

A wave of ice washed over me. What if my calling his name had pulled Pete right into the path of bullets?

I reached out to support myself against the roof of Luce's car. "Anna—"

"Pete's the one who called 911, Bob," she said in a low voice. "He's okay. As a matter of fact, he should be at the station now himself, waiting for us with his own police escort."

"A police escort?" I echoed. "I thought you said he was all right. Is he in danger?"

Anna shook her head. "He's fine, Bob. He's under arrest. Like you."

"I'm under arrest?"

I was beginning to sound like a parrot.

"Well, yeah," Anna said, a note of exasperation in her voice. "You were trespassing, and since I just arrested our assistant DA for the same thing, I can't exactly let you off scot-free, can I?"

I stared at her across the car roof.

"Wait a minute," I said. "Didn't you just tell me you'd forget about the trespassing if I came to the station and gave a report?"

Anna made a big deal of slowly nodding her head up and down. "Yes, but we're not there yet, are we?"

"Get in the car, Bobby," Luce said from the driver's seat, "before Anna has second thoughts and we both end up with an arrest on our records."

I gave Anna a two-fingered salute and got in the car. Luce spun the car around and came up behind Anna's vehicle, and we followed her out of the parking lot.

"I'm glad Pete's okay," I said as we drove through the dark neighborhoods on the way to the station. "He may be a pain in the rear when it comes to the records committee, but I'd never wish him any harm, let alone getting shot by a gunman while he was birding."

"You know, I've been thinking about that," Luce said.

"Getting shot by a gunman while birding?" Crap. I was still in parrot mode.

Luce nodded, her eyes on the road.

"How did Pete end up a target? I mean, unless someone's been following him, waiting to shoot at him, why would he be in someone's crosshairs at that particular place at that particular moment?" she mused.

"I don't know Pete Moss other than as a birder," I said. "Maybe he's just as abrasive to everyone he meets as he is to me and the other MOURC members. Maybe all kinds of people want to shoot him, and somebody finally got lucky."

"But he's a birder, Bobby," she reasoned. "He's probably in isolated places all the time looking for birds. Seriously, if you're going to kill someone, and you got to choose where, wouldn't you pick somewhere remote? Somewhere no one else would hear the gunshots?"

I looked out the car window and thought about what Luce had just said.

I decided I'd better never make her angry enough to kill me, because she'd know plenty of remote places to shoot me.

It was the first time I'd ever considered there might be a down side to marrying a birder.

Tucking that realization aside, I focused on the particular time and place piece of the night's adventure and the shots that had hurtled into the powerhouse.

Time: Charles and Camilla knew the police patrol schedule so they could get in and out of the brewery undetected. That had been on the side of the plant where we'd entered. Was there a security patrol on the ravine side where the shots had been fired? I'd have to ask our urbex experts, but since they hadn't seemed cautious about using their lights in the powerhouse, I guessed that part of the brewery really was a no-man's land that even the property owners didn't monitor. Only an empty expanse of land lay between the powerhouse and the lip of the ravine thanks to demolition of other plant buildings. There was nothing valuable or dangerous in that space to require surveillance.

Place: By the same token, that would make access to the plant through that side especially easy, as long as you didn't mind climbing up a steep ravine slope.

Pete must have come that way—up the slope.

I did a quick mental check of my birding experience in the area, and realized the Bruce Vento Nature Sanctuary lay not far beyond the bottom of that same slope.

"From the nature sanctuary," I said aloud, piecing together a scenario that would fit what had happened tonight. "Pete could have been birding in the Bruce Vento sanctuary—owling, most likely, since it's dark—when something brought him up the slope," I told Luce.

"And you know Pete knows the area," she added. "Wasn't this where he said he saw the Chimney Swift a few years ago in December? The report that was rejected?"

I turned from the window and stared at Luce's profile as she turned into the police station's parking lot.

"Yes, it was," I replied. "He claimed it was a Chimney Swift, in December, at the Hamm's brewery."

Without warning, a clear memory popped into my head of the photo Pheej had shown me of the Chimney Swift clinging to Ron's shoulder. The swift had grown tame in rehab, learning to rely on its human keeper. A bird that bonded to a person might easily hang around out of season as long as it continued to receive care. But if its keeper suddenly left or went missing, leaving the bird to fend for itself . . .

I suddenly knew how Pete's unseasonable report of a Chimney Swift sighting might have been possible.

Not probable, but definitely possible.

"You're not going to believe this," I said to Luce, "but I think there's a chance Pete's claim was real. But the swift he saw wasn't wild anymore. It had become used to humans, because someone was rehabbing it."

Luce put the car in park and stared back at me a moment before she caught on to where I was going with my theory.

"Like the Birdman of Alcatraz," she said. "You think someone was held prisoner in the brewery and took care of an injured Chimney Swift."

"Or maybe an abandoned juvenile because it was sickly or it hatched too late to migrate," I speculated, the pieces of my theory fitting neatly together as I shared it with Luce.

"Whatever the reason," I insisted, "there was a swift lost somewhere in the plant that was tamed by a human, so it was on-site out of season. The human left, the swift finally found its way out of the tunnels and the plant, and Pete happened to see it when it escaped."

Luce's gloved fingers tapped the steering wheel as she considered my conclusions.

"It could be possible," she finally conceded. "A long shot, but possible."

"If I'm right," I said, "then Pete might very well be the key to why Trisha was murdered."

Chapter Twenty-Three

"Run that by me again," Anna said, taking another sip of the police station's coffee, which really was as bad as she had implied that morning. I'd taken one taste of the brew poured into the cardboard cup in front of me and decided we taxpayers might pay for a lot of government office perks, but flavorful coffee was not one of them.

There were ten of us seated at a long table in a conference room: Charles/Andrew, Camilla, two detectives, Anna, Pete, two additional police officers, Luce, and I. After we'd all given our versions of the evening at the brewery, I'd pieced together my conclusions for the assembly to consider. Granted, there were a lot of conclusions, and I admitted that some of them were shaky at best, but I figured if we could hash it out together, then maybe someone in the room would have the key to what was going on at the old brewery and why Trisha had been killed.

I laid it out again.

"We have an abandoned complex of buildings that sprawls over such a big area that it's hard—if not impossible—to monitor, especially given that the buildings are connected by an underground tunnel system, parts of which are nearly impassable. Right, Camilla?"

She nodded. "Charles and I have explored a big chunk of it, but you never know if sections of it might have collapsed since your last visit. I don't know any urbexers that have a complete map."

"So it's easy to get lost underground, but it's also the best place to escape surveillance of any kind," I said.

"I got that part," one of the detectives piped up. "But how do you jump to someone using it as a place to stash undocumented immigrants?"

"There are clear signs people have lived there at some point," Charles said. "Within the last six months, in fact. The magazines we found tonight were from this summer, and they were Spanish-language editions, which, of course, leads me to think whoever was there was probably a Spanish speaker."

He directed his attention to the two detectives and policemen. "We all know we have a problem in the city with illegal immigrants in our Spanish population. We also know how hard it is to identify them and get them into social services because they don't want anyone to know they're here illegally."

The men nodded. Charles clearly knew how to work with his fellow officers of the law despite his own penchant for breaking it as an urban explorer. A thought began forming in the back of my mind about how some people want to play on two opposing teams at the same time: eventually, you have to make a choice.

For a split-second, I felt a sharp stab of urgency that if I could just finish that thought, I'd know how everything in the last few days fit together—but the feeling disappeared as quickly as it had come.

Something about playing on two opposing teams at the same time.

Charles, meanwhile, had turned to address Anna.

"On other trips," he explained, "I noticed food containers, or smelled recent—ah—waste, to put it nicely. But I never considered someone might be there against his or her will. I assumed anyone staying there was either homeless or transient. After what we found tonight, though, I'm not so sure."

"That's where Pheej's picture-taking comes in," I said. "His picture shows a face in a window."

Nine pairs of eyes landed on mine.

"What? You're saying the kid got a picture of someone held captive in the powerhouse?" Pete asked. "He thinks someone's in trouble and takes a picture? Why didn't he run to the police?"

"He was at the brewery counting Chimney Swifts," Anna told him. "And he thought he got a photo of a ghost. He's a kid, Pete, not a vice cop."

"And it wasn't the powerhouse," I corrected Pete. "It was the warehouse. The only windows in the warehouse are above the catwalk, so if someone was trying to get out, he or she would have to climb up the old rung ladders still in there and hope the catwalk would hold so she could get to a window to try to reach outside help."

I looked at Charles and Camilla.

"You saw the catwalk," I said. "It was busted right beneath the window in the warehouse. What would make it collapse, except for a sudden weight, like a person walking on it?"

"The crew is working on that right now," the second detective said. "They might be able to pick up fingerprints on the railing or ladder, or reconstruct how the catwalk failed."

"And why wouldn't a captive just bust out through the door of the warehouse?" one of the policemen asked.

"You couldn't get in through that door this summer," Camilla said, looking down into her own cup of bad coffee. "I know. I tried."

The policeman next to her fixed a stare on her. "How many times did you break the law trespassing on that property?"

Camilla looked at Charles for advice. "Do I have to answer that?"

"Not without your lawyer present," he told her.

He addressed the policeman on Camilla's other side. "Let's stay on task here. If we've got some kind of kidnapping ring, or human trafficking going on at the Hamm's brewery, I think that takes precedent over trespassing right now."

"You hope so," the policeman nearest me commented under his breath, "Mr. Assistant DA."

"I agree with Andrew," Anna said, throwing a silencing look at her colleague. "Let's keep focused." She looked at Camilla. "The warehouse door was locked this summer, you said?"

Camilla nodded. "In fact, now that I think about it, we always use another route to get into the plant in the summer. We come in from the ravine side, since you can get into more buildings on that side with no one seeing you. But in the winter, the slope up from the river gets too icy to climb up, so it's easier to use the warehouse side."

She threw a quick glance at Charles for him to comment, but he kept his mouth shut.

"Before tonight," Camilla said, "I didn't know anyone patrolled that side of the plant."

The policemen, the detectives, and Anna all exchanged a look.

"We don't," one of the detectives said.

"So who was shooting at me for trespassing?" Pete asked.

"I don't think it was for trespassing," Anna answered him.

"We don't shoot first and ask later," one of the policemen said, an undertone of frustration and resentment in his words.

"Pete," I said, "you're ruffling the man's professional feathers. Give these guys some credit. They risk their lives every time they go out on a call. They're not the targets here. You were," I pointed out. "Someone didn't like you scouting around on the edge of the ravine by the powerhouse so much that they tried to kill you."

"It's the Pipe," Camilla blurted out. "The Pipe! It's a hidden entrance we use on the ravine side—the one we don't use in the winter. It's an old concrete drain that leads to the caves they dug beneath the brewery for cooling the beer. You access the steam tunnels from the caves," she explained, her voice rising in the room. "From there, you can go anywhere in the plant."

"If you know the way," I amended her comment, "which isn't likely to be the case if you're kidnapped and hustled through the tunnels to some remote spot in this huge abandoned complex. You wouldn't have a clue where you were, no one's going to find you, and you're not going to find your way out—doesn't that make the brewery a perfect place to stash someone?"

"Or maybe store someone," Luce said, "like a stopover for human trafficking? It happens all over the world, so why not here?"

One of the detectives let out a string of expletives, and everyone at the table turned his way.

"The Pipe!" he bit out angrily. "Not a pipeline. The Pipe!"

"Okay, here's the deal," the other detective explained once his partner finished his swearing. "We've been trying to crack a trafficking ring we have reason to believe has been operating here in the state for a few years. You're right," he said to Luce. "It can happen anywhere, including here. Generally, the victims are young Asian females who've been snatched and sold into slavery, then smuggled into the United States, though we get children of all nationalities."

The first detective muttered another oath, then picked up the explanation.

"A few months ago, we finally had a tip about a pipe somewhere in St. Paul, but we took it to mean there was a pipeline, so we'd focused our investigation on tracking down a whole organization, not a place."

"The Pipe," Camilla said, looking at the two men. "At the brewery. A hidden entrance to what could be a prison if you don't know your way around it."

"It still doesn't explain why someone took a shot at me tonight," Pete groused. "So you found evidence of what you think might be criminal activity. But it was last summer. You're too late. Why is someone hanging around now outside this Pipe place?"

"Because we're on their trail," Anna said. "Whoever is—or was—running this ring knows we've got reason to be investigating the site for criminal activity, but they probably don't know exactly what we might find, so they're scared and trying to keep people away."

Pete glared at me from across the table. "And this is why you say I'm the key to Trisha's death? I still don't see it, White."

The others in the room focused on me again.

"You reported a Chimney Swift at the brewery in December, Pete," I reminded him. "It was rejected because the swifts leave at the end of summer. That means there's no reason for birders to be around the brewery before or after the Chimney Swift count—the place is abandoned except for urban explorers, who are involved in illegal activity themselves. If an urbexer saw anything criminal, he or she would have to risk arrest themselves for reporting it, even if they found something suspicious, which is doubtful since they're in the plant at night and not looking for evidence of crimes. But birders—"

"Have no reason *not* to report something suspicious," Anna continued. "So your presence, Pete, at the plant when birders aren't normally birding alerted our ringleaders they needed to be vigilant about someone other than urbexers near the property."

Charles shook his head.

"Not enough," he said. "There's still too many holes in that theory to connect Pete with what happened to Trisha."

"Except that Trisha was on the committee that rejected his sighting three years ago. She knew the details of exactly where Pete was when he made the claim," I pointed out.

"So did you," Pete said. "You were on that committee, too. But you're not dead, White. Trisha is."

"Which means that Trisha must have told someone about your location, Pete," I speculated, "and that particular someone wasn't happy about it, especially if it meant their criminal enterprise might be compromised because of it."

"If that was the case," Charles objected, "why didn't our mysterious 'someone' kill Trisha three years ago, right after the rejection of Mr. Moss's sighting?"

"Because there was no suggestion of anything criminal going on at the brewery?" I guessed. "At least, to my knowledge, there hadn't been any . . . until we found out that Pheej took a photo that included a face at a window in an abandoned warehouse."

The two detectives exchanged a glance, and then one of them abruptly left the room.

"I think we have something," the remaining detective said.

And I suddenly knew where Pheej's first photo had gone.

"Pheej counted Chimney Swifts at Hamm's this summer with Trisha," I said. "He gave the photo to Trisha."

I remembered Cai had accused Pete of calling the police on them for trespassing the night before, but Pete hadn't admitted to it.

Because he wasn't the one who made the call.

Trisha's murderer had.

The police weren't the only ones patrolling the Hamm's site.

More pieces fell into place in my mental jigsaw puzzle of Trisha's death.

Trisha must have just recently, and unknowingly, alerted our mystery criminal to the fact she had a photo with a clue to his illegal secret.

As a result, Mr. Bad Guy had kept the Hamm site under surveillance as a precaution to see if exposure was going to be a problem for his business. When he spotted Pheej and Cai trespassing last night, he'd jumped at the opportunity to get Pheej arrested, which would destroy any credibility the boy might have in the investigation into Trisha's death. In fact, coupled with the attack on my car today, it would lend support to the theory that Trisha's death was a result of Pheej's harassment by the street gang, and that his friendship with her had led to her murder.

But who would Trisha have recently talked with about Pete's rejected claim?

"We need to find that picture," the detective said. "It has to have some kind of key information in it that didn't make any sense to this kid, or even Trisha."

"I'll call Pheej," Anna said, "and ask what he did with the photo."

I reached under the table and found Luce's hand. I wrapped my hand around hers and gave it a squeeze, more to comfort me than her. The only people I could imagine who might be interested in talking about Pete's impossible December sighting of Chimney Swifts would be birders.

Great. According to the latest statistics I'd seen, that only included about seventy million Americans. Could I possibly narrow this down any better?

How about Minnesotan birders?

How about MOU members? Given that Trisha was killed at the annual meeting and that she apparently knew whoever was on the other side of her car door when she opened it to pass over the coffee carton, that was definitely narrowing the field.

Off the top of my head, I could think of a few people I'd seen at the meeting who might have talked with Trisha about Chimney Swifts in general, and Pete's claim about the Hamm site in particular: Birdchick, Ron Windingstad, along with the other, now deceased, members of the Records Committee: Harry Harrison and Nip Kniplinger.

And Pete Moss, of course.

"I give up," I whispered to Luce. "I know this is all going to be obvious once it gets figured out, but right now, my brain is mush. I want to go home."

"I got it!"

The detective who'd suddenly left the room earlier had returned, waving a sheet of paper in his hand. He passed it along to his partner, who read it out loud for the rest of us.

"Mariana Ribeiro. Female. Fourteen years old. Brazilian. Reported missing on June 23 this year by her parents who were in South St. Paul visiting relatives. Last seen getting on bus to downtown St. Paul." The detective looked up from the paper. "A missing child report. We never got any leads."

"Street art is big in Brazil," I said, then shared what I'd learned from our art teacher Paul Brand about graffiti.

"And this self-portrait you saw," Anna asked me, "could you find it again? We can get a photo of it to send to the parents. Maybe get an ID."

"I know where it is," Camilla offered. "I'll show you."

Moments later, only Luce, Anna, and I were left in the conference room. The others had all cleared out, heading back to Hamm's.

"Go home," Anna told us. "I'll let you know what we find. Just promise me you won't do any more trespassing tonight."

"Not tonight," I promised. "Tomorrow . . ." I shrugged. "A birder's got to do what a birder's got to do."

Anna gave me a little push out of the room. "Get out of here, Bob. Thanks, Luce."

Outside, I spotted my SUV with its new window parked in a far corner of the police station lot. Luce gave me a ride to it, and just before I opened the door to hop from Luce's car to mine, Luce grabbed my arm and pointed at a branch in the pine tree standing in front of my car.

Two yellow eyes separated by a white "Y" of feathers and a sharp little beak set in the middle of a small round head looked sternly back at us.

"He's guarding your car," Luce said of the Northern Saw-whet Owl sitting near the trunk of the tree, just above eye level.

"I know. I'm scared," I replied. "He's got to be all of seven inches tall and weigh a good five ounces. If I were a mouse, I'd be shaking in my tiny boots right about now, because I know I'd never hear him coming."

Luce leaned over and gave me a kiss on the cheek.

"Predators come in all sizes, Bobby. Unfortunately," she added, and I could tell she was thinking of a lost girl named Mariana and a predator no one had seen coming.

"They're going to get him," I assured my wife. "You'll see. Anna's on this case. Once she's set her sights on adding a bird to her life list, she gets it. I can't imagine she doesn't have the same determination at work."

I patted Luce's hand on the steering wheel before getting out and into my own car. "See you at home," I said.

But as I drove through the night following Luce's taillights home to Savage, I realized that, despite my confidence in Anna and her crew, there was still a murderer at large tonight, and he was probably a birder I knew.

I actually hoped Anna didn't identify the killer before I did, because I found myself really wanting to be the one to push this guy out of the nest for a long fall . . . right into jail.

CHAPTER TWENTY-FOUR

YOU KNOW WHAT THE UPSIDE to winter mornings is for a birder? The birds don't wake you up at dawn with their singing, because the sun rises so late.

You know what the downside to winter mornings is for a birder? It's that I'm so used to the birds waking me up the rest of the year, I forget to set my alarm clock, and I end up having to speed to work to make it on time because I oversleep.

Especially after spending a night tossing and turning, trying to figure out who, among my fellow MOU members, should be voted most likely to engage in human trafficking and kill a colleague who unwittingly stumbled across evidence of the same.

What? You don't have nights like that?

I pulled out of the driveway after an extremely rushed job of getting up and almost missed seeing the Pileated Woodpecker flying over our roof on its way to our backyard suet station. Woody, so named because he was clearly the inspiration for Woody Woodpecker of cartoon fame, was a regular visitor to our suet in the winter. Fortunately, even if I missed seeing his big crested red head, I couldn't mistake his black-and-white underparts and his irregular wingbeat. He was a big strong guy I felt I could count on, sort of like my brother-in-law, Alan.

Alan.

Crap. I'd forgotten his Secret Santa gift in my rush to the car. Part of me had given up the game with him this year since I'd already told him I was his gift-giver, but since he didn't believe me, I figured I could still have some fun with it. This morning I was going to give him a teething ring I'd bought for Baby Lou—his daughter and my niece—for Christmas, and ask him to pass it along to her since he already knew I was his Secret Santa. I figured he'd either finally believe me, or accuse me of covering up for his real Secret Santa, which would just give me more fodder for mercilessly teasing him later.

But I'd forgotten the gift, and since I was crushed for time, I decided I'd have to make a quick detour to the teachers' lounge on my way to the counseling suite to score more candy bags for Alan. I pulled open the school's parking lot door and came face-to-face with Paul Brand.

"Hey, Paul," I said. Mr. GQ was wearing a classy jacket with a woolen scarf tossed artfully around his neck. In comparison, my overstuffed parka made me look like I was wearing a sleeping bag. "You're leaving already?"

He stepped back to let me in. "No, I just left some things in the car. I thought I'd grab them now before class starts for the day."

"Thanks for the lecture about street art yesterday," I told him. "You may have helped solve a missing person case for the St. Paul police."

"Glad to be of service," he replied. He pointed toward the parking lot. "I got to go."

He ducked out the door into the cold, and I watched him run to the row of cars.

"Gee, he must help the police solve crimes all the time with his art knowledge," I muttered. "He didn't seem overly impressed, that's for sure."

I hustled down the hall, made a quick stop in the lounge for the peanut M&Ms, then walked into the counseling reception area.

"Why, look who's here!" Patty, our receptionist, cheerfully called out from her desk. "A day late, and a dollar short," she said playfully.

"I'm not that late," I corrected her, "nor am I a dollar short. At least, not that I know of."

Patty smiled like she knew something I didn't. Her blonde hair had sparkly green highlights today, I noticed, and her wool sweater would be a strong contender for any ugly Christmas sweater contest she cared to enter.

"Rudolph dressed as a ballerina," I said. "A gift from your favorite aunt?"

"I wish," she replied, "then I could get away with never wearing it. No, this one's my mom's handiwork."

"You are a dutiful daughter," I told her.

"You owe me chocolate, by the way," she added, fluffing her green highlights, "since Wanda the Wonderdog got your goose yesterday."

"Nice touch," I said, nodding at her dyed strands. "Very seasonal. And Wanda didn't get my goose, as you'll recall. She got my *duck*," I stressed. "Maybe my Secret Santa brought another one to make up for it. You wouldn't happen to have seen my Santa make a delivery, did you, Patty?"

No harm in going the direct route, I figured. It couldn't hurt to ask, right?

"Not today," she said, smiling.

"So that means you did see my Santa yesterday?" Maybe I was going to get lucky after all and solve this little mystery with one question.

"I didn't say that."

Okay, maybe it was going to take two questions.

"Patty, do you know who my Secret Santa is? I'll double the chocolate I owe you and never breathe a word that you told me."

Patty's eyes glazed over. I could tell she was on the verge of delirium imagining pounds of chocolate with her name on it, but she managed to snap herself out of it before she totally lost control.

"I meant," she said carefully, "that your Santa didn't leave you anything in your office this morning."

She gave me an exaggerated wink. "Unless Santa's running late himself, today," she added with a sly grin.

That clinched it. Patty knew who my Secret Santa was, but clearly wasn't going to let me in on it.

Wait a minute.

Running late.

I'd just bumped into Paul Brand going back out to his car for something he'd forgotten.

He was running late.

Not only that, but he was always trying to lecture me on art, like with the graffiti, and if I thought about my Secret Santa gifts so far, they could both qualify as types of art: a photo and a sculpture, even if it was made of chocolate.

Was Paul my Secret Santa?

He could certainly have recruited Patty to open my office door for his deliveries. And for all I knew, he'd left my Monday gift on my desk after I'd left work on Friday, since I knew Paul frequently stayed late working in the school's art studio.

Yes, Paul Brand definitely belonged on the short list of suspects, I decided.

The possibility I might be able to uncover my Santa's identity before the staff party gave me a much-needed mental shot in the arm. After my long night of wondering if Trisha's killer was a birder I knew, a Secret Santa search sounded much more appealing.

Not to mention less stressful.

And less dangerous.

"Oh, and I have a message for you," Patty called before I walked into my office. "Anna Grieg just called to tell you there'd be a memorial gathering late this afternoon for birders who knew Trisha Davis. She hoped you'd be able to attend. And she wants you to give her a call, too."

As I walked into my office, I wondered at the short notice from Anna. Last night, she hadn't said anything about a gathering for Trisha before we left the police station. Now it was going to take place in a matter of hours.

Something was up, unless I missed my guess. Like every skilled birder, Anna was adept at making changes on the fly if an unexpected opportunity presented itself to see a bird. She wasn't the first birder to dump a carefully plotted birding itinerary to one area when a rarity was found elsewhere. No doubt, she applied that same talent to her police work, so if Anna organized a last-minute gathering, she had a compelling reason to do so.

No way was I going to miss this gathering of birders.

I tapped in Anna's phone number, and she answered on the second ring.

"I need you to do me a favor," Anna said. "Could you pick up Pheej on the way to the memorial this afternoon? I want him there, but I'd feel much better if I knew you had an eye on him."

"Sure," I said. "I can do that. Give me his address, and I'll pick him up on my way. But," I bargained, "you tell me what's going on with the rush for this memorial today, first."

Anna sighed into the phone. "Okay. Here's what I think. You convinced me last night that Trisha's murder is tied to Pete's Chimney Swift claim from three years ago, when he apparently, inadvertently, almost exposed a human trafficking ring at the brewery. Because of that near miss, our traffickers have kept an eye since then on anyone who might be interested in the brewery."

"Legally," I qualified. We'd already agreed last night that urban explorers enjoying their illicit adventures wouldn't pose a threat to a ring using the brewery for their own criminal purposes.

"Which leaves birders," Anna continued, "and in particular, Chimney Swift spotters."

"And if I were trying to keep track of a group of birders with a specific agenda like monitoring populations," I interrupted her, "then I'd make sure I knew what they were doing by being in the group myself."

"Or had an informant reporting back to me," Anna added. "Either way, I think I smell a rat amongst the Chimney Swift counters."

I let silence fill the phone connection as another thought wrapped itself around Anna's comment.

Not a rat, but a Hammster.

"We're forgetting the Hammsters, Anna," I said. "They've got a big interest in the property. So big, in fact, they won't let anyone renovate it, right? They want it to stay just the way it is."

The light bulb exploded in our minds simultaneously, because Anna and I said it at the same moment: "A front."

"The Hammsters want the brewery for a cover." Anna's voice filled with certainty.

"I know this! Give me a minute," I said, frantically searching my memory for the name of the birder I'd met who was connected to the preservation committee for the Hamm's plant. I could recite the names of hundreds of birds at the drop of a hat for a trivia contest, but recall one little detail amidst the emotional and mental overload of the last few days? I hit the fast scroll on my memory.

I could do this. I just had to find the right moment . . .

"At the wake for Nip!" I said triumphantly. "He was there. It's Frank something."

Frank.

Frank the Hammster.

Frank who considered hiring Trisha to replace Sharon.

Frank who was interested in Chimney Swifts.

Frank who'd been called in years ago to inspect the Hamm's site . . . which meant he knew his way around the abandoned plant.

"Frank Quinn." Anna's voice was deadly calm. "I'll take you down," she promised.

Another silence on the phone.

"You think he killed Trisha," I said.

It was a statement, not a question.

"How do you prove something like that, Anna?"

"I'm not going to," she said. "You are."

CHAPTER TWENTY-FIVE

IT WAS ALMOST FOUR O'CLOCK when Pheej hopped up into my SUV outside Central High School in St. Paul.

"Thanks for the ride," he said, snapping his seat buckle into place. "Even if Officer Grieg hadn't asked me to be there, I would attend Trisha's memorial as a sign of my deep respect for her. She was a good friend, Mr. White."

"I'm sure she was, Pheej." I wheeled out of the school entrance drive and headed towards White Bear Lake, where the memorial was taking place at Evergreen Funeral Home. "I know I really appreciated the friendships I had with older birders when I was a kid. Those folks have been my friends my whole life."

We drove in silence while I navigated my way through afternoon traffic.

"Have you birded in this area very much, Mr. White?" Pheej asked me when we passed a sign for the White Bear Lake city limits. "I saw a posting on the MOU listing during lunch today for a Townsend's Solitaire near here."

I threw him a quick glance.

A Townsend's Solitaire.

Nice. The solitaire was a gray, long-tailed thrush that showed up sporadically throughout Minnesota in the winter. The birds were native in higher elevations out west, but with the winter months, they moved to lower elevations for food—primarily juniper berries. And unlike most other songbirds, Townsend's Solitaires sang through the fall and winter, but it wasn't for mating purposes. It was about food. The birds were extremely possessive about their juniper berries, so they sang to declare their territory and warn off other birds from their food source.

Sort of like defending your piece of the pie from your sweet-toothed relatives at a family reunion, except this was no picnic for the thrushes. It was a matter of survival: the Townsend's Solitaires with the bigger supplies of berries had a better probability of surviving the winter than their berry-poor brothers.

That was also why you didn't see a flock of Townsend's Solitaires in the winter: they didn't invite each other over for dinner.

"What time was the post?" I asked Pheej. I'd never seen a Townsend's Solitaire in Ramsey County before, and I had to admit it would put a bright spot in attending a memorial service.

"I eat during the second lunch period," he explained. "I always check my email then, even though I know I can't get out of school to go birding. It was almost one o'clock."

I glanced at the clock on my dashboard. Trisha's memorial was scheduled for 4:30.

"If it's close to here, we have time to swing by where it was sighted," I told Pheej. "If you're interested, that is."

He gave me a grin. "I'm very interested. If we see it, we could tell the others at the memorial, too."

Yup. The boy was a birder, all right. Birds trumped everything.

"Can you pull up that sighting on your smartphone?" I asked.

He bent to rifle through his backpack on the floor of the car and sat up again, phone in hand.

"It's about a half-mile from the funeral home," he reported after a few moments. "It was found in a stand of cedar trees near an ice rink in a park. I'll get us a map there."

Within minutes, Pheej had the route displayed on his smartphone and directed me to a small park that sat near White Bear Lake.

"Have you ever seen a Townsend's Solitaire, Pheej?" I stopped at a red light and looked at my eager co-pilot.

"No," he replied. "And I don't have my camera with me, either. This will be a missed opportunity to get a photo."

The word "photo" reminded me of the rest of my conversation this morning with Anna. After our little party last night at the police station, she and a detective had gone to speak with Pheej about his missing photo of the face in the brewery window.

"We told him the photo was a clue to Trisha's killer," Anna had explained to me on the phone, "and not a photo of a spirit at all. He told us he'd given the picture to Trisha because she'd asked to see it when he told her about his ghost theory. Trisha told him she was going to run it by someone familiar with the brewery to get his expert opinion. We figured whoever it was she was referring to was the one most likely to have seen Trisha as a threat, since she had the proof of illegal activity in the brewery. But we couldn't come up with a suspect."

"Until now," I said.

While we talked, my eyes had landed on my new photo courtesy of my Secret Santa, and I vaguely wondered again who had taken the picture.

Who took the picture?

I bolted upright in my desk chair.

"Anna, what exactly was in that picture? Did Pheej describe it in detail?"

She hesitated slightly. "Yes, but without the original, we're stuck. We have to rely on his memory."

My conversation with Bridget at the beginning of the week came back to me. She'd said that Pheej had told her the photo had a ghost in it, and that he refused to show it to anyone because it would bring a curse on them.

Why would he think the photo would curse someone?

"Anna, who did Pheej say was in the photo? I mean, other than the girl in the window."

For a moment, there was silence.

"How do you know there were people in the photo?" she slowly asked. "I didn't say that."

"Because a student of mine had heard about the photo, and she said Pheej thought it could curse someone," I told her. "That means something bad must have happened to someone in that photo, and since Pheej believes in spirits, he thinks there's a connection. Who was in the photo?"

"Trisha was," Anna finally relented. "and Pheej. And Sonny Delite."

I mulled over that information for a moment and began to see how Pheej had come to his conclusion that the photo was dangerous. Sonny Delite, a well-known Minnesota birder and member of our ill-fated Records Committee, had died in October in a freak accident. Pheej, however, had blamed the photo for Sonny's premature death because he thought he had captured the image of a ghost in it, and Trisha's murder had, no doubt, fueled that suspicion. I tried to remember what little I knew of Hmong belief in supernatural cause and effect, but something else nagged for my attention.

"Pheej was in the photo?" I asked.

"Yes," Anna said.

"Poor kid," I replied. "He must be freaking out by now, thinking . . . hold on. If Pheej was in the photo, he didn't take it," I reasoned, "unless he'd propped the photo on a stand and used a timer."

"He didn't say that," Anna said. "But I didn't ask, either."

The nagging feeling intensified.

"We need to find out who handled the camera," I said, "because that's one more person who knew about the photo."

The stoplight finally turned green and I drove through the intersection.

"Hey, Pheej," I asked, checking my rear-view mirror to move into the right-hand turn lane to the ice rink parking lot, "Officer

Anna told me a little about the picture of you with Trisha from the Hamm's brewery this summer. Who took the photo?"

Nothing like going the direct route, right?

Okay, it hadn't gotten me results with Patty about my Secret Santa, but I figured I'd give it a try with Pheej.

"A policeman," Pheej answered. "Trisha knew him, since he's often patroled the brewery. He offered to take the photo of us."

I wasn't sure what I'd hoped he'd say, but that wasn't it.

A policeman. An officer of the law.

I realized I'd hoped Pheej would have said, "Frank Quinn. He took the picture," because then I'd know for sure Anna and I were definitely closing in on Trisha's killer. Without more evidence to go on, I was beginning to feel nervous about Anna's plan for me to pin down Frank.

What if it didn't work?

I shot a quick look at Pheej, who was gazing out the front windshield, an unhappy look on his face. His mood had clearly shifted from the excitement of a birder anticipating seeing a new bird to one of serious gravity.

"I should have destroyed the photo as soon as I saw it," he said in a soft whisper. "Capturing a ghost on film is bad luck, especially a wandering ghost. They follow you, they cause trouble. Sonny died. I fell off a ladder and had to quit soccer. Trisha asked to have it, and she was killed."

Regret and self-blame rolled off him in almost tangible waves. The boy needed help, and while I might be only a sub-par detective, I knew I was a good counselor.

"Pheej," I said, "you are not responsible for any of those things. Crazy stuff happens, like Sonny's death. Everybody falls off a ladder sometime. And Trisha wasn't killed by a ghost. It's all bad stuff, but it's just coincidence that those things happened since you took the photo."

I turned off the engine and looked through the windshield to locate the stand of cedars and junipers where the bird had been found earlier in the day.

"Coincidence can go either way, Pheej," I said. "Good or bad. Bad as in people dying unexpectedly," which brought Sonny and Trisha to mind, along with Nip Kniplinger and Harry Harrison, "or good as in a Townsend's Solitaire showing up on our way to a memorial."

I pointed out at the trees. "It's right there."

I reached for the binoculars I keep in my car and handed them to Pheej. He put them up to his eyes and focused in on the bird perched in the cedar branches.

"We don't control what happens to other people," I assured him, "we can only control how we respond. Think about it, Pheej. You're a smart kid."

I socked him lightly on the shoulder.

"Even if you are a bird nerd like me."

We took a few more minutes to observe the bird before I started the car for the last half-mile to the memorial for Trisha.

"So are you working with Officer Anna to find out who killed Trisha?" Pheej asked.

"I am," I told him. "And you're going to help me."

I handed him what Anna had brought to me while I'd waited for Pheej to walk out of the high school.

"You want me to wear a bandana?" he asked.

"Yes. We're going to find out if anyone at the memorial recognizes it," I told him.

He turned it over in his hand.

"I don't recognize it," he said. "I've never seen any gangs wearing . . . turquoise?"

I smiled at his confused expression.

"I know. I'm guessing our bad guy must be colorblind or just stupid," I agreed. "Probably both. Anyway, here's the plan."

CHAPTER TWENTY-SIX

THE FIRST PERSON I SAW once we got inside the Evergreen Funeral Home was Steve Weston, one of the few birders in the state who can rival me with the size of his own collection of speeding tickets. Steve worked long hours as a courier making deliveries around the state, which allowed him to bird almost non-stop.

And, on long highway trips, at high speeds.

Rough translation: he'd become casually acquainted with some of the same highway patrol officers I knew.

"Bob! How you doing?" he said, shaking my hand.

Steve had never lost his native New York accent even though he'd been a pillar of the Minnesota birding community as long as I could remember. "Can you believe how many Snowy Owls are showing up around here?"

I shook my head in shared disbelief and told him about the Snowy Owl Luce and I encountered on our way to Birds & Beers a few nights earlier.

"It practically popped up out of nowhere, like a . . . surprise," I lamely added. I'd almost said "like a ghost," but in light of the conversation I'd just had with Pheej, I decided to downplay ghost-anything. I changed the subject with Steve.

"Are you going to play your Jew's harp for us?" I asked him. "We could use a little lively music in here. I heard you perform on Prairie Home Companion last month."

Steve brushed off my invitation. "Another time, maybe. Today is for Trisha."

He extended his hand to Pheej. "Aren't you the fellow who was supposed to give us the report on the Chimney Swift towers at the meeting last Saturday? Sorry you got cancelled."

Pheej shook Steve's hand and introduced himself. "I'm hoping I can do it another time."

I watched Steve's eyes drift to the bandana Pheej had wrapped above his elbow.

He leaned over to whisper in Pheej's ear, but I could still hear his words.

"Gangs don't wear turquoise," Steve informed my young partner-in-sleuthing.

"We know," I whispered to Steve. "It's an experiment for his sociology class," I improvised. "He's supposed to see how people react to symbols."

Steve nodded in understanding. "Got it. Catch you later."

He walked away to join another group of birders standing near a guest book on a table.

"That was quick thinking," Pheej commented. "I actually had an assignment like that for my social studies class last year. I learned that people are not always what they seem."

"Amen to that," I said, "and speaking of which . . ."

I nodded across the room at Sharon Stiteler and Frank Quinn. The Birdchick's back was to us, but Frank's profile was easy to recognize, thanks to the crest-like shape of his hair.

I expected he'd have to shave that down in prison. Jailbirds weren't known for stylish coiffures.

"I'm going to go talk with them, Pheej," I said. "Give me a few moments, and then I need you to interrupt us. I'll say something about the bandana, and we'll see how Frank reacts. If Anna and I are right, he's going to do a double-take when he sees the same bandana he planted at two places tied around your arm."

Yes, I knew this wasn't a brilliant scheme to trap a killer, but Anna had asked me to give it a try, so here we were, about to try to blindside Frank Quinn into making some kind of self-incriminating remark about a turquoise bandana. Since the police had deliberately withheld that piece of information when releasing their reports to the media, Anna and her colleagues were convinced only the killer would react to the strip of fabric.

"Just a few moments, Pheej," I repeated to him, "and we'll prove that a man, not a ghost's curse, killed Trisha."

I started to walk away and almost collided with a man who approached me from the side.

"Can I have a word with you?" Duc Nguyen said. "I'm not sure whom I can safely speak with about this, but I know that Cai and Pheej both respect you very much, so I'm hoping to impose on your kindness."

Crap. Just when I had myself psyched up to nail a Hammster, I got sidetracked by a Duc.

"Sure," I said.

What else was I going to say to a request like that? "Get out of my way, I've got a killer to trap"?

I moved with Duc to an empty corner of the room and threw a glance back at Pheej. I held up a finger to let him know this was only a brief interruption to our plan.

"What's up, Duc?" I said.

Ouch.

"I have a confession to make," he said. "I wasn't completely honest with you yesterday at the Swede Hollow Café. Yes, I was in the area to see the Trumpeter Swan, but I was also there to be questioned by the police."

I already knew about that thanks to Frank Quinn's comments at Nip's wake, but I waited for Duc to finish what he had to say.

"My plane wasn't late arriving on Saturday morning," he told me. "The reason I was late was because I met Trisha at the coffee shop where she picked up the coffee for the MOU meeting. I had called her after my plane landed, and we arranged to meet there for a private conversation. I needed to see her alone."

"You saw Trisha just before she was killed?"

Duc definitely had my full attention now.

"Yes," he said. "And the employees at the coffee shop saw us together. That's why the police called me in for questioning. They knew I was the last person to see Trisha alive."

I tried to read his emotions in his face, but I couldn't get past the bleak expression he wore. "And you're telling me this . . . because why?"

He wiped a tear from the corner of his eye. "Trisha is dead because of me."

"You killed her?" My throat tightened as I tried to comprehend what he was saying. I'd planned to ambush Frank at the memorial, not the Duck Man. What reason would Duc Nguyen have for killing Trisha Davis?

"No!" Duc protested. "No! Trisha and I—we were going to announce our engagement at the meeting."

I looked at Duc, stunned.

Engagement? Like in getting married?

Sure, I knew lots of couples who met while birding, but generally, budding romances between birders were nearly impossible to keep quiet. In the birding community, gossip could fly almost as fast as news of a rare bird sighting.

Duc nodded. "We kept our relationship very private," he said, apparently as much of a mind-reader as my wife. "We met on a birding trip last year in Ecuador, and it's been a lot of phone calls and weekend plane flights since then."

He wiped at another tear trying to escape.

"Trisha wanted all of her friends and birding colleagues to hear our news at the same time. That's why we met at the coffee shop—I wanted to have a moment alone with her to make sure her engagement ring fit."

He drew a small box from inside his jacket and popped it open for me to see inside. A diamond ring lay on a bed of blue velvet.

I'll be darned, I thought. Cai had called it correctly—Duc was here on a romantic mission after all.

Duc stared at the ring in the box. "Trisha was especially worried about Sharon's—the Birdchick's—reaction, since they are—were—such good friends, and Sharon and I were competing for the publishing contract."

I still didn't know where he was going with this, or why I was suddenly his confidant, but I could sense something just ahead in his confession was going to throw me for a loop.

"Trisha had told me about the threats to Sharon, but they had nothing to do with me, so I thought nothing of it. Trisha tried on the ring, and since it was a size too big, I decided to run by a jeweler and get it sized, even if it meant I would be late to the meeting."

He paused a moment and took a deep breath in, slowly blowing it out through his lips. He closed the little box and put it back inside his jacket.

"When Trisha pulled out ahead of me to return to the Bell Museum and the MOU meeting, I saw she had a different car than her own, and the license plate—it was BRDCHK1—I assumed it belonged to Birdchick."

He paused again, clearly struggling to finish his story.

"I had a terrible premonition I would not see Trisha again." He said. "I thought to myself, 'She is a sitting duck in that car for anyone who hates the Birdchick.'"

A sitting duck.

I couldn't help it. Call it a result of shock or grief or mental breakdown, but a snappy comeback popped into my head: "She wasn't a sitting Duc . . . yet."

Ow.

Talk about completely inappropriate. I was attending the woman's memorial, and talking with the man who loved her. Could I be any worse as a person?

Bad, Bob! Bad!

Although, in retrospect, yes—I could have been worse.

I could have been Trisha's killer, who I suspected was right in the room with us.

Duc struggled to speak. "I am convinced that my rabid fan killed Trisha, thinking it was Sharon."

No. That wasn't right.

I wanted to tell him Anna and I had it all figured out: Frank had killed Trisha because she had Pheej's photo, which was proof of a trafficking ring at the brewery. There was the shooting incident with my car at Bruce Vento Sanctuary. There were the bandanas at the two crime scenes. We'd put it all together and solved the crime.

And yet . . . Duc's conviction about Trisha's murder was like a solid presence hovering around him. I could practically touch it, it felt so strong. Could it be possible Anna and I were so off-base with our theory that we weren't even in the ballpark? Had Trisha been the victim of a mistaken identity, and everything else was just bad luck and coincidence?

"Why do you think that?" I carefully asked Duc, shaken by his certainty. Had the police arrested Trisha's killer unknowingly when they thought they were apprehending a harmless pie-thrower? "You don't have any proof of that, do you?"

Duc shook his head. "No, but after seeing the man throw the pie at Birdchick, I began to wonder. There was a man at the coffee shop—he kept looking in our direction, but I thought nothing of it. I don't remember what he looked like, either."

He shrugged and looked vacantly across the room of Trisha's mourners.

"Now I think it was Sharon's stalker watching Trisha," he said. "He must have gone to the Bell Museum early in the morning because he knew Birdchick would be at the annual meeting, and when Trisha drove her car, he followed her to the coffee shop and then back to the empty parking garage. If I had not worried about the ring size, I would have been with her in the garage, and she would still be alive."

Oh, man. I needed to send Duc along with Pheej for counseling. They were both swimming in guilt, and I didn't want to see either Pheej or Duc drown in it.

"Duc," I said, "You're not at fault here. Let the police do their work. I know it won't bring Trisha back, but they'll make sure justice is done."

I seized on a detail in his story in hopes I could give him some peace.

"The police think Trisha knew her assailant," I told him. "She opened her car door and was passing the coffee out to whoever was there. She was a smart woman, Duc. She wouldn't have opened the door to a stranger. It was someone she trusted."

I glanced across the room and saw Frank Quinn buttoning up his coat.

Someone like Frank Quinn, a birding colleague and possible employer. Was he getting ready to leave already?

If justice was going to be done, it had better be done quickly, I realized.

Swift justice.

Trisha would have appreciated that.

"I've got to go, Duc," I said. "I have to take care of something."

I made a beeline for Frank, stopping along the way only to grab Pheej's arm and drag him along with me.

"We're out of time," I said to him as we weaved through the crowd that was beginning to form in the room. "Frank has to see your bandana."

We stationed ourselves directly in Frank's path as he headed for the door.

"Frank!" I said, forcing a smile on my face. "Have you met Pheej Vang? He counted Chimney Swifts with Trisha last summer."

Frank brushed the crest of his hair and gave Pheej the once-over.

"No, I don't believe we've met," he said, offering his hand to Pheej. "A turquoise armband? Is that an Asian custom for a funeral?"

"I'm in a gang," Pheej said, just as we'd rehearsed.

Frank smiled knowingly.

"No, you're not. There are no gangs in Minnesota with a turquoise bandana. I ran for city council a few years ago, and I learned all the gang colors then. If you want to fool someone else with that, you might be able to," Frank conceded, "but it won't be me."

My smile was frozen on my face.

This wasn't going at all the way I had played it out in my head.

Frank sees the bandana on Pheej's arm and swiftly pulls me aside.

"The bandana," he says. "It's the same kind used by the gangs in St. Paul. I heard they found one near Trisha's car. We've got to call the police."

"Wrong, Frank," I say. "Nobody in St. Paul uses this bandana. And the police never released that particular information, either. But you are right about one thing: we've got to call the police, because you've

just identified the bandana you left at the scene of the crime. You killed Trisha Davis because she figured out you were running a human trafficking scheme, didn't you, Frank?"

Cue the dramatic music and the cops flood into the room to cuff Frank.

It wasn't happening.

Nothing was happening.

If Frank knew the turquoise bandana wasn't a gang color, then he wouldn't have left it at the crime scenes as a red herring for the police.

Would he?

I grabbed Frank's arm before he left the room.

"You told me you'd heard that gangs were involved in Trisha's death and in the car shooting," I said, desperately trying to recall our conversation from the previous evening. "Who told you that?"

Frank brushed his crest of hair. "I hear a lot of things," he said, "but I probably heard that from my brother-in-law."

Frank's brother-in-law.

Our conversation from the night before came back to me.

"He told you Duc Nguyen was at the police station being questioned the other morning," I said. "He's a sergeant, right? Your brother-in-law?"

"He is now," Frank said. "Although he's moonlighted for a security company for years. A policeman's salary isn't exactly extravagant," he added.

The pieces of my murder theory flew into a new configuration in my head.

The police did patrol rounds at Hamm's, along with a private security company. Together, they would be the first line of defense to breach in order to use the plant for criminal purposes.

Unless the criminal was already a part of that defense.

"What security company?" I said, releasing my grip on his arm. "In St. Paul? Does he patrol the old Hamm's plant?"

Frank brushed his coat sleeve where I'd grabbed onto him. He gave me a concerned look.

"Yes, he does," he said. "Why do you ask?"

"And you talk to him about the site, right?" My new theory took on a sharp focus in my mind's eye. "I mean, you're on that preservation committee, and you count Chimney Swifts, so you guys talk about the plant sometimes, right?"

Frank brushed his crest of hair, clearly confused where I was heading with my questions. "Yes, we do."

"And when Trisha showed you the photo Pheej took . . ." I prompted him, expecting him to say he'd passed it along to his brother—the man who knew the Hamm's site best—for his opinion.

"What photo?"

His question slapped me in the face with enlightenment.

Trisha told Pheej she was going to give the picture to someone familiar with the brewery. I'd assumed she was referring to Frank.

Not Frank.

Frank's brother-in-law, who probably made sure to be patrolling the Hamm's brewery every time birders, including Trisha, counted Chimney Swifts.

Frank's brother-in-law, who . . . Pheej said a policeman took the photo, a policeman Trisha knew! . . . had taken the photo.

The photo that proved something was rotten inside the Hamm's plant.

And the brother-in-law probably had no idea what he'd caught in the picture until Trisha handed him the print a few weeks ago . . . for his "expert opinion."

I called Anna on my cell phone, and she picked up on the first ring.

"The Hammster is not the rat," I told her. "But the Hammster's brother-in-law is. It's your desk sergeant, Anna."

There was dead silence.

"You're sure, Bob?"

"Yes," I said, looking directly at Frank. "Book him, Anna. Frank and I are on our way."

"What are you talking about?" Frank objected. "I'm not going anywhere with you. I've got a Hamm Heritage Group meeting to attend at City Hall."

Another piece in the murder puzzle fell into place.

"Is your brother-in-law part of this group?"

Frank smiled proudly. "He started it. More than five years ago."

Which would have been just before Pete Moss found an out-of-season Chimney Swift at the Hamm's brewery.

"You are so clueless," I said, grabbing his arm again and pulling him towards the door of the Evergreen Funeral Home. "Pheej, can you get a ride home with Duc?"

The boy nodded.

"And call Anna for me," I told him. "Tell her I'll meet her at the station in thirty minutes."

Frank pulled out of my grasp. "What's going on here? What does my brother-in-law have to do with Trisha's murder? And why did you tell Anna to book him? For what?"

I zipped up my parka to go back out into the cold.

"For murder, Frank. Your brother-in-law just became the primary suspect in the investigation into Trisha's death. And despite your obvious cluelessness, I think you might be able to provide some information the police will find helpful."

Frank's expression gradually changed from defiance to compliance.

"Okay. I can do that. For Trisha. She was a good woman. We'd even talked about her coming to work for me," he noted. "I don't know if you knew that."

"I'd heard something about it," I admitted.

I didn't bother to add his possible employment of Trisha had led to my initial suspicion he was somehow involved in her murder. Some things, I guess, really were best left unsaid.

"You know," Frank suddenly confided, "I always told my sister she deserved better than my brother-in-law."

No, no, no. My finely honed counselor instincts were setting off my interior warning bell: Frank was getting ready to tell me all about his sister and her now scum-bag criminal husband.

I gestured at the front door.

"Shall we?"

"Do you want to ride with me?" Frank offered. "We could talk on the way there."

No, no, no!

The warning bell was a lot louder this time

"Thanks," I told Frank, "but I don't want to have to come back for my car."

And I sure didn't want to hear about his sister and her husband, either.

I had a better idea.

"Hey, Frank, I know just the man you need to get in touch with. His name is Charles—I mean, Andrew—and he's this sharp young attorney. I'm sure he'd love to talk with you. But if he puts on this raspy voice, tell him he's not fooling anyone."

Frank gave me a confused look.

"Inside joke," I assured him. "Get in your car, Frank. We're going downtown."

CHAPTER TWENTY-SEVEN

"THE PACIFIC LOON IS STILL out at Lake Waconia," I told Luce the next morning as I kissed her goodbye before I left for my weekly before-school basketball game with Alan. "I checked the MOU listing. Can you break free today after lunch?"

"Are you going to stand me up, again?"

My wife wasn't one to let bygones be bygones without getting some ribbing mileage out of them first.

"I was saving my student from a life of crime," I reminded her, "or at least, from starting a police record before he goes off to college. Barring any similar emergency, I'll pick you up at one o'clock."

"How about you call me when you're on the way?" she suggested. "Just in case."

"Got it," I said as I went out the door into the garage.

Inside the car, I double-checked to make sure the bag of M&Ms for Alan was still on the passenger seat where I'd left them after purchasing them at the corner gas station late last night on my way home from St. Paul.

When Frank and I had arrived at the police station, Anna was waiting for us in the lobby and told us Frank's brother-in-law was already in custody. I shared with her what I'd learned from Frank and then left them both to compare notes. The last thing Anna said to me was that, as soon as they uncovered where Frank's brother-in-law had funneled his earnings from the trafficking ring, she was confident they'd get a conviction.

"Without an eye-witness, or indisputable evidence, it's going to be tough to convict him of Trisha's murder," Anna had admitted, "but he's going to jail one way or the other, I promise you that. I heard our new district attorney has a personal interest in the case," she'd added, along with a quick wink.

"Is that the Andrew fellow Bob mentioned to me?" Frank had asked. "You know, I ran for city council a few years back, and I know a lot of folks around here. Maybe I can help him navigate some of the maze of local politics—it can be pretty intimidating to a novice."

I had to stifle a laugh. Based on what I'd seen two nights ago of Charles/Andrew's ability to navigate through dark, winding tunnels—not to mention an embarrassing arrest and spontaneous strategy session—I guessed the intricacies of city politics might be right up his alley.

But I'd already decided it might be fun to sic Frank on him, anyway: Mr. Know-it-all patronizing the Prince.

Yup, that might be a lot of fun.

"I'm sure the DA would appreciate any directions you could give him," I'd told Frank. "Just don't tell him I said that."

I PARKED MY CAR in my usual space in the school lot and walked into the building. A pair of Northern Cardinals swept past me on their way to a perch in the bare branches of a maple tree, and beyond them, a glorious sunrise of reds and purples was waking up a frozen Savage. Winter birding in Minnesota certainly had its bleaker moments, but this wasn't one of them. With that sunrise for a backdrop, I wished I'd dragged myself and Luce out of bed an hour ago and driven straight out to Lake Waconia to see the Pacific Loon in the first rays of morning sun. If the bird was still there come the weekend, I decided, a sunrise trip out to the lake would definitely be on our schedule.

"Beautiful morning, Bob," Elway, our custodian, called out to me from where he was salting the apron by the school's auto shop at the end of the building. "I heard the bomb dog got a snack in your office the other day. A whole box of chocolates, huh?"

"It was an artisan chocolate duck," I called back. "I don't think the dog appreciated that aspect of it, though."

I took another step before I realized Elway had just ruled himself out as my Secret Santa.

He hadn't known that my chocolate wasn't in a box.

That left Paul Brand at the top of my Secret Santa suspect list. Given that I'd seen him running late yesterday morning—the one morning I hadn't had a gift waiting for me—and that my other gifts were art-themed, I concluded that the evidence was neatly mounting that our new art teacher was, indeed, my Santa.

I walked into the school and headed straight for the teachers' lounge to slide the bag of candy into Alan's mailbox. As I tucked the bag in, I was startled to see my own box overflowed with mail, until I remembered I'd never made it into the lounge yesterday for lunch, or for anything else, for that matter. When I hadn't been mentally occupied with the mystery of Trisha's murder, I'd been furiously attacking that stack of college recommendations I'd promised students.

Contrary to the old saying, time flies when you're *not* having fun, too.

I sorted through the materials in my box and discovered a neatly wrapped package at the very bottom of the pile. The tag on it identified it as another gift from my Secret Santa, but seeing as it was lying underneath the materials from yesterday, I reasoned that it had been delivered yesterday.

"I get it now," I muttered to myself. "When I asked Patty if she'd seen my Santa yesterday, she said she hadn't seen a delivery to my office. That's because the gift was left in my box here in the lounge."

I pulled the green ribbon off the box and opened the giftwrap to find a small box. Inside it was a brightly painted hand-carved wooden duck whistle.

I let out a low whistle of my own.

"Geez, Paul, you either do amazing work, or know someone else who does it," I commented to my Santa in absentia.

The whistle, though, made me pause.

Yes, it was as much a work of art as the other two gifts, but I honestly couldn't recall ever having a conversation with Paul about my passion for birding. Every time we talked, it was about art, or a student. Only my closest friends and co-workers knew the full extent of what birding meant to me, and I didn't count Paul Brand in either of those categories.

I turned the whistle over in my hand and studied it carefully. What did a hand-carved whistle, a chocolate duck, and a photo of student chickens have in common besides being forms of art and bird-themed?

I heard the lounge door open and looked up. Alan walked in.

"Hey, White-man," he greeted me. "Saw the very early newscast again this morning, courtesy of Lou's erupting teeth. You bagged another one, I guess."

He walked over to his mailbox and pulled out the candy I'd just stuffed into it.

"Yes!" he sighed, shaking the bag at me. "I love my Secret Santa. I'm living on this stuff this week."

"What did you see on the news?" I asked him.

"Corruption in the ranks in St. Paul. Human trafficking ring cracked. Local birder's murder key to scandal." Alan recited the sound-bites he'd heard as he tore open the bag of peanut M&Ms.

"Sounds like a private entrepreneur found a great, albeit completely reprehensible and criminal, use for the old Hamm's brewery and used a preservation committee as a cover for it. You want some?" He held the bag out to me.

I shook my head. "I try not to indulge in a thousand calories of sugar before 7:00 am," I said. "Besides, we've got some basketball to play."

"Suit yourself," Alan responded, tossing a handful of the red and green candies in his mouth. "I love sugar before I play. It wakes me up."

He shook out a few more of the candy pieces into his palm.

"I really hate it when bad people compromise the work that good people do," he said, this time picking the candy one piece at a time out of his hand to put into his mouth. "Like with this Hamm's Heritage Group the guy was using as a cover. The rest of the group members work hard to preserve the brewery as a piece of history for Swede Hollow. They've made some excellent decisions from what I've heard. But this guy hijacked their objectives: he found an illegal use that could be hidden by the legitimate work."

Alan ate the last candy in his hand.

"Now the whole historic preservation community has a black eye because of it," he noted. "Good intentions get twisted to serve bad ends. It's the human paradox, I guess. Why are you staring at my hand?"

His question broke my concentration. I realized I'd been focused on his hand because the bright colors of his M&Ms reminded me of the tinted coconut that had surrounded my doomed chocolate duck: sparkling green.

I glanced at the whistle still in my hand.

An electric red edged both ends.

It occurred to me that the photo I'd received on Monday sat in a bright yellow frame.

My gifts all had bright colors.

They were colorful.

I suddenly knew who my Santa was, and it wasn't Paul Brand.

In fact, I was sure I'd find clear proof of my Santa's identity when I walked into the counseling suite in another hour: if Patty Rodale had electric red streaks in her hair, I had my Secret Santa locked down.

"A day late, and a dollar short," she'd said yesterday morning when I'd slipped into the office just before the first bell. *A day late—* she was color-coordinating her hair dye with each gift the day after she delivered it.

Clever lady. She'd even found the will-power to resist the chocolate duck long enough to put it on my desk. She must have known that would make me rule her out as a suspect. No wonder she almost swooned when I said I'd give her half.

Before I confronted Patty, though, I had a basketball game to play with my brother-in-law. I followed him out the door to the gym, and sure enough, his sugar hit woke him up so well he outscored me three to one.

"Bad luck, Bob," Alan said as another of my long shots glanced off the rim of the hoop. He took the rebound and dribbled it up to the net for a perfect lay-up.

I picked off the basketball as it bounced past me.

"That," I said, nodding at his last basket, "was not good luck, Alan. That was skill."

The mention of luck reminded me of Pheej and his belief in curses and the supernatural. While it was true his photo had turned out to be evidence of kidnapping, and not a ghost-in-residence at Hamm's, it was ultimately leading to cracking a crime ring that exploited young girls. Even if Mrs. Hamm's spirit didn't haunt the brewery, I hoped wherever she was, she got a clap on her unembodied back for tipping off a young boy interested in ghosts and Chimney Swifts.

I ran up the center of the court and put the ball up.

Swish.

"Yes!" I put my hands up in triumph.

"It's about time," Alan commented. "I was beginning to think I was going to have to drag you back to the teachers' lounge and pump you full of coffee in order to get a game out of you."

"Heaven forbid," I said. "That stuff doesn't come close to being coffee, and you know it. Give me the strong stuff at the Stop-n-Go any day."

Alan took the basketball in for a final shot, but I managed to block it at the last minute.

"So you're not giving up the old joe, after all?" he asked as I went after the ball. "I thought maybe, after this last weekend, you might decide coffee was not your beverage of choice anymore."

I could suddenly hear the faint echo of Nip Kniplinger's voice from twenty-three years ago on a frigid morning on my way to see my first Mississippi Kite.

"There's nothing better than that first hit of joe when you've got a bird to find," he'd told me. *"But a lousy cup of coffee? That'll kill you every time."*

"Give up coffee?" I responded, bouncing the ball as I brought it back in bounds. "No way. I'm a birder, and birders live on coffee. Good coffee, preferably," I stressed.

I could feel a smile coming on as I repeated my old friend's words.

"There's nothing better than that first hit of joe when you've got a bird to find," I told Alan. I thought about all the birders I knew, all the birders I'd ever known, and the sheer pleasure each of us found in scouring the outdoors for birds.

I wouldn't give it up for anything.

Even if I did have to drink the occasional horrible cup of coffee.

"You know," I added, "there's a whole world of birds out there I haven't seen yet, Alan. So keep that coffee coming."

I faked to the right, peeled around Alan to the left and sent the ball flying.

Bob White's bird list for *Swift Justice*

Ivory Gull

Chimney Swift

Northern Shrike

Dark-eyed Junco

Great Horned Owl

Pileated Woodpecker

Northern Cardinal

Snowy Owl

Bohemian Waxwing

Trumpeter Swan

Pine Siskin

Northern Saw-whet Owl

Townsend's Solitaire

Acknowledgments

One of the things I love about writing the Bob White Birder Murder Mysteries is blending together fact and fiction. This book was no different. The real Ron Windingstad first suggested I write a book about Chimney Swifts several years ago, and thanks to his boundless enthusiasm and advocacy for the birds, I finally took the hint and tapped his expertise to get this manuscript started. Long before I finished writing the book, he also had the title for me, thanks to a conversation he had with another birder. Thanks, Kristin Hall, for coming up with an awesome title!

There are two more real birders who granted me permission to write them into my story: Sharon Stiteler, Minnesota's own Birdchick, and Steve Weston, a long-time member of the Minnesota River Valley Audubon Club. They both gave me free rein to do with them fictionally as I pleased, which was tons of fun, and I hope they enjoy their fictional counterparts as much as I did. Thanks for all you two do to bring the joy of birds to others!

Finally, in the course of writing this story, I was able to track down Barney Clark, aka Officer Friendly, who was the school police officer during my own years working at Shakopee High School. With his assistance, I was able to come up with a legitimate reason for a high school senior to spend the night in jail. Thanks, Barney. It helps to have experts in law enforcement on your side when you write about murder.